Praise for Simon Gervais:

"*A Red Dotted Line* reminds us of what thrillers are supposed to be: thrilling. Gervais, a former anti-terrorist agent, knows the world that he writes about and illuminates the dark threats we all face on the global stage. *A Red Dotted Line* will entertain, educate, and engage even the most jaded reader of international thrillers."
– Nelson DeMille, *New York Times* bestselling author

"Make a note: in the years ahead Simon Gervais is a name you'll be seeing on many more book covers."
– Steve Berry, *New York Times* bestselling author

"When Simon Gervais writes about the world of high-stakes global security, he knows what he's talking about. His world-class security expertise shines through in *The Thin Black Line*, a high-speed, break-neck, turbo-charged thriller that takes readers behind the scenes of the war on terrorism."
– David Morrell, *New York Times* bestselling author of *The Protector*

"With firm echoes of the best from Steve Berry and Christopher Reich, *The Thin Black Line* leaves its own indelible impression, as well written as it is told while establishing Gervais as a thriller force to be reckoned with."
– *Providence Journal*

"Gervais brings back covert agents Mike Walton and his wife, Lisa, in this stellar follow-up to *The Thin Black Line* . . .. The personal stakes involving his protagonists and almost nonstop action keep the pages turning; his improved prose style reveals that Gervais is a thriller writer to watch. The next book in the series can't come soon enough."
– *Library Journal*

"Simon Gervais is a born storyteller. He creates great convincing characters and his writing is underpinned with authenticity that shines through every page."
– Peter James, #1 international bestselling author

A Thick Crimson Line

A Thick Crimson Line

Simon Gervais

This is a work of fiction. Names, characters, places, and incidents are either products of the author's imagination or are used fictitiously. Any resemblance to actual events, locales, organizations, or persons living or dead, is entirely coincidental and beyond the intent of either the author or the publisher.

Studio Digital CT, LLC
P.O. Box 4331
Stamford, CT 06907

Story Plant Hardcover ISBN: 978-1-61188-252-0
Fiction Studio Books E-book ISBN: 978-1-945839-21-4

Visit our website at www.TheStoryPlant.com

First Story Plant Printing: April 2018
Printed in the United States of America

0 9 8 7 6 5 4 3 2 1

For Florence and Gabriel.
I wouldn't change either of you for the world,
but I wish I could change the world for you.

PART ONE
This Is War

CHAPTER 1

Ottawa, Canada

Newly promoted Royal Canadian Mounted Police Sergeant Khalid al-Fadhi came carefully down the stairs, hoping the creaking of the hardwood floor wouldn't wake his wife. He had kissed his eighteen-month-old twin boys goodbye but didn't feel the need to do the same to her.

His hand had barely touched the front door's knob when his wife's voice made him cringe. *Almost.*

"No kiss?" she asked, already halfway down the stairs.

"I didn't want to wake you," he lied.

She hugged him, and he had no choice but to embrace her back. He scratched the back of her neck and placed his lips next to her ear.

"I'm sorry, Julia. I should have spent the weekend with you and the kids," he whispered.

His wife of ten years gently pushed him back. "That's nonsense, baby. You deserve a break too. I'm glad you had fun fishing with your buddies."

"I don't deserve someone like you." He pulled his wife back toward him.

They had met twelve years ago at the RCMP training academy in Regina, Saskatchewan, when they were both newly hired police officers. It was love at first sight. At least, this is what he had repeated over and over to Julia for the last decade. The truth was that Julia's dad was a high-ranking member of the organization. This had meant much more to him than her blond hair and thick thighs.

"I'll see you tonight," he said before closing the door behind him.

He unlocked the door of his five-year-old Audi A4 sedan and waved one last time as he accelerated away.

At six in the morning, the traffic was light, and the drive to his office took less than ten minutes. He showed his credentials to the rent-a-cop manning the front gate of Canada's federal police service headquarters. He was waved in immediately. He could have shown a Costco card and they would have waved him through. It was a farce. With everything that had happened in the world in the last five years, it was beyond him why the RCMP didn't assign real police officers to man the entry points to its headquarters.

He parked his car in his designated spot and forced himself to relax. It was going to be a busy morning.

He had a sitting prime minister to take out.

CHAPTER 2

Athens, Greece

Mike Walton looked through his spotting scope.

"Confirmed," he said to Zima Bernbaum who was standing next to him in their sixth-floor suite at the Grande-Bretagne Hotel. "Jupiter is walking westbound on Vasilissis Sofias toward the Danish embassy."

"Just like he did yesterday," Zima replied. "Maybe this time the intel is good."

"Maybe. But we've been in Athens for more than forty-eight hours. I don't want to push it."

Mike and Zima were members of the International Market Stabilization Institute, a privately funded covert organization whose sole purpose was to protect the North American financial markets from any direct or indirect terror attacks. That sometimes meant chasing terrorists after the fact. Following the latest attacks in Paris, Charles Mapother—the IMSI director— had tasked Mike and Zima to pursue those responsible. It hadn't been easy. With so many agencies after the same targets, the risk of being caught in crossfire was high. In the last two months alone, Mike and Zima had stumbled three times upon a Mossad kill team going after the same targets. This has prompted Mapother to ask his friend Meir Yatom—the head of the Special Operations Division of the Mossad—to send a liaison officer to his team. Yatom had chosen Eitan David. Mapother didn't usually work with outsiders, but Yatom's team—and Eitan in particular—had conducted operations with his crew in the past with extraordinary results. Mike was confident they'd get the job done again. Eitan was not only a world-class operator; he was also Zima's boyfriend. Mike wasn't sure how he felt about Eitan and Zima working together in the field. He had voiced his concerns to Mapother, who had wasted no time in pointing out to Mike his own success in the field working with his wife Lisa. Mike had to acquiesce.

Jupiter's real name was Zaid al-Menhali. He was ISIS's chief recruiter in Greece. He had personally drafted two of the Paris terrorists into the fold. Both Mapother and Yatom wanted him dead.

"He doesn't seem to watch his back too much," Mike observed. "You'd think he'd at least change his route. You see anything, Eitan?" he added into the microphone clipped to his collar.

"Negative," the Mossad operative replied. Eitan was positioned on his scooter two street corners east of the target. "It's too early to say for sure though."

"Copy that," Mike said. "Be ready."

Next to him, Zima was taking pictures of everyone and every car passing by al-Menhali as he continued his walk toward the embassy.

With his Schmidt & Bender scope glued to his eye, Mike continued to observe al-Menhali, while Zima and Eitan busied themselves looking for counter-surveillance. Mike remained focused on the target. His feed was being transmitted live to the IMSI headquarters where a bunch of analysts, including Lisa, were assessing al-Menhali's every move.

Three angry knocks at the door startled him.

What the hell? The *Do Not Disturb* sign should have kept all hotel employees out. Whatever it was, Zima would have to take care of it. He couldn't afford to lose sight of al-Menhali.

. . . .

Zima had her Beretta in her hands before the third knock. She pulled her cellphone out of her jean's pocket and scrolled to the application linked to the sticky camera she had positioned across the hallway.

On the other side of the door was a slim woman, dressed in a summer dress under a white light jacket, her hair up on her head. She wore a scarf around her neck and appeared to be in her twenties.

"This ain't funny, damn it! Open the door!" the young woman yelled in English.

Can't she read the sign hanging on the doorknob?

"I said I was sorry, okay? Please open the door," the woman continued, loud enough that Zima recognized an American accent.

Wrong room, lady. C'mon, go away.

Zima's hopes of a quick resolution evaporated when the woman started banging on the door with both fists.

"I know you're there, you piece of shit! Open the goddamn door!"

The woman gave Zima no choice. Another minute of this and someone would notify hotel security.

If it's not already done.

Zima unlocked the door but kept the security chain in place. She opened the door, just a crack, but it was enough. The foul odor of liquor reached her.

The woman was drunk.

"I think you knocked on the wrong room," Zima started. "I'm with my husband."

"You're with my husband? I knew it! You slut!" The woman took two steps back, clenched her fists, and rushed the door.

Zima, guessing what was about to happen, had already removed the security chain. She opened the door wide. The drunk woman, expecting to encounter a solid door, almost flew into the room. Zima dropped to the floor and scissored the woman's legs, bringing her down with a sickening thud as her head hit the floor. Zima kicked the door close and bent next to the limp woman, worry lines wrinkling her forehead.

Oh shit!

She checked her pulse. Strong.

Thank God.

Keeping a close eye on the unconscious woman, Zima fished a pair of heavy-duty plastic zip ties out of Mike's backpack. Mike hadn't moved one inch during the incident. He was still immobile behind his rifle.

Zima tied the woman's hands behind her back before doing the same with her ankles. She then grabbed the woman by her feet and dragged her into the bathroom. She searched the woman for clues to her identity. Inside the jacket, she found a California driver's license, an American Express card, a two-euro coin, but no weapons.

. . . .

Mike sensed Zima next to him. "What happened?"

"Someone drank too much. I'm calling headquarters to check her out."

It had taken Zima less than two minutes to handle the situation. During that time, al-Menhali stayed in the same spot and burn through half a cigarette. In the background, Mike heard Zima talking to someone at headquarters. This incident changed their timing. What were the chances someone had heard the commotion and called security?

"Her name's Jane Fonseca. She's an American, and she and her husband are indeed checked in at this hotel. She had the right room, but one floor too high."

"Credit card?"

"Last processed payment was for a one hundred and ninety euros at a bar nearby."

So this was a fluke? How long could they stay in position?

Not long.

"Call back Mapother and put him on speaker," he asked Zima.

Either Mapother gave them the green light to take down al-Menhali now, or Mike's next order to his team would be to pack up and leave.

CHAPTER 3

New York, New York
IMSI Headquarters

Lisa Walton stood up from behind her desk and grimaced as pain shot up her left leg. She sat back down, out of breath. Three months had passed since the shootout in Koltsovo, Russia. Since then, she'd had good days and bad days. Today was one of the latter. Nevertheless, she was grateful to be alive. She shivered as thoughts of the Sheik played with her mind. She tried to block them out, but the smell and taste of his urine always seemed to barge through her defenses. It was a vivid reminder of how close she had come to dying at his hands. She took consolation in knowing that Mike had kicked his ass back in Mykonos, and that the Sheik was now in an underground prison without any chance of seeing the light of day again.

"You okay, Lisa?" Mapother asked, placing his hand gently on her shoulder.

"I will be," she replied. A medical doctor herself, Lisa appreciated how long the human body needed to recuperate from injuries. Wounds from bullets that tore through muscles and ligaments wouldn't heal overnight. The psychological wounds took even longer.

It was her third day back in the office. She had jumped at the opportunity to get back to work the moment the doctors cleared her. She had had enough of staying home. And she was worried about Mike. A lot. She had gotten used to being in the field with him. From Africa to Europe to Russia, they had made a great team chasing down the terrorists responsible not only for the death of their unborn child and their two-year-old daughter Melissa, but also for the worst terror attacks since 9/11. Sheik al-Assad—the man who had orchestrated these attacks—had killed their entire family during the first phase of his assault on the North American financial markets two and a half years ago. If it had not been for Mike and a few other heroes, the economic consequences would have been even worse.

She pushed the unpleasant memories of her time in the Sheik's captivity out of her mind and focused on the video feed Mike was sending to the main flat screen of the control room.

"Start cross-referencing today's feed with yesterday's," Mapother said.

Lisa's fingers danced over her keyboard. It was difficult not to marvel at the capabilities of the IMSI. Even though the IMSI's existence was known only to a select few, Mapother's organization had grown into a redoubtable counter-terrorism force. But the IMSI's many achievements had been overshadowed by some monumental failures, and Lisa wasn't sure what would happen after the next presidential election. Mapother had assured her that everything would remain the same, but she wasn't convinced. Director of National Intelligence Richard Phillips, who had previously been a staunch supporter of the IMSI, was now an unknown player. Lisa could hardly fault him for it. DNI Phillips's main job after protecting the country was to shield the president from any repercussions caused by the possible implosion of the IMSI. If the IMSI's true purpose was brought to light, the president's involvement with the IMSI would be more than enough to get him impeached. Operating under the cover of a foreign-market analysis center working for nine of the biggest corporations in the United States, the IMSI's cover was solid but had come under pressure recently when it was discovered that Steve Shamrock—one of the IMSI's founding members and the CEO of Oil Denatek—had been a traitor and the financier behind the Sheik's terror network. Charles Mapother had cleaned up the mess, but DNI Phillips had never fully regained his confidence in the organization. But he still called on the IMSI to execute the missions he felt should stay at arm's length from the United States government.

"I got something here," Jonathan Sanchez said, walking into the control room. Sanchez was a close friend of Mike and Lisa and had played a major role in bringing them to the IMSI. A former member of the 1st Special Forces Operational Detachment-Delta, he had fought alongside Mike in Serbia during Operation Picnic. A round had shattered his knee and forced him out of the field.

"What?" Mapother asked.

Sanchez took a picture out of a blue folder and showed it to Lisa and Mapother.

"That's Anja Skov," he said. "She's the lady Zaid al-Menhali had lunch with yesterday."

Lisa looked at the picture. Anja Skov was strikingly hot. Tall, blond hair, big blue eyes. She could have been a Victoria's Secret model.

"What do we know about her?" Lisa asked.

"She's the personal secretary of the Danish ambassador."

Lisa scratched her head. "Why would he go after her? She seems of little value. Unless she has the ambassador's ear . . ."

"You're right," Sanchez said. "I doubt her security clearance alone is enough to warrant al-Menhali's attention. But she's an activist, and her boss's brother is an influential member of the Danish parliament."

"What do you mean by 'activist'?" Mapother asked, taking a closer look at the picture.

"She's very active on social media," Sanchez replied. "Mostly on Facebook. She believes the Danish government should do much more to accommodate the Muslim community and she wants it to repeal the 2002 law that made it harder for immigrants to bring their families over."

"The Danish Aliens Act," Mapother said. "I remember when this was voted in. It raised an uproar within the United Nations Human Rights Council—"

"Really?" Lisa interrupted her boss. "What doesn't raise an uproar these days?" She wasn't a big fan of the United Nations. In her opinion, the United Nations had been hijacked by political self-interest and had become a global talkfest. It was too big, consisted of too many endless bodies and committees and was good only at producing thousands of reports that nobody cared about.

"I don't disagree with you, Lisa, but that's not the point, is it?" Mapother said.

"Didn't the UN actually come up with a report condoning the Aliens Act just last May?" Sanchez asked.

Mapother nodded. "So you think she's in love with him?"

"He represents everything she's fighting for," Sanchez said.

"And we shouldn't forget that al-Menhali is a local celebrity within the Muslim community," Lisa added. "It's because of his thinly veiled threats of violence that the Greek parliament voted to speed up the taxpayer-funded mosque they'll build in Athens."

"So where does that leave us?" Sanchez asked, looking at Mapother.

"It doesn't change anything. At best, she doesn't know anything about his involvement in the Paris attacks, and, at worst, she's a minor player."

Lisa agreed with this assessment. "If al-Menhali were to die in Athens, I don't think the Greek authorities would launch an international investigation, but even if they do, we'll make sure it doesn't gain any traction."

"But if an employee of the Danish embassy is killed, that's another story. So we stick to the plan and let Mike and Zima take him out at their discretion. She lives," concluded Mapother.

That's it? Did we just decide who lives and who dies? The feeling was frightening and empowering at the same time. In the field, Lisa never had an issue taking down a target. In fact, Mike had recently told her he thought she was a bit too eager to pull the trigger on some occasions.

She disagreed.

She had to.

Telling him the truth would have ruined her chance of getting back in the field.

"Sir?" This was from Anna Caprini. She was holding a phone against her ear. "Mike says you either give him the green light on al-Menhali now or he pulls the plug."

"Why? Did I miss something?" Mapother asked.

Lisa wondered the same.

Caprini continued, "A drunk crashed their party at the Grande Bretagne."

Lisa swore under her breath. She looked at Mapother. He was the one calling the shots, and he didn't delay in making his decision known.

"Execute."

CHAPTER 4

Royal Canadian Mounted Police Headquarters
Ottawa, Canada

RCMP Sergeant Khalid al-Fadhi strolled into the briefing room and waved to Corporal Mason Quinn who was chatting with Superintendent Serge Caron, the officer in charge of the prime minister's protective detail. As always so early in the morning, the briefing room smelled of coffee and burnt toast. Most officers preferred to eat their breakfast at work with their peers rather than alone at their residence while the rest of their family was asleep. Al-Fadhi often did the same, but the knot in his stomach told him it wasn't a good idea to force anything down this morning. Instead, he poured himself a coffee and added two packets of sugar. He looked for a stirrer but couldn't locate one, except for dirty ones in the small garbage bin next to the coffee table.

"Looking for one of these?" asked Superintendent Caron, holding a stirrer in his hand.

"Thank you, sir."

"Saw the pictures you posted on your Facebook page," Caron continued. "One hell of a catch that rainbow trout."

"The biggest I ever caught," al-Fadhi replied.

"What lure did you use?"

Al-Fadhi was momentarily caught by surprise and his mind raced to remember what he had read about the subject. A lure? He didn't know anything about fishing. Fishing was only a pretext he used to leave the house to prepare his extra-curricular activities. It wasn't even him who had posted the picture on Facebook. Someone far away did that for him. Aware that Caron was a hardcore fisherman, he had to tread carefully.

"I used an orange floating trout worm," he finally said.

"Really? I heard about those orange ones but never tried one myself. We should get together sometime. Maybe you could show me where your best spots are?"

"That'd be fun." Al-Fadhi smiled.

"All right then." Caron looked at his watch. "Drink up. We'll start the briefing in two. You're the PSO for this morning's move. Are you ready for this?"

Al-Fadhi's heart skipped. He couldn't believe it. The officer in charge of the prime minister's protective detail had just entrusted him with the most vital position. The personal security officer—or PSO—was in charge of the whole protective detail while in the field. He had authority over all the bodyguards and the other officers attached to the four-car motorcade. During a road movement, the PSO sat in the passenger seat of the armored limousine carrying the prime minister. Wherever the prime minister went, the PSO went. Al-Fadhi hadn't expected to be trusted in this position so soon after his promotion. His hard work and dedication had finally paid off. And just at the right time. It would make everything so much easier.

"So?"

Al-Fadhi realized he hadn't responded to his boss.

"Yes, sir. Thank you, sir."

Caron nodded and slapped him on the shoulder before taking his position at the head of the huge table in the middle of the briefing room.

Al-Fadhi had always known he was going to be called upon. In fact, his whole life had been dedicated to the successful completion of the mission Ayatollah Khomeini had entrusted to his father more than three decades ago. As committed as he was to his task, it wouldn't be easy. He had never loved his wife, but he had come to love his twin boys. They'd never understand what their father was about to do, and that bothered him. Still, he was a soldier of Iran, and a soldier of God. He would do his sacred duty. Whatever the cost.

CHAPTER 5

1979 – Iran

Ayatollah Khomeini made eye contact with each of the seven SAVAK—the Iranian Organization of Intelligence and National Security—colonels seated in front of him. These were men he trusted. These were men who shared his vision for Iran. These were men who had put their careers and their lives in jeopardy to serve him. And they had paid a heavy price. To convince the CIA these seven men were in real danger, the ayatollah had ordered that at least one member of each colonel's family be killed. It was a price the colonels had been willing to pay to one day see Iran as the beacon of Islam and the only superpower in the Middle East. With the help of number "8"—a covert American asset he had recruited years ago—these seven warriors would all be in the United States within days, officially commencing the first phase of Operation PERIWINKLE. The second phase wouldn't be initiated for another two or three decades, but the Ayatollah was a patient man. A visionary, some people said.

His victory here in Iran was inevitable. Prime Minister Shapour Bakhtiar was a fool not to see it. With the shah in exile and the SAVAK imploding, he could have taken the country in less than a week. Months of protests had loosened the grip of the central government on its populace. Yes, he could have taken power already. But at what price? Not that he cared much about the death of civilians, but he did care about the future of his country. He needed to retain the confidence and respect of the population to achieve his objectives. He wouldn't strike before he had all his peons in place. The men in front of him were his knights, his secret weapons. The second and third phases of PERIWINKLE, if used at the right time, would allow Iran to influence and even manipulate the United States' foreign policy.

His gaze stopped on the most senior colonel and he asked, "Are you ready?"

"Yes, I am. I've made contact with the Americans. We're meeting tonight."

A rare smile appeared on Ayatollah Khomeini's lips.

"I'm told the list of names you put together and that I forwarded to them is working miracles inside their counter-intelligence section," the colonel continued. "One name has already been scratched off the list."

That was a surprise. Ayatollah Khomeini had not expected the Americans to be so blunt. The list he had put together was meant to eliminate the last elements within the SAVAK that could cause harm to the revolution. It included the names of many high-ranking officers still loyal to the shah.

"So soon?" he asked.

"Let's just say I convinced them that these officers represented an imminent threat to Prime Minister Bakhtiar."

Ayatollah Khomeini knew that wasn't the case. In fact, the names of the officers on the list were the current government's last line of defense. But the Americans had no way of knowing that. The fact that they had already taken out one of them—one of their own really—indicated they had no clue what was really going on within the SAVAK.

"You know what to do, my dear friends," the ayatollah said. "You were chosen to carry the torch of Islam into the entrails of our greatest enemy. The road ahead of you will be long and perilous. You'll have no contact with me or with any of my aides. But know this. One day I'll call upon you, and you will be ready"

CHAPTER 6

Ottawa, Canada

Sergeant Khalid al-Fadhi paid extra attention during Superintendent Caron's briefing. The prime minister's wife had decided to ride with her husband that morning. She usually traveled with her own motorcade, albeit a much smaller one than the prime minister's, but since she was headed to Parliament Hill too, she wanted to ride with her husband. Her regular vehicle, a black GMC Yukon, would trail behind the prime minister's motorcade.

"Any questions?" Superintendent Caron asked.

There were none. It was a pretty routine movement. The prime minister would motorcade from his official residence at 24 Sussex Drive to the parliament building. Usually, this would be over within ten to twelve minutes, but since the City of Ottawa was repaving part of Sussex Drive, it would take them an extra five or six minutes.

"All right then. Have a good day, and have a safe shift."

As everyone rose, Corporal Mason Quinn approached al-Fadhi. "Congrats, man," he said. "Do you think it has anything to do with what happened last month with Vespa-2?"

Vespa-2 was the code name for Justine Larivière, Prime Minister Adam Ducharme's wife. It had been given to her because prior to the election of her husband—Vespa-1—a little less than a year ago, she used to own a red Vespa. A month ago, while assigned to Vespa's protective detail at the official summer residence of the prime minister at Harrington Lake in the Province of Quebec, al-Fadhi had saved the life of Sylvain Larivière, her fifteen-year-old nephew, when he attempted to swim across Harrington Lake. Sylvain was a strong swimmer and a part-time lifeguard but nearly drowned when a severe cramp in his leg surprised him in the middle of the lake. Al-Fadhi, who had been standing close to Vespa and keeping an eye on Sylvain with a pair of binoculars, saw him struggle midway through. Al-Fadhi knew right away something was wrong. Sylvain had swum across the lake the day before without any difficulties. Al-Fadhi never hesitated. He dropped his duty belt, his suit jacket and his shoes and sprinted to one of the four waverunners the first family kept at their dock. By the time al-Fadhi reached Sylvain, the young man was already underwater. Al-Fadhi dove and managed to drag Sylvain to the surface and onto the waverunner. A minute later they were ashore and other members of the protection detail started CPR. Thanks to al-Fadhi's quick reaction, Sylvain was still alive. That, of course, had put him in good standing with the officer in charge and the entire prime minister's family.

"Thanks," al-Fadhi replied. "I'm sure it did."

"As I said, well deserved. And the good news keeps coming."

"Why's that?"

"Caron asked me to be your L1 driver," Quinn said, referring to the armored limousine.

"Did he now?"

Al-Fadhi wished it wasn't the case. He had grown fond of Quinn. He was a good, honest cop with four young kids at home. Still, al-Fadhi had a job to do. The two men headed outside and climbed into one of the four black minivans the protective detail used to travel to the secured RCMP garage where all the motorcade's vehicles were kept. Al-Fadhi pulled his cellphone from his jacket pocket and dialed dispatch.

"Dispatch," said a voice belonging to a French Canadian woman named Emily.

"Hey, Emily, this is Sergeant al-Fadhi."

"Good morning, Mr. PSO. What can I do for you?" Emily's voice betrayed her excitement.

Emily would have known that al-Fadhi had been selected to be today's PSO. It was customary for the officer in charge to forward a copy of everyone's position first thing in the morning. Emily was also one of his wife's friends, and al-Fadhi was pretty sure she had a crush on him. He never understood why, since he never gave her any indication he was attracted to her.

"We just left HQ and we're on our way to the garage," al-Fadhi said. "Anything on your screens?"

"Way ahead of you, Khalid," she replied instantly. "Nothing to report as of now. Traffic is light and your primary route is clear."

"Thanks, Emily. I'll talk to you again once we're at 24 Sussex."

Al-Fadhi got the attention of the officer seated in the passenger seat by touching his shoulder. His name was Guy Blanchard. He was a quiet, serious guy who had recently transferred from Halifax.

"You're the A30, right?" asked al-Fadhi. Advance 30 or A30 was the member who ran the route the motorcade would take thirty minutes before the actual departure. There were also an A15 and an A5. Anything suspicious or a dramatic change in traffic pattern would be communicated to the PSO who'd then make a decision to continue with the original route or switch to one of the alternate routes.

"Yes, Sergeant," Blanchard replied.

"Since the guys from counter-surveillance are on another detail, I want you to run the primary once and then take a position close to Parliament Hill," al-Fadhi said.

"Understood," Blanchard said.

Al-Fadhi's smartphone chipped in his pocket. "Sergeant al-Fadhi," he said.

"Khalid, this is Emily. Prime Minister Ducharme's assistant just called. The PM wants to leave in fifteen minutes."

Al-Fadhi consulted his watch. It was going to be close.

"Roger that. Thanks, Emily."

Al-Fadhi asked the minivan driver to lower the volume of the police radio so he could speak to everyone on that channel without interference.

"Good morning, everyone," al-Fadhi said into his mic. "For your information, Vespa-1 and 2 will leave a bit earlier than scheduled. There's no time to stop for coffee."

One after the other, the lead officers of each vehicle replied that they had copied al-Fadhi's message. Schedule changes were frequent. This was why vehicles needed to be cleaned and gassed up before the end of every shift. A minute later, the minivans entered the underground garage. The moment they were parked, the drivers of each of the vehicles belonging to Vespa-1 and Vespa-2 details went to work. They inspected their vehicles and watched for signs that someone had tampered with them. This would be surprising since they were in the most secure garage in the city. Once they were satisfied, al-Fadhi conducted a radio check and ordered the motorcade to head toward 24 Sussex.

"Vespa-1 detail from ERT," came in the voice of the Emergency Response Team leader.

"Go ahead for Vespa-1 detail," replied al-Fadhi.

"We'll be in the area for your first move of the day."

"Copy that. Thanks."

It was customary for the ERT to provide a counterassault team to the protective detail. The ERT—or SWAT—members were well trained in a multitude of high-risk environments including hostage rescue and VIP protection. They could be deadly if they needed to be and everybody was confident that, with their support, an attack on Vespa-1 motorcade wouldn't be successful.

Everybody was wrong.

CHAPTER 7

Athens, Greece

Mike Walton had put the crosshairs in the middle of Zaid al-Menhali's chest, but his finger wasn't yet on the trigger even though he had just received the green light to engage from Charles Mapother.

"Target has stopped," Mike said.

"He's in front of the embassy. If he does like yesterday, he'll wait for her to step out," came in Eitan, who was still on his scooter and keeping a watchful eye for any other surveillance or counter-surveillance team working the same target.

"I won't take him out in front of the embassy," Mike said. "That could spell trouble."

"Wind is still from the east at fifteen miles an hour," Zima said.

Upon their arrival in Athens, Zima and Eitan had reconnoitered the area while Mike had drawn his range card. It allowed him to know exactly the distance between him and his target. The flags on top of the numerous embassies and government buildings provided Zima the info she needed to assess the wind conditions.

"Someone's coming out," Zima said. "It's Anja Skov."

Mike angled his rifle toward her. Dressed in an expensive sleeveless jumpsuit, Anja Skov descended the stairs of the embassy, smiling and waving at al-Menhali. What a gorgeous girl like her found attractive in a piece of shit like Zaid al-Menhali was a mystery to Mike. Then again, if he was to trust the intelligence Mapother had shared with him, she was a radical. Still, he would have thought al-Menhali would have preferred his women to be covered. Was al-Menhali playing her? Or maybe she was playing him?

Anja Skov hugged al-Menhali and he kissed her cheek.

"You got that?" Mike asked Zima.

"Sure did," she said. "Wanna blackmail the sonofabitch, don't you?"

Mike knew a man like Zaid al-Menhali couldn't be turned simply because there was a video of him hugging and kissing a girl on the cheek. But it did raise the question why al-Menhali, a high-profile Muslim in Athens, didn't mind being seen in public with a non-Muslim woman.

There's more to this than meets the eye, Mike thought. But at this point he didn't really care. There were only two things he wanted. The first was to get out of this hotel as soon as possible, and the other one was for al-Menhali to meet his creator. And he, Mike Walton, would see to that.

CHAPTER 8

Athens, Greece

Zaid al-Menhali watched her walked toward him. He felt helpless. He was addicted to Anja Skov. He just couldn't get enough of her. There was something exotic about her and he couldn't wait to spend more time in her company. He had always regarded women as accessories, and he had certainly intended on doing the same with this one, but she'd surprised him. Yes, she had enchanted him. She was so passionate, and not only in bed, but in all aspects of her life. It was impossible to fight her magnetism. He was drawn to her, and there was no doubt in his mind it was the same for her. You couldn't fake what had happened the night before. It had been magical.

Of course, he'd have to be careful not to show her the *real* Zaid al-Menhali. She wouldn't be drawn to *him*. He'd have to be cautious moving forward or he would lose her.

"Zaid," she squealed, "how I missed you."

She gave him a big hug and he brushed his lips against her neck. He felt her tension and assumed it was from desire. He felt an erection coming and wondered how he was going to resist dragging her into an alley and having his way with her. Maybe he was going to do exactly that. He shivered in anticipation.

"I was looking forward to this too," he said.

She slipped something into his hand.

"What is this?" He looked down at a flash drive.

"A little something," she said. "A little something just for you. You know, something to keep you warm at night."

They had talked about it the night before. She had promised him pictures of her that she swore would have him dream of her every night they weren't together. He didn't expect it to have them so soon though.

"I took them this morning," she said. "I think you'll like them."

Her face had become red. That was another thing he liked about her. She was confident—not a trait he was used to in women—but timid at the same time.

The palms of his hands grew sweaty. He hated that. He pocketed the flash drive and wiped his palms against his pants. It pissed him off that a woman—even one as beautiful as Anja—could make him lose control over his body. Suddenly he wasn't so sure about her. He didn't feel safe. She was controlling him, and that he couldn't stand.

I should teach her a lesson. Show her who's in charge.

But he had his orders. They'd been in the back of his mind all along. He had to continue to play nice with her. She knew the right people within her government, and his superiors wanted him to transform her into an ISIS asset.

"Shall we?" he asked.

She took his arm and squeezed it. "You make me feel good, Zaid," she said as they walked toward the restaurant. "We have so much in common."

Yes, she was perfect. As long as *he* knew who was on top, maybe there was nothing wrong with her being in control for a while.

. . . .

Anja Skov fought not to throw up her breakfast right there and then on the pavement. Zaid al-Menhali sickened her. The fact he'd been inside her yesterday night repulsed her. The moment he had fallen asleep, she'd gone to the bathroom. After turning on the shower to cover up any sound, she had violently thrown up in the toilet. When she had volunteered for this assignment she hadn't thought she would have to sleep with the man partly responsible for the death of so many innocent people. Her superior officer at DDIS—the Danish Defense Intelligence Service—had wanted her to infiltrate ISIS when they had come across intelligence suggesting a potential terror threat against Danish interests in Greece. Never before had a Danish government official been so close to getting raw intel from a reliable source. The counter-intelligence division of the DDIS had worked hard to fabricate elaborate stories to provide her with a background cover. And it was working. Zaid al-Menhali had fallen hard for her. With any luck, he'd love the naked pictures on the USB drive she had given him. He only had to click on one of them to download the Trojan program the DDIS techies had embedded in every photo. Once downloaded, the Trojan would collect passwords, logins and machine-specific information from al-Menhali's computer. With the collected data, the techies would have full access to everything al-Menhali had on his computer, including emails he had sent and received and the passwords to his bank accounts.

The next few months weren't going to be easy. She knew that. But if sleeping with al-Menhali helped save Danish lives, well, that would be her way to serve.

CHAPTER 9

Athens, Greece

"She gave him something," Mike Walton said. Anja Skov and Zaid al-Menhali were now on the sidewalk heading east on Vasilissis Sofias. In thirty seconds, Mike wouldn't have a shot anymore.

"Couldn't see what it was," Zima replied.

"Me neither," added Eitan from his position on the street.

Mike had to make a decision. "Eitan," he started, "once he's down, I want you to get whatever she gave him. He slipped it in his left pocket."

"Understood," Eitan said.

Mike took a few deep breaths and concentrated on his target. He trusted Zima to warn him if the overall situation changed. "Wind?"

"No change."

Mike was now in his zone, making one with his Sako TRG 42. A headshot wasn't necessary. At this distance, the 308 Winchester round would be just as deadly punching through his target's back, and chances of over penetration were almost non-existent.

Mike gently pulled the trigger.

CHAPTER 10

Athens, Greece

Anja Skov felt al-Menhali pitch forward. Then his knees gave and he fell face first on the sidewalk. Because their arms were entangled, his weight dragged her down with him. Though she'd never been in a gunfight before, she recognized what had just happened. Zaid al-Menhali's eyes locked with hers and he tried to speak. But only blood came out of his mouth. His body jerked twice and then remained still.

She screamed for help, as any sane person would. And then she stepped back, furtively looking for cover while hoping it would appear to any observers like a move made by a frightened woman. The DDIS had an officer tasked with watching her back. She had never met her protector, but now would have been a good time for him to show up.

Her mind was spinning. *Am I a target to? Where did the shot come from?* She looked at where the dead terrorist had fallen and concluded the shooter had been at the Grande Bretagne Hotel. A few pedestrians, who had no idea the man on the ground had just been shot, approached al-Menhali. They took out their cellphones but instead of calling for help, they started filming the scene. A man on a scooter stopped close by and rushed to al-Menhali's side. *Is it him?* She tried to make eye contact, but he didn't even look at her. Plus, he kept his helmet on, which was odd. Almost no one in Athens wore a helmet while riding.

"What happened?" she heard him ask the small crowd gathered around the dead man. When nobody answered, he rolled al-Menhali on his back and checked his pulse. He started CPR but stopped almost immediately when a huge amount of blood erupted from al-Menhali's mouth. Then she thought about the flash drive. She had to get it back. Before she could move, another man approached the scene. His eyes moved left and right and stopped on hers for a split second. This and his demeanor told Anja he was the DDIS agent responsible for her safety. He kneeled next to the man who had started CPR and grabbed his wrist as he started to get up.

. . . .

Eitan David hated being out in the open like that. He had counted no less than five people filming the scene with their smartphones. He needed to leave. Now. But he also needed whatever Anja Skov had passed to the dead terrorist.

His right hand slipped into al-Menhali's left pocket. He felt the contour of what seemed to be a flash drive, but before he could examine what he had found, another man knelt in front of him and grabbed his wrist.

There was a chance the man was a Good Samaritan trying to prevent what might have looked like a thief pickpocketing someone in distress, but Eitan couldn't take the chance. Instead, he used his left hand to chop the inside of the man's forearm. He did it with such force that he broke the man's radius. The man's eyes opened wide, in shock. Eitan used his advantage to pull the man toward him using his right hand and delivered a powerful punch to his solar plexus with his left. The man doubled over and went to his knees, desperately struggling for breath. Not knowing who the man was, Eitan did not intend to cause him any lasting damage. He grabbed the flash drive he had dropped during the altercation and was about to climb back on his scooter when he heard Zima's alarm in his ear.

"Behind you!"

. . . .

Anja Skov had rarely seen someone move as fast as the scooter man. He had incapacitated the agent in charge of protecting her in less than two seconds. She watched him pick up the flash drive. She had to get it back.

She followed him to his scooter and was about to try to subdue him with a carotid artery choke from behind. She never made it. The man suddenly dropped down and performed a perfectly executed foot sweep that sent her crashing to her side. By the time she got up, he was already gone.

"C'mon, we need to go," said the other DDIS agent, holding his injured arm. "The police are on their way."

"He has the key," Anja Skov said.

"Is it really a bad thing? Maybe we'll learn something we don't know about these assholes."

Anja Skov doubted it. She didn't think the scooter man worked for ISIS. He was probably part of a kill team, and if she was right about this, she was lucky to be alive. All this work, all this pain. All for nothing.

Shit.

CHAPTER 11

Athens, Greece

Eitan half expected to be shot in the back as he accelerated away and only breathed a sigh of relief when he made a right at the first intersection. He sped up the street, trying to put distance between him and the dead terrorist. More than one person had his description. They might not have seen his face, but he'd need to find new clothes and a new method of transportation before meeting up with the team.

"Eitan, this is Jonathan," came in Sanchez's voice.

"Go ahead."

"Go to location Alpha-Niner," Sanchez said. "There's a white Hyundai Getz parked in lot P2. Key's in the exhaust pipe."

"Copy. I'll advise once I'm on site."

Eitan promised himself to thank James Cooper, the Support 6 team leader, for that. That was another thing Eitan loved about the IMSI: they were well prepared. Sometimes even more than the MOSSAD. Almost anywhere they went, IMSI assets had a support team with them. While the assets focused on the actual mission, the support team made sure the assets had everything they needed to complete it. Preparing weapons caches and positioning exfil vehicles were all part of the job they performed to ensure mission success.

Alpha-Niner was a two-hundred-and-seventy-four-slot multistory underground parking garage located in the downtown area of Kerameikos. Eitan smiled at the thought that the Greek authorities had spent more fifteen million euros to build the parking structure. That meant that each parking spot had cost the taxpayers more than fifty-five thousand euros. *No wonder they're broke.*

The Hyundai Getz was where it was supposed to be and so was the key. Eitan opened the trunk and unzipped the carry-on suitcase. Inside were three changes of clothes—one for each operator—fifteen thousand euros, three genuine Canadian passports, two thermite grenades, and three Glock 19s with one spare magazine each.

"Jonathan from Eitan," he said, trying to reach the IMSI headquarters. No response. He was about to try again when he realized there was no way he'd reach them from the underground garage.

Eitan jumped in the cramped rear seat of the Hyundai and changed his clothes. He was almost done when he saw a man in uniform walking from car to car. His heart stopped when he recognized the patch of the Hellenic police on the officer's shoulder. Had he been followed? He doubted it. More than likely, the description of his scooter had been broadcast at large and an officer must have seen him and called it in.

Of course they had no way of knowing whether he was still in the garage. And it was not as though he had been seen killing the man. They probably only wanted to question him. Eitan watched as the officer moved from car to car, looking for anything out of the ordinary. Another forty seconds or so and the officer would reach the Hyundai. Eitan would have a hard time explaining what he was doing alone in the backseat of a car.

He had to move.

He stepped out of the vehicle, glad he'd had time to change clothes. He sat in the driver's seat and started the engine. He put the transmission in reverse, but the police officer was standing behind his car, blocking his way. A look in the rearview mirror told him the officer meant business. His hand was on his weapon and he was yelling at him to stop. Eitan wasn't sure to whom the vehicle was registered and he didn't want to find himself facing questions he couldn't answer. Not willing to plow through a police officer, Eitan obeyed and turned off the Hyundai. The officer slowly approached his window and, although Eitan didn't speak Greek, it was clear the officer wanted him to exit his vehicle.

Eitan was delighted to see the officer's gun still in its holster. Making sure not to make any move that could jeopardize this fact, Eitan opened the door and smiled at the officer. He kept his hands well in sight. He was halfway out of the car when he sensed something change in the officer's demeanor. It only took a quick look at the backseat of the car for Eitan to understand. In his rush to get out of the garage, he had left the soiled clothes on the backseat and the officer had seen them. The blood on the white t-shirt was hard to miss. The officer already had his pistol three quarters of the way out of the holster when Eitan reached him. Then the first shot rang out.

CHAPTER 12

Athens, Greece

Even though Zima kept an eye on the target as he went down, Mike knew it was a good shot. He started to disassemble his rifle. The armorer at the IMSI headquarters had customized it so that the Sako could be stored in a gym bag. Mike had no problem fitting it in his carry-on suitcase.

The clear line of sight from his sniper nest to his target had facilitated his shot, but that also meant it would be easy for anyone trained in ballistics to know where the shot had come from.

"Eitan's off," Zima said. "Looks like he had to fight his way out."

That wasn't good. They needed a clean exit, and an altercation made that much more difficult to achieve.

"First there was a man," continued Zima. "I don't know why he got involved but Eitan pushed him off. Skov tried to stop him too. Then she left the scene with the man."

"Did they go to the embassy?" Mike began to wipe the room clean of fingerprints.

"No. They went north on a side street and I lost visual."

That was strange. The first thing she should have done was rush back to the embassy. Who was the man Eitan had to take down? Clearly, he was a friend of Anja Skov. Was al-Menhali being played by the Danes? It didn't matter anymore. The next ten minutes were spent making absolutely sure they didn't leave any trace of their presence. The woman Zima had secured in the bathroom was still unconscious.

"Could she identify you?" Mike asked.

"Unlikely."

"Okay, then. Let's go."

"I'll get the car," Zima said, her gloved hand on the door handle. "Give me ten minutes and wait for me at the corner of Xenofontos and Filellinon."

Mike waited another minute and then followed her out of the room. The room had been rented using an alias and paid for with cash, which wasn't at all suspicious in Greece. Businesses in Greece loved cash. In fact, it wasn't unusual for them to claim that their interact or credit card payment processing machines were broken so their clients had no choice but to pay with cash.

"Mike from Jonathan," came in Sanchez as Mike called the elevator.

"Go for Mike," he replied once he made sure no one else was around.

"We've lost comms with Eitan. Can you reach him?"

Mike tried to reach him on the alternate channel. Nothing.

"Negative."

"The last contact was when he was on his way to Alpha-Niner."

This was the underground parking garage where James Cooper had set up one of the exfil vehicles.

"Eitan will be fine. He'll meet us at the airport. We'll wait for him there," said Mike. "We need to bug out."

"Roger that," Sanchez replied. "I'll make sure the Gulfstream is ready to go."

Mike knew the pilots well. Martin St-Onge and William Talbot were solid. They'd be ready. Eitan had better show up.

CHAPTER 13

Athens, Greece

Eitan cursed out loud. The officer had shot himself in the foot trying to get his weapon out. Eitan had then easily wrestled the pistol away from the officer and used the man's handcuff to secure his hands behind his back.

"You speak English?"

The officer was in shock but managed to nod. "What's your name?" Eitan asked, removing the officer's shoe.

"Manos."

"I'm no threat to you, Manos," Eitan replied. He was now taking the officer's sock off. He was pushing his luck staying in the garage for so long but he needed to make sure the officer would be okay. He didn't want to have a police officer's death on his conscience. It was a small miracle that nobody had come to investigate the commotion.

The round had taken out half the man's toe. "You'll be all right. This is superficial, okay?"

Manos didn't look convinced. "Don't move," Eitan told him. He opened the trunk and grabbed the first aid kit. He bandaged the wound as well as he could.

"I'll call for help the minute I'm out of here, understood?"

Manos didn't reply. No doubt he wondered how he had ended up with his hands behind his back and half a toe short.

Eitan started the engine and backed away from his parking spot, careful not to hit the officer. He hadn't even shifted the transmission to drive when a round punched through the windshield and embedded itself in the passenger seat. Eitan saw a muzzle flash and the next round hit the engine block. The shooter was another police officer. He was using a concrete pylon as cover. Someone had heard the gunshot after all.

With only one way to reach the exit, Eitan was stuck. With backup surely on its way, there wasn't much time left for Eitan to escape.

The stairs. That would mean leaving the suitcase behind. Eitan put the car in reverse and pressed the gas pedal as another round went through the windshield. The bullet deflected into the dashboard but Eitan had had enough. Using his left hand, he pulled the Glock out of his pocket and fired five rounds in the general direction of the officer, making sure to miss him by several feet. The moment the officer sought cover, Eitan place his pistol between his legs and pressed trunk release. He stopped the car and jumped out, pistol in hand. He fired two more rounds toward the officer and ran to the rear of the vehicle. He opened the suitcase and pocketed the two spare magazines. He grabbed one of the thermite grenades, removed the safety pin and left it next to the suitcase. He closed the trunk lid and peeked to see if the police officer had remained in the same position. Eitan didn't see him and assumed he was still behind the pylon. He fired one more time in his direction and then sprinted to the staircase sixty feet behind him. He hated being out in the open, but it was better than staying close to the car with the thermite grenade working its wonders. There was no point looking back; he knew the car was on fire by the reflection of the flames on the walls of the underground garage.

Eitan was less than five feet away from the door leading to the staircase when it opened and another police officer materialized in the doorframe. He must have been close to six and a half feet tall, and his biceps threatened the fabric of his shirt. Even though the officer had his pistol out, it was pointing to the ground. As big as he was, a look of panic appeared on the police officer's face when he realized he wouldn't have time to do anything before being hit by the man who was racing toward him. Eitan rammed him at full speed and they tumbled together to the ground, with the Greek officer taking the brunt of the impact. Both men dropped their weapons and, for a second, their eyes locked. The Greek pushed Eitan off and got back to his feet with the agility of a hardened pugilist. The men circled each other, but Eitan didn't have the leisure to wait around.

He fainted a right hook but jabbed the Greek on the nose with his left before delivering a powerful uppercut to the other man's chin. The Greek didn't even flinch, and his right fist connected with Eitan's jaw. Eitan thought he was going to pass out and took a few involuntary steps back. If it hadn't been for the wall behind him, he would have fallen. He couldn't remember ever being hit so hard.

He was in trouble.

The Greek took a step forward, blocking any escape routes. There wasn't going to be an easy way out of this fight. Another hit like this and he'd be out.

A smirk appeared on the Greek's lips as he grabbed his expandable baton from his duty belt. This was his first mistake as it would force him to remain at a certain distance from Eitan. Distance was exactly what Eitan needed. He actually had doubts about being able to take the bigger man down. But he had only one shot. If he missed, it would be all over. Just as he had anticipated, the Greek swung his baton in a wide arc aimed at his upper body. Eitan stepped in and blocked the blow by striking the inside of the Greek's forearm and then rammed his knee into the police officer's groin. The reaction was immediate and the Greek loosened his grip on his baton. Eitan clutched it with two hands and twisted it away from the Greek by turning it counterclockwise. He then whacked the baton against the outside of the Greek's left knee. A loud crack echoed in the tight space of the stairwell when the Greek's kneecap fractured. The officer fell to his side, and Eitan used the baton to secure the doors leading to the garage. Through the small window, Eitan saw that the officer with whom he had exchanged gunfire was now heading in his direction. Eitan picked up both pistols.

"Me have child. Many child," pleaded the officer in broken English. "Not kill me you. Parakalo!"

"Believe it or not, my friend," Eitan said as he disassembled the Greek's pistol, "we're on the same side."

He threw the gun on the floor and climbed the stairs two by two, leaving the confused Greek police officer behind.

CHAPTER 14

Ottawa, Canada

Sergeant Khalid al-Fadhi looked at his men deployed around the motorcade. They were good men who took their job seriously but somewhat lacked the alertness and vigilance they exhibited when deployed overseas. It was true that the threat toward the prime minister was at an all-time low. Newly elected, Prime Minister Adam Ducharme enjoyed one of the highest ratings of any Canadian prime minister in history. His party controlled the House of Commons and the Senate. They had swept the last election and sent the Conservative Party of Canada back to official opposition status.

The Canadians had bought into Ducharme's rhetoric of high taxes and high spending. Within months of taking power, the deficit for the fiscal year had grown to close to thirty billion dollars. But the great people of Canada couldn't care less; Ducharme promised them prosperity and had already started sending checks to a large percentage of the population. The fact that high-income earners—people earning more than two hundred thousand dollars per year—were taxed at fifty-three percent for every dollar earned about that threshold and that entrepreneurs and small business owners were squeezed like never before didn't matter to them. *They* were getting more money in their pockets and they'd continue to elect him until he stopped sending them checks. The media was also going the prime minister's way. They absolutely loved him, and you'd have a hard time finding any negative news about him or his wife. They were like rock stars, even overseas. Everybody loved them. Word at the office was that since there were no term limits in Canada, it was entirely possible that Ducharme would remain prime minister for the next two decades.

But al-Fadhi knew better. It would be a very, very short reign.

It had taken a decade longer than Ayatollah Khomeini had envisioned, but the second phase of PERIWINKLE was a go.

And it was al-Fadhi who would strike the first blow.

CHAPTER 15

Official Residence of The Canadian Prime Minister
24 Sussex Drive, Ottawa, Canada

Prime Minister Adam Ducharme looked out the window. His motorcade had arrived and the men and women in charge of protecting him were standing outside their vehicles, scanning the horizon. All of them were dressed in suits and ties, and most wore dark raincoats. The sky had gotten cloudier and rain was soon expected.

"The RCMP is here," he said to his wife. "We should go."

"They can wait a little longer," Justine Larivière replied. She wasn't fully dressed yet, and Ducharme couldn't help wondering if they had time for a little quickie.

He grabbed his wife by the behind and kissed her neck. It felt good to be so powerful. He could do what he wanted and his minions would wait for him. No matter what.

"Not now, Adam," Larivière said, pushing his hands off her. "There's no time."

"They'll wait," Ducharme replied, his hands already loosening his belt.

"We need to talk," she said.

He didn't like the sound of that. That meant there was no chance he'd get what he wanted. At least not this morning. He sighed. "What is it?" He glanced at his watch.

"I'm late," she said, smiling.

"That's okay," he replied. "I told you, they'll wait. They work for us, not the other way around."

"No, Adam," she said, taking his hands in her own. "I'm late."

It struck him harder than lightning. His knees wobbled, and he had to grab the top of his dresser to prevent himself from falling. His wife must have seen the terror in his eyes because her demeanor changed. She slapped him on the cheek. Hard. A swing full of hate and disgust. It stung, and Ducharme felt the blood rush to the area. Before he could say anything, she slapped him again, this time on the other cheek.

"Say something!" she yelled at him, her famous short temper roaring back to life.

Words had always come easily for him. That was one of his strengths; he could bullshit his way through pretty much anything. But this time he was speechless.

"Whatever," his wife said. "I'll go to a private clinic and take care of it."

That brought him back to reality and he grabbed her wrist. "No."

"Let me go, Adam," she warned him, "or I swear to God I'll hit you again."

He let her wrist go. It was question period today. He had to look good for the cameras. A bloody lip or a broken nose wouldn't do.

"You clearly don't want it, and I'll certainly not take care of another child all by myself," she continued.

Ducharme's mind was racing. If the radicals across the aisle got wind Justine had gone to an abortion clinic, he'd never hear the end of it.

"Wait, baby. I'm sorry," he said, doing his best to sound sincere. "You surprised me, that's all. Are you sure?"

She nodded.

Maybe it wasn't so bad. The press would go crazy. He'd be the first prime minister to have a baby while in office. Plus, thanks to the taxpayers, he could get a couple more nannies to help with the kids.

"You know I love you, right?" he said, pulling her close.

CHAPTER 16

Ottawa, Ontario

"Heads up, guys," Sergeant Khalid al-Fadhi said. "Vespa-1 and 2 are coming out."

Al-Fadhi walked to the prime minister to greet him.

Is that a handprint on his cheek?

"Good morning, Mr. Prime Minister, and to you too, Mrs. Larivière. How are you this morning?"

"They bumped you up to PSO, Khalid?" replied Ducharme. "Good for you."

"Thank you, sir."

The prime minister took his seat at the back of the armored limo. Once Justine Larivière was seated next to her husband, al-Fadhi ordered the bodyguards into their vehicles.

"XJD-85 from Vespa detail," he said to the radio operator.

"Go ahead for XJD-85."

"Vespa-1 and 2 are 10-17 to Site Eighteen. We have a 10-26 of ten to twelve minutes."

"10-04, Vespa detail."

Al-Fadhi replaced the radio in its cradle. While in movement, the four-vehicle convoy would follow the directives of the motorcade commander seated in the lead vehicle. Behind the lead vehicle, also called C-1, was the first security vehicle—S-1. Behind S-1 was the armored limo followed by S-2—or security vehicle two— the last vehicle of the secured package.

"Khalid, I know it's not on the schedule, but Justine and I will visit her parents tonight," Ducharme said, opening his laptop computer. "Will you still be on shift?"

"No, sir," al-Fadhi said while opening the bag in which his MP5 was stored. "Sergeant Flory will take over at four o'clock. I'll make sure to let him and the officer in charge know as soon as we're at Site 18."

"Thank you."

Justine Larivière's parents lived in Montreal. It was an easy two-hour drive from Ottawa. Not that it mattered.

"I was wondering, sir," al-Fadhi said, his right hand tightening around the grip of the Glock 19 he had packed with his MP5. "Is that a handprint on your cheek?"

Baffled, Ducharme looked up from his laptop. "Excuse me?"

Khalid turned around in his seat so he could face the prime minister.

"No seriously, I noticed it the moment you guys came out."

Ducharme's face grew red but Larivière's remained unreadable. Al-Fadhi figured she was so shocked she didn't know what to do. These two were used to being treated like royalty. This was unfamiliar territory.

"Khalid, for Christ's sake," Quinn hissed. "What are you doing?"

CHAPTER 17

Ottawa, Canada

Prime Minister Adam Ducharme was furious. "How dare you talk to me like this, you piece of shit? I'm the prime minister!" he spat as the motorcade came to a stop at a red light.

The way al-Fadhi looked at him sent a chill down his spine. Deep down, Ducharme knew he was in trouble, but since he had never been a man of action, he froze. Even when al-Fadhi pulled a gun out of his bag, never did he think about his wife's or unborn child's safety, only his own. Ducharme had never seen such a long pistol in his life. Guns had always scared him.

Ducharme watched helplessly as al-Fadhi shot the driver—weren't they friends?—in the head. Ducharme expected the gunshot to be much louder.

He wanted to do something but he couldn't move. He couldn't breathe. He couldn't form a sentence with the deluge of words that ran through his mind.

"Ayatollah Bhansali sends his regards," al-Fadhi said, a faint smile appearing on his lips.

CHAPTER 18

Ottawa, Canada

It was too bad good people—like Quinn—would die protecting this poor excuse of a man. Until the end, al-Fadhi hoped Ducharme would try to defend himself, or at least shield his wife, but no.

Nothing.

He clung to his last seconds of life like the true coward he really was. Al-Fadhi shot Larivière once in the heart and once in the head. He then turned his pistol toward the prime minister and shot him only once. Ducharme's head snapped back and the rear window became crimson with blood and brain matter.

Al-Fadhi hurried to insert a new magazine in his Glock before grabbing the MP5. A quick look at the traffic light confirmed they'd be moving soon.

"All units, all units, this is the PSO. Vespa-1 has suffered a medical emergency," al-Fadhi said in a controlled voice over the radio. "All bodyguards out of the vehicle. Now! Meet me at L1. Someone bring me a defibrillator."

"I have the defib, Sergeant," responded the bodyguard seated in S-2.

"A-Five and A-Fifteen, I want you to run routes to the closest hospital. Report back to me," al-Fadhi ordered to his advance team.

This was it. Al-Fadhi wished his father was still alive to see this. He would have been so proud. His life's work, really. Al-Fadhi took three long breaths to calm his nerves. His hands were shaking. *Allah, please give me the strength to carry on.*

Al-Fadhi remained in the vehicle until the four bodyguards were within twenty feet of the armored limousine. When he opened the door, he kept the MP5 at his side and brought it up only once he was in a stable firing position. The first man he took out was Carl Desjourdy, one of the two bodyguards in S-2. Al-Fadhi always hated the know-it-all-I-am-better-than-you officer and actually took pleasure in sending him to his death with a double-tap. The first round hit him in the vest but the second one went through his throat.

Al-Fadhi had many things going for him. One was surprise. By the time Desjourdy hit the ground, he had already pivoted forty-five degrees to his right and engaged the second bodyguard, the one carrying the defibrillator. One round to the head was all it took. His next six rounds—fired in quick succession—were for the S-2 driver. The bullets smashed the windshield and the officer's body jolted with every impact.

His second advantage was that while his colleagues were stuck in the open between vehicles, the opened door of the armored limousine protected him. It was an unfair fight. Al-Fadhi did an about-turn and took aim. The third bodyguard froze in place less than ten feet away, his pistol still pointed to the ground when al-Fadhi shot him in the head too. Al-Fadhi spun to his left in search of Sebastian Joanis, the last of the prime minister's bodyguards. He caught a glimpse of him retreating to his vehicle. Al-Fadhi fired two rounds but missed. Joanis was quick, and al-Fadhi wondered if he should have engaged him first. Joanis was a former Emergency Response Team member and one of the best marksmen of the unit.

"Drop your weapon!" someone screamed behind him.

He took a second, but al-Fadhi recognized the voice. *Renée Villadelgado.* She was Vespa-2's bodyguard.

You should have taken the shot, Renée.

Al-Fadhi turned around. Villadelgado was fifty feet away and seemed unsure what to do next. Vespa-2's driver was still in his seat, as he had been trained to do in case of an emergency. Al-Fadhi brought up his MP5 and actually had time to bring his sight on Villadelgado before she gathered enough courage to fire. She snapped the trigger and her round went wide. *Not even close*, thought al-Fadhi as he fired twice. Both rounds found their marks. Villadelgado collapsed. To keep the ex-ERT member's head down, al-Fadhi sent a few more rounds toward Joanis. He then switched his aim to Villadelgado's colleague who had finally exited his vehicle. He died when one of al-Fadhi's bullets struck him in the side of the head.

Al-Fadhi needed to move. Joanis was a dangerous man. If he wanted to get out of there alive, he couldn't afford to be bugged down. He still had the advantage though. With the prime minister in the backseat, it was Joanis's duty to get to him.

. . . .

Corporal Sebastian Joanis crouched behind the engine of S-1. He signaled the driver to stay low. What the hell was going on? Al-Fadhi had lost his mind. The odds were that he had killed the prime minister and his wife, but Joanis couldn't do nothing. He had to get to the prime minister. It was his job.

He tried to call for backup using the radio but couldn't get through. Al-Fadhi had kept his mike open, making it impossible for everyone else to cut through. Joanis's cellphone was plugged in the car.

Damn it!

Loud cracks told him al-Fadhi had opened up on S-1. Windows shattered and S-1's driver yelled in pain. Joanis angled his body so he could look. Al-Fadhi was reloading. He didn't hesitate. He sprinted and fired his pistol at al-Fadhi.

. . . .

Al-Fadhi fired rapidly into S-1. The driver's head popped up and he adjusted his aim. He fired until he emptied his magazine. He ejected the spent magazine and was inserting a new one when he saw Joanis running toward him firing his pistol.

He's nuts. Al-Fadhi didn't panic. He made himself a small target by hiding most of his body behind the armored door. Round after round smashed into the window. Spiderweb cracks appeared.

How many shots had Joanis fired? Al-Fadhi looked through the window. Joanis had changed course when he realized he wouldn't make it to al-Fadhi in time. He was now running perpendicular to the armored limousine. In another second, Joanis would have a clear shot at him.

. . . .

Eight, nine, ten . . . Joanis was getting low on ammo but he couldn't afford to slow his rate of fire. He needed al-Fadhi pinned down in order to move to a position where he'd have a clear shot. Just a few more feet . . . *Eleven, twelve, thirteen* . . . He was almost there when he saw the barrel of al-Fadhi's MP5 creeps past the armored door. A bullet grazed his right leg. *Fourteen.* Joanis dove as the next round pierced his right bicep and lodge in the side of his vest. He hit the ground hard and dropped his pistol on impact. He rolled to a stop and tried to locate his firearm. It was five feet behind him.

He knew it was all over when al-Fadhi came out from behind the limo's door with his MP5 pointed directly at him.

Damn it! He'd been so close.

. . . .

Al-Fadhi admired Joanis's courage. The prime minister didn't deserve men like Joanis on his protective detail. Al-Fadhi smoothly squeezed the trigger at the same time he was hit from behind. His shot missed and al-Fadhi tried to spin around, but his left leg buckled the moment he shifted his weight. The excruciating pain came right after. Al-Fadhi fell on his bum just as he was hit again. This time the bullet shattered his right hand and he dropped the MP5.

Villadelgado. The bitch. She wasn't dead after all. Squatted next to her open door, she fired at him with her pistol. Her next round hit him high on the left shoulder. Al-Fadhi crawled back to the armored limo, looking for the Glock, but stopped when he remembered his service pistol on his hip. With his right hand ruined and his left shoulder on fire, he had difficulty drawing his issued Smith & Wesson. His lack of speed cost him another round in the chest. Even though his vest stopped it, it knocked the wind out of him. He still managed to return fire but it wasn't accurate. Nevertheless, it was enough to send Villadelgado back into her vehicle to seek cover.

Then Joanis reappeared, his pistol pointed at al-Fadhi's head.

His main objective completed, al-Fadhi saw no point in surrendering. He tried to bring his gun around but never really had a chance. Joanis was too quick and didn't hesitate. Al-Fadhi didn't feel a thing when the 9-mm round entered his mouth.

CHAPTER 19

Tehran, Iran

Major General Jalal Kharazi eyed the man standing at attention in front of him. Colonel Asad Davari was a tall man who wouldn't look out of place in *GQ* magazine. But as handsome as the colonel was, he wasn't to be underestimated. Davari had proven himself many times over in Iran's secret wars. He had served his country with distinction and had risen through the ranks, not because of whom he knew, but because of his accomplishments on the battlefield. Still, perspiration appeared on the colonel's forehead. This pleased him very much. Colonel Davari hadn't yet said a word as Kharazi pondered whom he should blame for the debacle that threatened years of work and planning. As the commanding officer of the Quds Force, Kharazi was one of the most powerful men in Iran and answered only to the supreme leader. His organization was responsible for all the Iranian Revolutionary Guard Corps'—IRGC—extra-territorial covert operations, with its two main focuses on the training of Islamic fundamentalist terrorist groups and the implementation of companies and institutions that acted on behalf of the Iranian government. These activities included providing cover for intelligence operations and support to terrorist and insurgent groups in the West. Kharazi was known as a man who rewarded success but had a low tolerance for failure. Colonel Davari had never disappointed him. His promotion to brigadier general was only a matter of time.

"Congratulations, Colonel Davari. You are my new deputy," Kharazi said once he had made his decision about what to do with the man.

"Sir?"

"General Adbullahi is gone. You are now the second-in-command of the entire Quds Force."

Davari met his gaze, a rare look of confusion on his face. "There are officers who are much more senior than me—"

"I trust you, Asad. Which is more important than seniority, wouldn't you say?"

"Yes, sir. Thank you, sir."

It was clear to Kharazi that the colonel didn't want the position. Which was exactly why Kharazi wanted him. Davari would be a good leader, but without the ambition needed to ascend any higher than Kharazi was willing to let him go. General Adbullahi—the cause of the problem—had been his previous deputy. He was the only other man in the Quds Force to know the entire operational plan for PERIWINKLE, a plan Ayatollah Khomeini had spent decades building and that the current supreme leader, Ayatollah Bhansali, had continued to support. With the second phase of PERIWINKLE initiated, General Adbullahi's treachery could have dire consequences. Quds Force leader or not, Kharazi's position didn't preclude a bullet in the back of the head. Fortunately, he was high enough on the food chain that he'd hear about it before it actually happened and would probably have time to escape before it was too late. Was that what had happened with General Adbullahi? Did he fear for his life? The timing of his treason—less than a week after he had learned of the ayatollah's plan—made that a possibility. He had made a grave mistake entrusting Adbullahi with the ayatollah's secret. The more he thought about it, the more worried he became. Leaving the country because he feared for his life was one thing, but seeking exodus because he was a full-fledged traitor was another. Did General Adbullahi have another master? Just the consideration was enough to send Kharazi into full panic mode.

Two of the five combative cells had already been activated. They'd do what was expected of them. The Canadian component of the operation had produced results far exceeding the predictions. It had been a complete success, and the American and Canadian media weren't talking about anything else. Surprisingly, the stock markets were holding on, and Kharazi wondered if the assassination of the Canadian prime minister—a known socialist—had some investors cheering in secret. The problem was with the American side of the operation. There was a strict schedule to follow, one that required finesse and patience. General Adbullahi's treachery was forcing Kharazi to move faster than he wanted to.

But Allah was merciful. Kharazi had the most capable and lethal man of the entire armed forces of the Islamic Republic of Iran in front of him, and he would use him as such.

"Please, Colonel Davari, have a seat," Kharazi said. "I'd like to hear your thoughts on General Adbullahi."

CHAPTER 20

Tehran, Iran

Colonel Asad Davari felt awkward sitting in front of the Quds Force commanding officer. He enjoyed being in the field with his men but hated every minute he spent in the company of people like Major General Kharazi. In combat, you usually knew who were your enemies. Inside headquarters, you could only guess. Everybody had an angle, and Davari would have to learn how to play the game. And he'd have to be a quick learner. His ascension inside the elite Quds Force hadn't been spectacular. His whole career had been spent fighting Iran's many clandestine wars. Every promotion he had ever taken was so he could be a better advocate for his men to the higher echelons. Truth was, he had never expected to become a colonel. He never wanted it. He was very good at what he did but he didn't belong behind a desk. Outside the Quds Force, he was no one. But within it, he was already a legend at thirty-five. The question Major General Kharazi had asked him was dangerous. Rumor had it that the deputy commander of the Quds Force had done something to piss Kharazi off. Nevertheless, he remained Davari's superior officer, and Davari didn't find talking about another officer while he wasn't present appealing.

Colonel Davari shifted in his seat. "What do you want to know, sir?"

"Let's start with this," Kharazi said. "Did you know that General Adbullahi had deserted?"

Davari felt as if he had just been punched in the stomach. His expression must have answered Kharazi's questions because he said, "Good. You didn't know."

"Where did he go?"

"He took one of the SJ30s and headed to Greece with his family and his security detail."

"Sir, I have to ask," Colonel Davari said. "Are we one hundred percent sure he actually defected?"

"Yes, Asad, we are." Kharazi replied. "His plane took off from the VIP terminal at the Tehran-Mehrabad airport. By the time we realized this was an unauthorized flight and sent a pair of MiG-29s after it, it was too late. Secrets documents were downloaded from his office. His assistant is presently being interrogated, but I'm told she didn't know anything."

Colonel Davari was shocked. The defection of such a powerful man within the Quds Force couldn't be tolerated. The reason General Kharazi had asked for him was now apparent.

"You want me and my men to go after him," Davari stated.

"General Adbullahi knows certain things that could bring down the entire regime. An important operation is presently underway. An operation conceived by our supreme leader that will reshape the entire Middle East and bring prosperity to our nation. Adbullahi needs to be taken out immediately."

Davari stood up. "I will personally travel to Greece and bring him back here so he can face the wrath of the ayatollah."

"As much as I'd like to make an example of him, we can't allow this treason to be public. You'll take care of him and his family in Greece."

"As per your wishes, sir," Davari said. In his mind, he was already putting his team together. He'd traveled to Greece only once before so he'd have to pick his team carefully as he didn't speak the language. "Do we have any assets already in the country?"

Kharazi smiled. "No operators *per se*, I'm afraid, but there are two mid-level intelligence officers operating from the embassy who will be in position to help you. But, more importantly, one of Adbullahi's bodyguards is my son-in-law, and, like all members of my family, he wears a tracker."

Davari had to be cautious about how to ask his next question. "General Kharazi, is your son-in-law aware of General Adbullahi's treason?"

Kharazi nodded. "I suppose he is, and this is why he activated his tracker. He wants us to find him."

"Very well, sir," Davari said. "We'll bring him back safely."

"I appreciate the gesture, Colonel, but you won't. He will die in Athens. His death will help to convince the rest of the world that this attack was perpetrated by a foreign nation with hostile intentions toward Iran. Understood?"

"Yes, sir." Davari didn't care one way or the other. He had his marching orders.

CHAPTER 21

Athens, Greece

Mike Walton had been waiting at the agreed location for more than fifteen minutes when Zima finally parked the small black Audi A3 hatchback seventy-five feet away. She waved at him and he headed in her direction with his backpack and carry-on. The police had responded even quicker than anticipated and closed many of the downtown streets.

"Sorry, traffic is a bitch. Anything from Eitan?" she asked as he placed his luggage in the trunk.

Zima did a good job hiding her concern, but Mike sensed she was worried.

"Nothing yet," Mike said. There was no point lying. "Headquarters is trying to reach him."

"So we're going to the airport?"

"We have to, Zima," Mike said. "We can't stay here. Eitan knows what to do if he misses the plane."

Charles Mapother couldn't have been clearer during the initial briefing. If the hit was successful, they would have to leave Greece within the hour. The Hellenic police might not have the same resources as the FBI but they weren't clueless. With the assassination being so close to their parliament, they wouldn't take any chances. Each of them had a protocol to follow in case the initial exfiltration plan didn't work.

The traffic continued to be an issue but at least they were moving. But Mike was getting anxious. There was a lot of incriminating evidence in the car. If they were stopped, it could turn ugly fast. They couldn't reach the airport fast enough. In the back of his mind, he wondered what had happened to Eitan. The Israeli agent could take care of himself, but memories of his recent mission in Russia with his wife Lisa were reminders that there were no guarantees in the field.

The secure satellite phone rang.

"It's in the glove box," Zima told him.

Mike extended the antenna of the Iridium phone before accepting the call. Only the IMSI headquarters and the members of his team had the number.

"I'm listening."

"Any news from Eitan? We still can't reach him."

"Nothing. We're halfway to the airport. Maybe he'll join us there."

"You're not going to the airport anymore, Mike," his wife said.

"How come?" His tone of voice caused Zima to look at him.

"Not sure yet. Mapother just texted me to tell you to stay put. I'm sure he'll contact you shortly."

Mike shook his head. "That's crazy, Lisa. There's no way we're staying in Athens. We don't even know where Eitan is or if he's been compromised. The Greeks might decide to close the airport or strengthen its security at least."

"Trust me, Mike, I don't like it any more than you do. I'm just relaying Charles's message."

Damn it! Charles Mapother wasn't stupid. He knew the risks of he and Zima staying in Athens. What could force him to make such a decision? He prayed that it wasn't because of Eitan. If that was the case, and Eitan had indeed been taken, Mike would do anything to get him back. And so would Zima.

"It's Eitan, isn't it?" Zima asked, her knuckles turning white from holding the steering wheel too tightly.

"You don't know that," Mike said. "Charles has ordered us to stay put for now."

"Should I head to the safe house?"

Mike thought about it. Their support team had set up a safe house in case of an emergency. Unfortunately it was located northwest of the city while the airport was southeast. Going back meant driving through the city again. Mike wasn't ready to take the chance. He was about to suggest they find a quiet place to eat when the satellite phone came alive.

It was Charles Mapother.

"Let me first tell you that we haven't heard from Eitan directly but the police channels have lit up in the last half hour or so."

"Can you be more specific?"

"There was an exchange of gunfire in the parking garage where one of our escape vehicles was parked."

"Shit," Mike murmured. That was enough for Zima to glance at him, her eyes tight and worried.

"We all know how resourceful he is, so unless we hear something to the contrary, let's assume he's fine and following his secondary exit protocol."

"You're monitoring—" Mike started, but Mapother cut him short.

"Trust me when I say we're doing everything we can to locate him."

"We're headed back," Mike said to Zima. "Eitan needs us."

"You'll indeed head back to the city, Mike, but it isn't to render assistance to Eitan," Mapother said.

"Then for what?"

"Put me on speaker so Zima can hear me too."

Mike pressed the button and told Mapother he could speak.

"For yet unknown reasons, the deputy commander of the Iranian Quds Force and his close family fled Tehran earlier today—"

"That's General Zamyad Adbullahi," Zima said. "I know who he is."

"That's correct, Zima," Mapother said. "You've actually met him before?"

"He came to Ottawa years ago before their embassy was closed. He wasn't the deputy commander of the Quds Force then but he was high enough to warrant around-the-clock surveillance while he was in Canada. I was one of the agents on the detail."

"Can I assume you'll recognize him right away if you see him?" Mapother asked.

"Unless he's changed his appearance drastically, this shouldn't be a problem."

"Good to know," Mapother said. "Anyway, the general allegedly used one of the Quds Force SJ30s for an unsanctioned flight to Athens. He landed half an hour ago. And before you ask, yes, the intelligence is good. It came from Meir Yatom's office."

It was no secret that the MOSSAD kept a close eye on the Iranians. After all, Iran's supreme leader had publicly vowed to destroy their country. General Adbullahi was a prime target. He might have been safe and protected in Iran, but not so much anywhere else. "Who knows about this?" Mike asked.

"It's hard to know," Mapother replied. "Yatom told me he had only shared the intel with me but you know as well as I do, Mike, it doesn't mean he didn't speak to anyone else."

Mike and Zima had dealt with Yatom in the past. He and his team had been key players in Mike's father and Lisa's rescue operation. Yatom was a true spymaster and his main mission would always be the protection of the state of Israel. Mike nevertheless believed they could trust Yatom on this matter. Embedding Eitan—one of his best men—with them proved he was willing to play fair with Charles Mapother.

"What do you want us to do, Charles?" Mike asked.

"The general is on his way to the King George—"

"You've got to be kidding me," Mike said. "The place is crawling with police officers."

By now, the police must have realized the shooter had taken his shot from the sixth floor of the Grande Bretagne. And since the five-star King George hotel was right next door to the Grande Bretagne, access to the King George would be limited.

"He's too big a target to pass on, Mike," Mapother said. "You know this. Bringing him in would be a huge deal. Since he became the deputy commander of the Quds Force, I don't think he's set foot outside Iran."

"There's no way we can pull that off covertly," Zima interjected.

Mike was glad to know he wasn't the only one not sharing Mapother's enthusiasm.

"I don't think he'll resist much to be honest," Mapother said.

That surprised Mike. A man like General Adbullahi would travel with a security detail. They wouldn't let their boss out of their sight.

"You'll have to explain this one to me," Mike said.

"Shortly after his jet took off, two Iranians fighters were scrambled to intercept it. They weren't quick enough, though, and they had to turn around when General Adbullahi's plane crossed into Azerbaijan."

That could mean only one thing. Someone powerful enough to scramble two jets wanted him dead. And it looked as though they were prepared to kill everyone aboard to do so.

"I think, and Meir seems to agree, that Adbullahi wants to defect," Mapother added.

That would be something.

"Why on earth would he want to do that?"

"Who knows what's going on inside the regime? One thing I need to add, though, is the fact that another jet belonging to Quds Force left Tehran around the time Adbullahi's jet landed in Athens."

"And they're on their way here too?" Zima asked.

"That seems to be the case, yes."

"Do we know who the passengers are?" Mike asked.

"For now, we don't," Mapother admitted. "But if I had to guess, I'd say they're Quds Force."

"So if he really wants to defect, we'd better get to him before they do," Mike said.

"That would indeed be preferable, Mike," Mapother said. "Unless you want to face off against a bunch of angry Quds Force soldiers."

"Rules of engagement?" That was from Zima.

"You guys do whatever you need to," Mapother said. "I want to know why he left Iran in such a hurry."

CHAPTER 22

The White House, Washington DC

United States Secret Service Supervisory Special Agent Yash Najjar's heart was racing as he rushed into the Oval Office, gun drawn. Two more agents were on his heels and ten more would join them within the next thirty seconds.

President Muller looked up from the document he was reading. His eyes registered surprise and then became alarmed when he saw Najjar's gun.

"What's going on, Yash?"

"Forgive us, Mr. President, but you need to follow us."

One of the agents threw a bulletproof vest over the president's shoulders and secured it around his chest. When Najjar exited the Oval Office, with President Muller in tow, a contingent of heavily armed Secret Service agents formed a protective pocket around them.

White House staffers made way for the advancing men. Those who weren't fast enough were shoved aside.

"We're fifteen seconds out," Najjar said over the secured communication system.

"Elevators are green. Ready to receive," replied one of the two agents posted next to the elevators.

Najjar and the rest of this team had practiced this kind of evacuation more than a dozen times. But this time, it wasn't a drill and Najjar's sweaty forehead was a testament to how he felt about the whole situation. The Canadian prime minister had just been assassinated by one of his bodyguards.

Was President Muller next? He knew his men were thinking the same thing as they bunched up in the elevator. Was the man standing next to you a traitor? Najjar doubted it. His men were the best of the best. He knew every one of them personally. They were warriors who'd willingly take a bullet for this president. But again, he was sure Prime Minister Ducharme had felt the same way toward his protective detail.

"We're going to the PEOC?" Muller asked him.

"Yessir."

The PEOC—Presidential Emergency Operations Center—lay underground beneath the East Wing. It served as a secure communication center and shelter in case of emergencies. President Roosevelt had it built so that it could withstand a nuclear attack on Washington DC.

"What about my family?"

"I'll have an update for you shortly, Mr. President. We have teams with them as we speak."

"What happened?"

"We're not one hundred percent sure what took place, sir, but we believe Prime Minister Ducharme was assassinated."

"My God," President Muller whispered. "And his wife?"

"We're not sure of that either, sir," Najjar said. That wasn't a complete lie, but Najjar knew Justine Larivière was with her husband when Ducharme's bodyguard shot him in cold blood. There was no point letting Muller know this tidbit of information just yet. Najjar doubted Larivière was still alive, and so did his RCMP contact in Ottawa. But what was the point in sharing what was only a suspicion with the president? He'd only get anxious. No, Najjar would wait until Muller's wife was safe.

"Let me know the moment we find out, Yash," Muller insisted, as the group marched out of the elevator and into the PEOC.

"Absolutely."

"And get DNI Phillips down here as soon as possible. We need to figure out who's behind this."

CHAPTER 23

Across the Aegean Sea

It had taken Colonel Davari less than one hour to assemble his team. Out of the six Quds Force soldiers he had selected, two of them spoke Greek fluently and had already spent considerable time in-country, and all of them looked Caucasian. Davari was the only exception.

General Kharazi had insisted on a quick in-and-out, but Davari's job was to ensure that Adbullahi's death could be pinned on the Israelis, the Americans or the British. Blaming one of Iran's enemies for the assassination of a high-ranking member of its military would play perfectly into the ayatollah's plan. What the exact plan was, Davari didn't know. And he didn't care. He was a soldier, not a politician. He only needed to be given an objective. Now that he had it, he would do his absolute best to complete it. And so would his men.

Davari felt the plane change its trajectory. As if on cue, the pilot said, "We're twenty minutes out, Colonel. We're starting our descent."

Davari walked to the back of the plane where his men were seated and talking among themselves. Laptops were used to study and memorize the streets of Athens and the layout of the King George Hotel.

"Upon arrival," Davari started once he had his men's attention, "two vans will be waiting for us. The drivers are intelligence officers attached to the embassy. They will provide transportation to the King George and will wait for us until we've completed our mission."

"What kind of weapons will we have?"

Davari looked at Captain Khalil Yavari, who had asked the question. His second-in-command for the operation, Yavari was a true warrior who had spent most of his career in special operations. He was dressed in a pair of dark jeans, a blue t-shirt and a pair of gray running shoes.

"Our men were able to get their hands on C8 carbines and Sig Sauer P226s," Davari said.

"SAS weapons of choice, yes?" Yavari said.

"General Kharazi's orders are to make it look like a Western nation assassinated Adbullahi. This will help."

"Do we know where the general is, Colonel?" asked another of his men.

"One of his bodyguards has a tracker. The moment we land, we'll reconfirm his location via his tracker."

Davari looked at his watch. "By now, General Adbullahi should be on his way to his hotel. If at all possible, this is where we'll take him and his entourage out. We leave no survivors."

CHAPTER 24

Athens, Greece

Mike Walton prayed for the traffic to get lighter. They needed to reach the King George before General Adbullahi and his party. For this mission to have any chance of success, he needed to establish how many foes he and Zima would be up against. His wife Lisa had forwarded him recent pictures of the general to help him identify the Iranian since he and Zima were going to split to cover more ground.

Mike understood the necessity of returning so close to the crime scene but he hated doing so. The three of them should have been on a plane and on their way to London by now.

"My cell's ringing," Zima said. "Hold the wheel for me."

Mike complied as Zima reached inside her pocket for her smartphone. She showed the screen to Mike. It was an unknown caller.

She put the smartphone on speaker. "Who is this?"

"It's me," Eitan said. "Can you talk?"

"Yes!" It was easy to see she was relieved. "Where are you? Are you all right?"

"I'm fine but I had a close call. I'm on foot and in the clear."

Mike took a deep breath and realized he had been holding it in anticipation of Eitan's answer. He took the phone from Zima and asked, "Can you make your way to the Syntagma Square?"

"Syntagma Square? Why? Aren't you on your way to the air—"

"I'll explain later. Can you make it or not?"

"I can be there in ten minutes."

"Call me when you get there. I'll wait for you at the S2 café."

. . . .

What the hell went wrong? Why were Mike and Zima heading back to downtown, so close to where he had taken the shot? It made no sense. They should have been at the airport by now.

And I should have been on my way to the seaport. Things were not going according to plan, but that wasn't what worried Eitan. He was used to having to improvise on missions. But what about Zima? She could take care of herself, but the alpha male in him wanted her to be out of the danger zone. Out of Greece.

Zima. He had fallen hard for her. Harder than for anyone he had ever been with before. He had met her in Syria during an operation. She'd been injured, even lost one of her fingers to a sniper. He liked to think he had saved her life, but the truth was that she had opened his eyes on what life had to offer. Eitan had spent his entire adult life fighting the enemies of Israel. Never did he consider doing anything else. He always expected to die a violent death. He wasn't so sure anymore. Zima had changed his perspective. He could see himself settling down with her somewhere peaceful, far away from the war he'd been waging for the last twenty years.

Children? Wouldn't that be nice? The mere thought of being a father used to scare him. Not anymore. Last night, in a moment of passion after he had slipped into Zima's room, she had held on to him tightly as they came together. She had looked into his eyes, the way only she could, and said, "I love you."

Her work with the IMSI was important. He'd have to be blind not to see she enjoyed every minute of it. And so did he. But how long could they cheat death? A driver honked at him as he was about to cross the street. He wasn't paying enough attention to his surroundings. His head was filled with thoughts that didn't belong in the field.

Since he had lost his communication system in the car fire, he had stopped at a small shop to buy three cellphones, with fifteen prepaid minutes for each, and a pack of cigarettes. He might have been overly cautious but he didn't want to use the same phone twice. He removed the sim card from the phone he had used to call Zima and discarded it in a storm sewer. Prior to the start of the operation, he had studied the layout of the Hotel Grande Bretagne and all the streets within a half-mile radius. The closed-circuit television system in Athens was massive so he had to be careful. Chances were his actions at the crime scene had been recorded. He wouldn't be shocked if his description had been sent to the police. Since the Athens Olympic Games of 2004, the Greek authorities had relied more and more on their CCTV apparatus. Public areas like parks and transport stations were heavily monitored, and Syntagma Square was no exception. During his research, Eitan had learned that the square had been designed and constructed in the early nineteenth century and had, since its inception, been the epicenter of Greek politics. That held especially true between 2010 and 2012 when the Square was the site of mass protests during the debt crisis. As many as fifty thousand people had occupied Syntagma Square to demonstrate their opposition to the economic policies of the Greek government.

Eitan entered Syntagma Square by the southwest corner. At this time of day, the square was packed with workers waiting for their commute home, and more than a few onlookers were trying to see what had happened on Vasilissis Sofias. Eitan lit a cigarette and stopped to observe what was going on around him. The emergency lights of numerous police vehicles could be seen on the northwestern tip of the square as they blocked access to Vasilissis Sofias. Uniformed officers were going in and out of the Hotel Grande Bretagne. But so were the tourists. Surely the authorities had found the room from which Mike had taken the shot. Why the police hadn't closed the hotel, or at least ordered its guests to remain in their rooms, Eitan couldn't say.

A teenage girl bumped into him and mumbled something in Greek without taking her eyes off her smartphone. Eitan threw the remainder of his cigarette on the ground and extinguished it with his foot. As he approached the S2 café, it became apparent he wouldn't be able to sit down inside. The place was filled with students and tourists who were either unaware of what had taken place two blocks away or simply didn't care. Eitan tried to spot Mike in the crowd but couldn't. He joined the queue of patrons and waited his turn. Although it smelled as if smoking was allowed inside, a faint odor of baked bread reminded Eitan he hadn't eaten in a while. The sight of freshly made sandwiches made his stomach growl so he ordered one with his Americano.

He walked out of the café and saw Mike standing next to the exit with a coffee in hand. He gestured to Eitan to walk with him.

"Tell me what happened," Mike asked.

"I got into a firefight with a few Hellenic police officers at Alpha-Niner," he replied. "I think it was bad luck. Nothing more."

Mike stopped walking. "Please tell me you didn't kill a cop."

"Seriously? I would never do that," Eitan said, pissed that Mike would even think that was a possibility. "Shit, man, who do you think I am?"

"Sorry, I had to ask. I need to know what's going on and if the police will be looking for a cop killer anytime soon."

"One of them shot himself in the foot, though," Eitan said. "Nothing I could do about it."

"Damn it! We don't need any more heat than we've already got."

"Why aren't you and Zima gone by now?"

Mike pointed to a bench that had just been vacated by an elderly couple.

"Let's sit down for a minute and I'll bring you up to speed."

. . . .

Mike talked while Eitan ate his sandwich and drank his coffee.

"I can't believe it," Eitan said, swallowing the last of his sandwich. "I have to agree with Mapother on this. We can't miss the opportunity."

"We won't," Mike answered. "But we need to act fast and we won't proceed unless I say so. Zima is already inside the lobby of the King George. I want you to stay in the square and keep an eye on the front entrance."

Eitan nodded. Mike gave him a new cellphone and a cordless mini-headset. "It's already programmed into our channel."

Eitan put it on.

"Try reaching Zima," Mike told him.

Eitan turned the device on and said, "Zima from Eitan."

"It's nice to hear your voice, Eitan. You're five by five."

"Copy. And it's nice to hear yours too," Eitan replied, genuinely happy.

Mike touched Eitan's shoulder to get his attention.

"Depending how big is his entourage, and if his family is with him or not, I'll make the call to go in or not."

"Got it."

"Zima has the keys to the car and will drive us out of here. I'll take her place in the lobby. Whatever happens, we can only take the general. His family will be left behind."

CHAPTER 25

Athens, Greece

General Adbullahi ordered his wife and two children to climb into the second SUV with two of his five bodyguards, one of them being Sanjar Behak, General Kharazi's nephew. Adbullahi wasn't without his own resources within the Quds Force. It had taken him a little less than three months to figure out whom within his protective detail he could trust and who had pledged their loyalty to another master. Sanjar had never wavered. It was entirely possible he didn't know his own uncle was using him, but Adbullahi couldn't take the chance. In fact, he had brought Sanjar on the trip as bait, hoping it would give him a few extra hours to do what he had to.

His family wouldn't go to the King George. Adbullahi had rented a small apartment on the outskirts of Athens for them.

"I'll see you tomorrow," he said to his wife as she hurried inside the SUV. "Take care of the children."

He grabbed the elbow of Tarapore, a trustworthy member of his detail, and whispered, "You know what to do, Sayed."

The bodyguard nodded and closed the door of the vehicle. Adbullahi watched his family drive off and wondered if he'd ever see them again. He had never loved his wife the way she deserved to be loved, but he'd always been nice to her, showed her the proper amount of affection while keeping his extra-conjugal affairs to himself. She knew, of course, but he never talked about it, thus, in his mind, respecting her. He hadn't shared with his wife the reason behind their sudden departure, but she had been with him long enough to know something was wrong. Her demeanor showed him she was uncomfortable. But she was a good woman and would do what he asked of her. He wished he could spare them the dangers coming their way but he couldn't. The fighter jets that had pursued them out of Iranian airspace were proof he had to hurry. His original plan had given him twenty-four to thirty-six hours to make contact with someone from a Western intelligence agency, but he doubted that was still the case.

Adbullahi didn't see himself as a traitor. On the contrary, he was a patriot who deeply loved his country and its people. When General Kharazi had shared with him the supreme leader's plan, it had shaken him to his core. How could Kharazi not see how potentially hazardous this could be for Iran? Of course, if successful it would allow Iran to once again control its own destiny, free of the sanctions that had crumbled its economy, but was it worth the risk? Adbullahi's knees had weakened when he learned the high-ranking positions achieved by some of the sleeper cells inserted by the former supreme leader. PERIWINKLE's first and second phases worked perfectly, but if the United States were to figure out the end game, its response would be swift and deadly. When he had voiced his concerns, Kharazi had assured him that Russia would stand by Iran, effectively limiting the Americans' military options to a long, expensive and bloody war no one wanted. It was a big risk, with huge upsides, yes, but, in Adbullahi's mind, the pitfalls were even greater. The ayatollah and General Kharazi had bet everything on this, forcing Adbullahi to wonder if Iran wasn't even closer to the brink of economic collapse than he had thought.

But even if that was the case, PERIWINKLE was too much of a gamble. He couldn't in good conscience move ahead with the operation.

So here he was; in a race against time to save his country.

He trusted his protective detail but, like everything else in Iran, nothing was what it seemed. He had to be careful. The clock was ticking. His protective detail didn't know the real reason they were in Greece. Loyal to him or not, Adbullahi didn't think they would hesitate to shoot him in the head if they had any idea what he planned to do.

He climbed into the lead SUV and told his driver to take them to the hotel. He had chosen the King George because of its proximity to the Greek parliament. A kill-team would have to be much more careful there than anywhere else in Athens. It also gave him a semblance of legitimacy to anyone who'd meet him at the hotel. How long the façade would last was another story.

In the plane, he had used a secured SAT phone to reach the American embassy, hoping to talk to the CIA station chief or at least an intelligence officer who'd be bright enough to recognize the urgency of the situation. No such luck. The only person who would take his call was the consular officer on duty. Clearly, the man had had no idea who he was but had nevertheless promised to pass along the info to someone else who'd be in a position to help. If Adbullahi didn't hear from him by the time he arrived at the King George, he would call the Israelis directly. They would know who he was. The question was: Would they let him talk or send someone to kill him?

CHAPTER 26

Athens, Greece

Colonel Davari was the first out of the airplane. The vans were waiting for them on the tarmac and Davari figured the customs agents had already been bribed to stay away. One of the two van drivers exited his vehicle and trotted to Davari.

"We have the equipment secured in the van, sir. Where would you like to go?"

Davari powered up his phone and clicked on the application that would allow him to follow the bodyguard carrying the tracker. He was surprised to see the dot outside the city limits. He gestured Captain Yavari to join him while the other soldiers transferred the luggage from the plane to the vans.

"Colonel?"

Davari showed him his phone. "Looks like the general isn't going to the King George after all," he said.

"If I may, sir?" the driver said.

"Please. Anything you can tell us is welcome."

"We were ordered not to intervene and to wait for you, but my colleague and I were already in position when General Adbullahi's two-vehicle motorcade left the airport. The vehicles were SUVs that didn't belong to the embassy."

"Did you see anything else?" Captain Yavari asked.

"Not much, sir, but I know General Adbullahi was in the lead vehicle."

"You didn't follow them?" Davari asked.

The driver scratched his head. "We were told to hold our position, sir. I'm sorry."

"What are you thinking, sir?" Captain Yavari asked the colonel.

"I'm wondering if we should split our force. If we're wrong and end up in the wrong spot, we'll miss our opportunity to catch him. Am I forgetting something?" he asked his second-in-command.

Captain Yavari took a moment to think and then shook his head.

"Then it's settled. You'll take two men with you and you'll head over there," Davari said, his finger on the flashing green dot on his screen. "We stay on comms and I want a SITREP every fifteen minutes. I'll head to the King George."

The men shook hands. "Good luck, Captain."

CHAPTER 27

Athens, Greece

Eitan found a bench with good views of the King George's front entrance. The traffic had dramatically improved since the police had reopened Vasilissis Sofias to circulation. He wasn't close enough to the entrance to identify who was entering the lobby but he had no difficulty assessing the vehicles that stopped in front of the hotel.

"Mike from Eitan," he said over their comms system.

"Go for Mike."

"A black SUV with tinted windows just stopped. Three men are getting out and are heading your way. They're all wearing dark suits. They'll be in the lobby in thirty seconds."

"Roger. Stand by," Mike replied.

. . . .

Mike was impressed with the King George's spacious lobby. It was magnificent, just like the rest of the hotel. The eye-catching period furniture and chandeliers, offset by remarkable modern art, gave the lobby an attractive look that made it a great place to sit or converse. Built in 1930 and located within walking distance of the Acropolis, the King George represented the best Athens had to offer. Mike had also heard about the Tudor Hall Restaurant on the hotel's seventh floor. It supposedly had the best Greek cuisine in town, while offering gorgeous views of the Parthenon atop the Acropolis to the diners lucky enough to get a table at the upscale breakfast buffet in the morning or a candlelit dinner at night.

Mike wasn't the only one in the lobby. Four people waited in line at the check-in desk and another six were seated in various locations across the lobby. They looked like tourists, but he would keep an eye on them to gauge their reaction to General Adbullahi's arrival.

"Five seconds, Mike," Eitan said through his earpiece.

Mike scanned the lobby but nobody else seemed interested in the three men dressed in dark suits who had just entered. The three men were laughing and appeared too relaxed to be anything else than businessmen on a sales trip.

"None of them are who we're looking for, Eitan," Mike whispered in his mic.

"Could they be part of his protective detail?"

Mike took another look at the three men. They had stopped next to a coffee table where chocolate truffles were offered in a bowl. They were pigging out by stuffing the expensive chocolate in their mouths two at a time.

"No chance of—" Mike started but was interrupted by Eitan.

"Stand by, stand by," the Israeli said. "I have a possible match for Adbullahi."

Mike unconsciously sat straighter. Eitan's tone suggested this might be the real deal.

"Two Persian-looking men exited an SUV. They're scanning their surroundings. Driver is still in the vehicle."

"Copy," Mike replied, scanning the lobby once more. He spotted a man and a woman getting up from the seat they had occupied since his arrival and watched them moved toward the entrance. The man carried a backpack that seemed heavier than usual while the woman only had a map in her right hand. She was wearing a windbreaker that made it difficult for Mike to assess whether she was carrying a weapon.

"It's him, Mike," Eitan said. "Adbullahi is climbing the steps to the lobby. He has one bodyguard in front of him and two behind. Adbullahi is wearing a gray suit and his protective detail are wearing navy-blue suits."

"Got it."

The front bodyguard entered the lobby the same moment the couple was leaving. He smoothly placed himself between them and his charge and deflected their trajectory with his right arm. The bodyguard positioned behind and to the right of Adbullahi stepped forward and caught up to the general until the couple was behind them and out of the lobby. The other bodyguard, the one still behind Adbullahi, scanned behind him twice to ensure the couple didn't represent a threat.

The whole sequence was lost to everyone but Mike who was an expert in protective operations.

"They're in the lobby," Mike confirmed. He took the time to observe all the other people in the lobby, but nobody else seemed interested in the four men.

"Copy," Eitan replied.

"I copy too," came in Zima. "For your information, I found a parking spot thirty seconds out."

"Mike copy your last, Zima," Mike said before adding, "One of the bodyguards is now at the check-in counter".

It was evident Adbullahi was stressed. His eyes were shooting toward the entrance every second or so and he was speaking rapidly in Farsi to the tallest of his bodyguards. A couple of minutes later, the bodyguard who had taken care of the check-in process walked back to the general and handed him a white keycard. The men spoke together for a few more seconds before calling the elevator. Adbullahi let one member of his protection detail enter the elevator first before following him. The two other bodyguards stayed in the lobby. One of them sat in the chair next to Mike and the other took position next to the entrance.

"Status check, Mike," Eitan asked over the air.

When Mike didn't reply, Eitan tried again, "Mike, what's your status?"

Mike didn't dare to look at Adbullahi's bodyguard. Even though he knew he was the only one able to hear Eitan, it felt as if the sound coming from his earpiece was being broadcast to everyone inside the lobby.

"I'm coming in, Mike," Eitan said.

Mike got up and mumbled an apology in French. He casually walked toward the bathroom.

"Negative, Eitan, negative," Mike said the moment he was out of earshot. "Stay in your position."

"Copy," immediately replied Eitan. "Staying put."

Mike entered the bathroom and listened for any noise that would tell him he wasn't alone. When he didn't hear anything, he peeked under the stalls just to make sure.

"Two bodyguards remain in the lobby," Mike said. "One stands next to the elevator and the other sits in the lobby."

"What about the general?" Zima asked.

"Adbullahi went to his room with one bodyguard. I'll ask headquarters to find out the room number. In the meantime, stay in your positions and advise me if you see anything remotely suspicious."

Once Eitan and Zima confirmed they had understood his directive, Mike used the sat phone to call Lisa at the IMSI headquarters.

"Good to hear your voice," his wife said. "I have Charles and Jonathan next to me. What can we do to help?"

"I need to know the general's room number."

"How long ago did he check in?"

"Between four and five minutes."

"We're on it. It shouldn't take long. Is there anything else?"

"Any way of knowing if there are any other exits than the front entrance? I didn't see any that were easily accessible."

"Call us back in ten minutes," Charles Mapother replied. "We'll have the info you need."

CHAPTER 28

IMSI Headquarters
New York, New York

Lisa Walton sat in the control room looking at a blown-up map of Athens on which she could see the three blue dots representing the three IMSI assets in the field. The wall to her right was covered entirely with flat screens showing the latest closed-caption news from the United States and around the world. The IMSI had three direct-action missions running at present and had at least two analysts attached to each asset in the field. Four rows of desks accommodated the team of analysts, with state-of-the-art computers that had direct access to most of the intelligence available to the United States government. When she had joined the IMSI following the tragedy that had altered the course of her life forever, Mapother had explained to her that President Robert Muller had authorized the IMSI to gain access to such a wealth of intelligence. Very few people within the federal government were aware of this, and she knew Mapother was afraid the IMSI could be shut down the moment this became public knowledge. It was no secret that there was friction between Mapother and the Director of National Intelligence Richard Phillips over this issue.

Being in the control room wasn't as exciting as being in the field, but she felt the pressure nonetheless. Her husband's team needed info and they needed it quick.

"You want a hand?" Jonathan Sanchez asked.

"You bet," she said. He pulled over a chair and sat in front of the computer next to her.

"An analyst has already found the general's room number," Sanchez said. "He's on the second floor. His room is facing the square."

"That was fast."

"It wasn't difficult. The room was booked through an outside travel agency over a network armed with a weak encryption code. Once he was able to hack the hotel's network, he used the reservation number to find the room that had been assigned to the general."

"What about alternate exits?"

"It doesn't look promising," the former Delta operator confessed. "The other exits are used by the staff and lead either to a courtyard at the back of the hotel or to another smaller entrance just off the lobby."

That wasn't good. Even if the team was able to snatch General Adbullahi from his room on the second floor, it would be next to impossible to bring him outside the hotel without being seeing by the two bodyguards in the lobby.

The phone on her desk rang. It was Charles Mapother.

"Yes?"

"General Adbullahi contacted our embassy. He wanted to speak to the CIA station chief."

"Did he?"

"No, they needed to vet him before doing so. I called DNI Phillips the moment we caught this. I briefed him on our intentions and why we were there in the first place. We have his support."

"That's good news. I'll let Mike know."

"I doubt his protective detail know about his plan. They might not welcome Mike with open arms."

"He'll find a way, Charles. Mike always does."

CHAPTER 29

Athens, Greece

"We're two minutes out, Colonel," Captain Yavari said over their secured communication system.

"Good. Let me know what you see before moving in," replied Colonel Davari. "We're still a good ten to fifteen minutes from the King George."

"Yes, sir."

Captain Yavari looked at his smartphone. They were half a mile away from the green dot. They weren't in the countryside *per se*, but they weren't in the city either. Houses weren't as close together as those you would see in downtown Athens, but the yards remained small or nonexistent. Most buildings were two to four stories high and their white paint had started peeling long ago. Detritus was everywhere, and graffiti adorned the doors of the few businesses that were open. Cars with tires or whole axles missing had been left on the side of the road. Their broken windows were proof that thieves had already taken anything of value left behind by their owners.

Yavari adjusted the sling of his C8 carbine so that the weapon couldn't be seen by someone walking on the street. The Sig Sauer was in a shoulder hostler with two extra magazines.

"We're not in the best part of town," the driver said, hitting the brakes to avoid killing a stray dog.

"Obviously," Yavari replied, glancing at his screen once more. They were getting close. "We'll drive once by the house. Don't slow down."

Why would General Adbullahi come here? It didn't make sense to him, but who cared? The general was a traitor and would be treated as such.

"We're here," Yavari said to his men. "If I'm to trust the application, they're in one of the buildings on the left side of the road."

It was hard to know for sure which building sheltered the person with the tracker. The application was good, but not as precise as Yavari would have liked. It would have been nice to have the time to set up surveillance, but the colonel had been adamant; they had no time to lose.

"Park here," Yavari said to the driver, pointing to a large space between two abandoned vehicles. "We'll walk back."

Yavari looked at the two Quds Force members who were riding in the back of the van. They were ready. He could see the resolve in their eyes. They were pros and didn't need a pep talk, so Yavari got right to the point.

"Iman, you'll walk with me. Pistols only," he said, placing the C8 at his feet. "There's too much foot traffic for us to carry anything else."

"You want me to stay back?" asked Musa, the other soldier.

"You'll stay in the van with the driver," Yavari told him. "Iman and I will assess the situation and I'll call you if needed. If we do need you, you'll come with the C8."

Yavari then turned his attention to the driver. "You do whatever he tells you, understood?"

"Yes."

"Good. Let's go."

CHAPTER 30

Athens, Greece

It was no secret that Sanjar Behak was General Kharazi's son-in-law. Sayed Tarapore would take no pleasure in killing Sanjar. None whatsoever. But Tarapore's loyalty lay with General Adbullahi and had done so since the general had called in a favor to give Tarapore's wife access to cancer treatment. It hadn't saved her life, but at least she'd died in relative comfort. For that, Tarapore couldn't betray Adbullahi's trust. With the love of his life gone, Tarapore didn't fear reprisals. He was alone in this world. Forty-five minutes ago, he had ordered Sanjar to stay at the apartment while he and the general's family went to the grocery store to buy enough food to last a few days. It had made sense for one of them to stay behind and keep the apartment secure. While it was true they'd stopped at the grocery store, Tarapore had no intention of taking them back to the initial location. The general's wife and children were now safe in another rental property a few blocks away. The general had thought this through.

Tarapore knocked six times on the door of the apartment, waited three seconds, and knocked again four times. Sanjar opened the door and Tarapore went in.

"Close the door," Tarapore said.

"Where are the others?" Sanjar asked, closing the door and holstering his weapon.

"There's a change in plans," Tarapore replied. "The general called to let me know a car was on its way to pick up his family."

"So they're gone?"

"Yes. The car was already in the neighborhood when I got the call. It made more sense to stay at the grocery store than to come back here to wait for them."

"So what do we do?"

"We're to take the SUV and make our own way to the King George. So grab your stuff. We're leaving now."

Sanjar came back less than a minute later with his backpack.

Tarapore opened the door. "Follow me. I moved the SUV further down the road."

He led the way down the stairs and waited for Sanjar to join him.

"Go ahead," Tarapore said, pointing to the alleyway to his right. "I'll be right behind you."

Tarapore scanned around him, and once he was sure nobody was in a position to see, he drew his dagger with his right hand and drove it hilt deep into Sanjar's neck while covering his mouth with his left hand. Sanjar's body tensed as Tarapore twisted the dagger left and right. Once Sanjar's legs collapsed from under him, Tarapore went through his pockets and relieved him of his pistol and extra magazines but left the smartphone behind. Tarapore then lifted his former colleague on his shoulder and carried him to a large garbage container a few feet away.

Tarapore opened the garbage container lid, but before he could dump the body inside the container, the lid closed with a loud bang. Tarapore's eyes caught movements in a window from the building across the alleyway. If someone had seen him kill Sanjar, there was nothing he could do about it now. He briefly considered running to the apartment to take care of whoever had been behind the window but dismissed the idea. He would lose precious time, and by the time he reached the apartment, the citizen would have most probably already called the authorities.

Tarapore grunted as he struggled to keep the garbage container's lid open with his right arm while keeping Sanjar's body balanced on his left shoulder. He twisted his body to the right and bent forward, allowing the body to slide off his shoulder. The corpse landed softly on the garbage bags. Tarapore closed the lid and hurried back to the rental property where a side window offered him a perfect view of the garbage container where he had left the body, about eighty feet away.

Tarapore had promised the general's wife he'd be back and he intended to keep his word. He placed Sanjar's pistol and the two extra magazines on the coffee table next to him. He pulled the curtain halfway across the window and took a step back. There was nothing to do now but wait for the men General Kharazi had sent after his boss.

CHAPTER 31

Athens, Greece

Mike gave Mapother and the rest of the analysts the ten minutes they had requested before calling him back.

"There are no other exits you can use, Mike," Mapother said. "To be honest, and with everything that has happened in the last two hours, I'm not sure you should proceed. His protective detail will be on high alert."

Mike didn't see a clear path either. Even if he managed to gain access to the general's room, it would be impossible to leave the hotel with two bodyguards in the lobby.

Unless . . .

"I'll be fine, Charles," Mike said. "What's his room number?"

Mapother told him. "What's your plan?"

"I'll call you back once we have the general."

Mike placed his smartphone back in his pocket and switched to his local comms.

"Eitan from Mike."

"Go."

"Stay in the square. I'm going to the general's room. I'll keep my comms open so be ready to back me up."

"Roger."

"Zima copy too," added Zima. "With the traffic, I'll need two minutes to make my way to you."

"Got it," Mike said.

He exited the restroom and took the stairs to the second floor. He opened the door leading to the second-floor hallway and took a peek. At the end of the corridor was a housekeeping cart. Mike didn't see the maid but figured she'd be cleaning a room close to her cart. Seeing no one else, Mike stepped out of the staircase and casually walked to the cart. He passed General Adbullahi's room and was glad the other bodyguard wasn't standing outside the room. It would have complicated things.

Mike reached the housekeeping cart. The door to his right wasn't completely closed and rested on the security latch. He knocked on the door and pushed it open. The housekeeper was making the bed and let out a small yelp when she saw him.

"I'm so sorry, sir," she said in perfect English. "You scared me."

"No worries," Mike said, noticing the keycard attached to the retractable reel clipped to her breast pocket.

"Is this your room?" she asked, and then continued without waiting for him to reply. "They shouldn't have checked you in. I need another half hour."

"Oh, this isn't my room," Mike said. "I'm right across the hallway. I misplaced my room key and was wondering if you'd be kind enough to open it for me."

Mike flashed her the most sincere smile he could muster.

"I'm not supposed to, sir," she said. "You'll have to contact security. You can use the house phone at the end of the hallway, if you wish."

"Can you show it to me?"

"Of course," the maid replied. She seemed relieved Mike didn't push the issue. "It's just around the corner." She walked around the bed and Mike placed his back against the wall to let her through. The moment she passed him, he slipped his right arm around her neck, grabbed his left bicep with his right hand and pushed her head forward with his left hand. Mike tightened his grip and the maid went limp in a matter of seconds.

He scooped her up and placed her on the bed. He used the two bathrobe belts to tie her hands and feet. She would wake up any second and he needed something to keep her quiet. He saw two pillows on the floor. He removed the pillowcases and used one to gag her and the other to wire her mouth shut. He unclipped the keycard from her belt and stood by the door.

"Eitan from Mike."

"Go ahead, Mike."

"Any changes?"

"Negative."

"Go into the lobby and confirm the bodyguards are still there."

"Copy. On my way."

Mike figured it would take the Israeli agent about thirty seconds to walk from Syntagma Square to the King George's lobby. Mike used the time to screw the SilencerCo Osprey silencer to his Glock 19. The Osprey broke away from the traditional cylindrical design and used a modified rectangular shape, allowing the user to use the conventional sight picture without altering the firearm.

"They're here, Mike," Eitan said.

"Copy. You let me know if they move. I'll get the general."

Mike visualized what he was about to do and took two deep breaths to calm his nerves. His holster didn't allow for the Glock with the silencer screwed in so he had to peek outside the room to ensure there were no hotel guests in the hallway before heading to the general's room. He approached Adbullahi's room with his firearm at the low-ready position and was about to use the maid's keycard to enter the room when Eitan broke the air.

"Mike, the bodyguards are heading up. They're running up the stairs. They'll be on you in ten seconds."

Damn it!

Things got worse when the door to the general's room suddenly opened.

Mike didn't hesitate. Couldn't hesitate. Things weren't going down as he had planned but he had to act. The man's eyes found Mike's pistol. His right hand moved to his hip where his own weapon was holstered. Mike muzzle-punched the man in the sternum to make sure he'd fall inside the room before shooting him in the head once. The bodyguard fell backward, and Mike stepped over him. The door closed behind him and Adbullahi turned in a stupor toward him.

CHAPTER 32

Athens, Greece

General Adbullahi was starting to think it had been a mistake to flee Iran. Nobody from the CIA had gotten back to him and the call he had placed with the Israelis had been met with skepticism. The person from the Israeli embassy he had spoken to on the phone had known who he was but had nevertheless insisted on a face-to-face meeting to assess his value.

Was it a trap? He'd know soon enough. Chances were the Israelis would take him to one of their safe houses in the city. They had to be curious. It wasn't every day a general of the Quds Force wanted to defect.

"Anything?" Adbullahi asked his bodyguard.

His man was looking out the window. He shook his head. "Nothing yet."

One of the four cell phones on the nightstand rang. Adbullahi had purchased a bunch of pre-paid phones and distributed them to his security detail so they could communicate without Tehran knowing exactly where they were.

"Go outside," he ordered his bodyguard. He didn't want him to listen to the conversation that was about to take place. "And ask the others to come up. I'll brief them on what to do next."

"Yes sir," the bodyguard replied before calling his colleagues on the radio.

Adbullahi picked up the phone and walked to the window.

"Yes?"

"This is Tarapore, General. It is done."

"My wife and children?"

"They're safe. For now."

Adbullahi swallowed hard. *Allah, please keep them safe.* He looked at his watch.

"Be ready, Sayed," Adbullahi said. "They'll be coming soon."

"I know," Tarapore said. "Goodbye, General."

Adbullahi wondered if he'd see his loyal man again. Probably not. In a way, he wished he'd never see him again because it would mean Kharazi's men had taken the bait.

A popping sound followed by a loud thud made him turn around. What he saw sent a shiver down his spine. His bodyguard was sprawled on the floor. His eyes were open but there was a hole in his forehead, right above his eye. Blood was already staining the beige carpet. A man stood above his bodyguard with a silenced pistol pointed in his direction.

"Get on the ground!" the man yelled.

This was the moment of truth. "More of my men will be here in seconds," he warned, hoping this would show how committed he was.

The man nodded. "I know. Get on the ground".

Adbullahi obeyed.

CHAPTER 33

Athens, Greece

Captain Yavari consulted his smartphone for the third time in the last minute. Something was amiss. The application showed the general's nephew to be in an alleyway sandwiched between two nearly identical apartment buildings. Why would Sanjar Behak be outside the building? To conduct a reconnaissance? Were they expecting company? Or maybe, just maybe, Sanjar knew they were coming and was there to help them.

Yavari paused and let Iman catch up with him.

"He's in the alleyway right here," he said, pointing to the flashing dot on his smartphone's screen. "We're two hundred feet away. I'll lead the way."

"Yes, sir."

Yavari couldn't shake the nagging feeling that they might be walking into a trap. His eyes moved from left to right, looking for threats, but he couldn't see any. There were a few pedestrians but none of them seemed to pay attention to him and Iman. His hand moved to the butt of his Sig when he turned the corner of the alleyway where Sanjar was supposed to be.

With the exception of a dog eating from a garbage bag left open, there was no one else in the alleyway. Yavari tensed and a small knot formed in his stomach. He pulled his Sig out of its holster and walked toward the center of the alleyway while holding his smartphone in his left hand.

. . . .

Tarapore saw Captain Yavari first. He recognized him immediately since they had briefly served together a few years back. Yavari was a good officer, and Tarapore pondered if he had chosen the wrong side. What was General Adbullahi really up to? With Sanjar's corpse resting in the garbage container, it was too late to change course. Plus, he owed this much to General Adbullahi. A man—especially a high-ranking officer—willing to help a subordinate's wife without asking anything in return couldn't be that bad. Right?

Another man walked behind Yavari. Like Yavari, he was holding a pistol. Yavari had a smartphone in one hand and periodically glanced at it as he walked deeper into the alleyway. Tarapore didn't see anyone else. That didn't mean there weren't more soldiers coming after him, but he didn't have the luxury of waiting longer before engaging the man in his sight. Taropore moved closer to the window to get an angle for his first shot.

He aimed at Yavari's head just as he reached the garbage container. Tarapore's finger moved to the trigger. He wouldn't miss.

. . . .

Yavari knew nothing good would come from opening the commercial garbage container. He signaled Iman to back off in case it was rigged with explosive. Yavari knelt to look under the container when someone opened fire. The first round struck him square in the back and knocked him to the ground. The second tore through his left calf, shattering his tibia and ripping flesh. Yavari yelled in pain. He heard more gunshots then felt someone—Iman?—roll him onto his back.

Yavari tried to speak but only managed to spit blood. Iman was yelling into his comms system for Musa to come over. Yavari felt as if he was drowning. But how could he be? There was no water around. Breathing became impossible and his body started to shake uncontrollably.

. . . .

Tarapore's first and second shots hit their intended target. He adjusted his aim but had to break contact when two bullets hit the window frame inches from his face. Two more followed half a second later. Tarapore left his position and rushed to the exit door. He ran down the stairs and landed on the sidewalk less than twenty seconds after the start of the gunfight. He had to finish this. Tarapore negotiated the corner leading to the alleyway by "slicing the pie." The man who had fired back at him was trying to drag Yavari out of the danger zone. Unfortunately for him, he had to holster his weapon to do so. The man must have sensed someone moving behind him because he suddenly dropped Yavari and turned on his heel with his weapon magically appearing in his hands. Before he could fire, Tarapore double tapped him in the chest. The soldier flew backward and landed on top of Yavari. Weapon extended in front of him, Tarapore advanced toward the downed Quds Force soldiers. He kicked the man's pistol away before shooting him again in the head. Yavari was still alive and Tarapore took a knee next to him.

. . . .

Yavari was drifting in and out of consciousness. His last memory was of being dragged by Iman. But when he opened his eyes, he saw someone else. He had seen the man before but couldn't remember exactly who he was. One thing was certain; he was one of General Adbullahi's men.

"Sir, my name is Sayed Tarapore," said the man. "How many of you are in Athens? And why are you here? What did General Adbullahi do?"

Yes. Sayed Tarapore. He remembered now. Yavari didn't even try to respond. Breathing was difficult and painful enough without speaking. Did Sayed know he was helping a traitor? Yavari heard police sirens. He had heard them before but now they seemed closer. Tarapore must have heard them too because he looked behind him.

. . . .

I knew there were more than two, thought Tarapore as the soldier that had appeared behind him holding a C8 carbine opened fired. At this distance, he would have been hard pressed to miss. And he didn't. Bullets slammed into Tarapore's torso, killing him instantly.

CHAPTER 34

Athens, Greece

Mike heard the lock mechanism cycling behind him. He pivoted in the direction of the door just as it opened. The first bodyguard stopped dead in his track when he saw his colleague's body sprawled on the floor. He then looked at Mike who shot him in the head. The second bodyguard ducked back into the corridor before Mike could fire again.

. . . .

Eitan charged the stairs two by two.

"I'm on the second floor, Mike," he said, his heart racing.

He turned the corner in time to see one of the bodyguards step outside the room and reach for his firearm. Eitan already had his pistol out and pointed at the man's center of mass.

"Hands up, hands up," Eitan yelled, not wanting to fire his unsuppressed pistol without having to.

The man turned his head toward him and seemed to hesitate for a fraction of a second before pulling his pistol out. Eitan fired twice. His two rounds found their marks and the man fell to his side.

Shit!

"It's me, Mike," Eitan said, announcing his arrival. "Coming in."

When he entered the room, Mike was already on top of the general.

"Do you have a pair of zip ties?" Mike asked.

Eitan looked around the room. There were two dead bodyguards, not counting the one he had killed in the corridor. Within minutes, the place would be crawling with cops.

. . . .

"Goddamnit, Eitan," Mike said, "do you have a pair of zip ties or not?"

Eitan reached into his side pocket and threw him a pair. "Sorry. We need to go, Mike."

"Call Zima and tell her to meet us in front."

While Eitan did just that, Mike secured Adbullahi's hands.

"We're here for you, General. The Athens station chief sent us," Mike lied. "Our orders couldn't be clearer. You either come with us or you die right here. It's your choice."

"I'll come with you. But we need to stop for my family."

"Where are they?" Mike asked.

"Everything you need is in my briefcase," Adbullahi said. He turned his head toward the work desk. "It's right there."

"Get the briefcase, Eitan," Mike said. Then to the general, "We'll get your family but we need to get out of here first."

"I won't fight you but we have to hurry," Adbullahi pleaded. "The head of the Quds Force knows where I am and he sent men after me and my family."

A strident noise suddenly filled the air. *Fire alarm.*

Mike grabbed the general. "Get up." He said to Eitan, "Walk behind him. If he does anything stupid, shoot him."

"Zima from Mike," he said on the radio.

"Go."

"What's your ETA?"

"I'm here now. But the cops are too," Zima said. "People are pouring out of the hotel. There are only four of them now and they can't handle the crowd. If you come out now, you might have a chance."

He looked at Eitan who gave him a thumbs-up to let him know he had understood. Mike removed the silencer and put it in his pocket. There was no need for it anymore. Mike was the first out of the room. Half a dozen people were hurrying down the corridor toward the emergency staircase. The staircase was full of people and it took longer than expected to reach the lobby. Hotel employees were urging the guests to exit the premises. Mike spotted two police officers positioned next to the exit. Their sidearms were holstered, but one of them was holding a piece of paper.

If General Adbullahi wanted to screw them over, he'd do it now. Mike glanced at the officers and was relieved to see they were wearing body armor. If the shit hit the fan, he and Eitan could fire at the officers without killing them. It was certainly not the way he hoped it would go down, but he'd do whatever needed to be done to bring General Adbullahi back to the United States. The lobby was filling up quickly, with more guests pouring out of the emergency staircase. They were less than twenty feet from the exit and Mike could see Zima through the glass door. She had parked the car perpendicular to the entrance with the front of the car pointing toward the street.

Movement to his left caught Mike's eyes. One of the officers was reaching across the crowd, yelling at someone behind Mike to stop. That was when Mike saw what was on the sheet of paper. It was a sketch of a man's face.

Eitan's.

. . . .

Eitan took half a second to assess the tall police officer yelling at him but didn't make eye contact. The officer was using his elbow to make his way through the thick crowd while keeping his free hand on the butt of his pistol. The fact that he didn't have his pistol out told Eitan there was a chance the officer wasn't yet sure he had the right man. Eitan would use that to his advantage.

"You," the officer said. "Stop."

The moment the officer placed his beefy hand on Eitan's shoulder, Eitan clutched the officer's little finger with his thumb and brought the knuckles of his index finger over the second joint of the officer's finger. He then moved his wrist in a circular motion toward the floor as he applied pressure. The officer went down to his knees to avoid getting his finger broken. Eitan struck him in the face with his knee before the officer's other hand reached his gun. The officer's hand shot to his face but Eitan wasn't done. He kneed him again, this time just below the jaw. The officer fell to his side.

Eitan didn't waste time. He needed to move quickly. The other officer had seen her partner go down. Eitan was on her in five strides, but the officer had her weapon drawn. Her eyes were wide open and the fear of missing her shot and hitting a bystander made her hesitate long enough for Eitan to deflect her weapon toward the ceiling. Eitan kicked the inside of the officer's leg, and then easily twisted the pistol out of her hands before kicking her again, this time in the solar plexus. The female cop staggered backward and tripped over a large oriental mat.

Eitan exited the hotel and ran to the waiting car. Mike was already in the back with General Adbullahi. Eitan also climbed in the back, sandwiching the general. Zima accelerated away before Eitan could fully close the door.

"Thanks for waiting," Eitan said, looking through the rear window. The female cop was now outside but he didn't think she had seen him get into the Audi.

They were in the clear.

CHAPTER 35

Athens, Greece

Colonel Davari was furious. He had lost men in combat before but he hadn't expected to take any casualties on this mission. General Adbullahi had played them all.

"Get out of there, Musa," Davari told the only surviving member of Captain Yavari's team. "Go to the safe house and call me back once you're there."

Davari slammed the dashboard with his fist. He wasn't one to easily lose control but he had just lost two good men. It pissed him off no end. He'd get his revenge.

"Sir," the driver said, "there seems to be a commotion at the King George."

"Pull over here," Davari told him, pointing to a parking space reserved for tour buses. They were in front of the Greek parliament and had an unobstructed view of the King George.

Davari looked through his binoculars to see what was going on. Hotel guests from the King George and the Grande Bretagne were exiting through all the available doors. Even though they were still some distance away, Davari could hear the fire alarm in the background. Did it have anything to do with the general? In the back of his mind, he knew it did.

"Are there any other exits?" Davari asked.

The driver knew the answer. "I'm afraid not, sir. These are the only ins and outs someone could use to escape. The other exits only lead to a small courtyard at the back of the hotel."

Raham Vevai, his most experience assaulter, confirmed this seconds later after consulting his smartphone. "That's correct, Colonel. If our target is still inside, and he decides to come out, he'll have no choice but to use the main—"

"I see him," Davari said, interrupting his man. "He's exiting the King George. He's wearing a gray suit."

Are his hands behind his back? And where's the rest of his protective detail? So many people were exiting the two hotels that it was challenging to determine whether Adbullahi was alone. He seemed to follow a Caucasian male. The man wasn't tall—less than six foot—but his head was on a swivel, scanning left and right, his movements light and precise. Davari had found his enemy. He grabbed the camera. He wanted to identify whom he was dealing with. There was no point attacking them now with so many witnesses around.

"He's climbing into a black Audi," Davari said, unable to snap a picture of the man walking with Adbullahi. *Why aren't they leaving? They're waiting for someone else.* He got his answer when another man came down running the steps and climbed into the backseat of the Audi. This time Davari was ready. He took many pictures of the second man. The Audi accelerated away and passed in front of the Grand Bretagne, less than two hundred feet away from their van.

"Follow the Audi," Davari ordered the driver. He removed the sim card from the camera and put it in his pocket. He inserted a new one and made sure the camera was off. He had no spare batteries.

Davari turned to his men and said, "Get ready. We'll take them as soon as we get the opportunity."

CHAPTER 36

Athens, Greece

Mike dialed Charles Mapother's number on the Iridium SAT phone.

"For the love of God, Mike, what's going on?" Mapother said. "The Hellenic police are reporting shots fired at the King George."

"We have the general," Mike said. "We're thirty to forty-five minutes away from the airport."

"You have him?"

"That's what I said."

"Did he resist in any way?"

"Not really. But we had to take out his protective detail. And Charles, he wants us to get his family."

"We've discussed this before. We can't."

"Roger that. I'll call you back."

The general stirred in his seat. "Do you really have to cuff me? The zip tie is cutting through my skin."

Mike placed his hand behind the general's back and asked him to move forward. He retrieved his Gerber Ghostrike tactical knife from his ankle sheath and used it to cut through the zip tie.

"Thank you," Adbullahi said, massaging his wrists. "If you didn't lie about getting my family out of here, I'll tell you where to find them."

Mike locked eyes with Adbullahi. "C'mon, General. You know how this works. You'll have to give us something first."

"Is being here in Athens not enough? I'm the deputy commander of the Quds Force. I'm the biggest fish you ever caught."

"I couldn't care less about you, General. As far as I'm concerned, you're a terrorist."

Adbullahi took a deep breath, and then said, "The Canadian agent that killed the prime minister is one of ours. And there are many more like him."

Mike felt as if he had just been hit by a bus.

He's lying. He has to be. But the general didn't flinch.

Mike had served with the RCMP prime minister's protective detail years ago. His father, Ray Powell, had been its commanding officer before being named Canadian ambassador to Algeria.

"If you don't get my family, General Kharazi will execute them," Adbullahi continued. "And then you'll never get anything from me."

Mike grabbed Adbullahi by the back of his neck and squeezed. "You're lying."

Adbullahi grimaced in pain. "It's the truth. What do I have to lose? Why would I lie?"

Mike's head was spinning. Could it be an elaborate plot? It seemed far-fetched, even for the Iranians.

"If I find out you lied to me, I'll personally see that your family is sent back to Tehran."

"Guys," Zima called out from the driver's seat. "We're being followed by a dark van. It's a few cars behind."

"Are you sure?" Eitan asked, twisting in his seat to get a better look.

"Yes, I'm sure, Eitan, and they're making a move," Zima said, her voice pitching higher.

Mike looked out the window too. The van was indeed making a move.

"It's the kill-team Kharazi sent after me," General Adbullahi said. "I'm sure of it."

The Iranian looked terrified. That told Mike there was a possibility he was telling truth. If that was the case, he had to take him back to the IMSI headquarters. Whatever the cost.

. . . He's one of ours . . . There are many more like him . . .

The traffic was getting heavier. If these men were indeed Quds Force commandos sent by General Kharazi, they couldn't afford to be trapped on this road. They'd be sitting ducks.

"Take the next exit, Zima," Mike said. "We need to create some distance."

Mike was dialing Mapother's number when the first bullet smashed through the rear window.

. . . .

Colonel Davari half expected his first shot to miss. They were still traveling at over thirty miles per hour and the road wasn't the smoothest. Even more problematic was the fact he had to shoot through the van's windshield. He planted one foot against the dashboard and trained his sights on the Audi.

His objective was to disable the vehicle either by killing its driver or by shooting at its engine block. Once it was immobilized, the rest of his team would move in and ensure all the occupants were killed. They would then take the next exit, and take advantage of the monster traffic jam that was sure to result to drive to the safe house where they would reconnect with Musa. Depending on the fallout their aggressive actions generated from the Greek authorities, they would either fly back to Tehran the next day or wait it out for a week or two.

Davari moved his sights to the driver. *It's a female. Mossad?* He pulled the trigger the same moment his driver was forced to hit the brakes. His round missed its intended target and instead shattered the rear window of the Audi. With his ears ringing, Davari continued to pump round after round at the Audi. He had emptied half of his magazine before he realized someone was returning fire.

. . . .

The bullet that had shattered the rear window had also grazed General Adbullahi's neck. It was a superficial wound but it was bleeding profusely, and by the incoherent Persian curses coming out of Adbullahi's mouth, it was painful too.

"Get us out of here, Zima!" Mike yelled. He tried to turn around in his seat but he was stuck between the door and the general.

"Move to the front, goddamnit!" he said to the general.

Eitan had started to engage the van with his pistol but the rounds kept coming in.

Mike was angry with the general for not moving fast enough. The thumping of bullets hitting the car's metal frame didn't help his mood.

"Reloading!" Eitan said.

Mike unbuckled his seatbelt and pushed the general out of the way. The van was two hundred feet away and gaining rapidly. With Zima zigzagging between vehicles, it was hard to get a shot off. Mike fired five rounds in quick succession but to seemingly no effect. The van kept coming.

"Hang on," Zima said as she made a sharp left toward the exit.

Eitan was thrown into Mike who, in turn, was shoved into the door. Before they could recover and reengage the threat, a hail of bullets smashed into the car, shredding its front left tire to pieces. Zima yelled a warning as she lost control of the Audi and smashed it into a low cement wall.

. . . .

Davari felt a bullet zap past his head, followed by the sound of metal hitting flesh. Davari fought the urge to look back as he concentrated on his next volley. The Audi suddenly veered left, offering Davari a perfect shot as it passed between two cars. He squeezed the trigger and didn't let go until his magazine was empty. A second later, the Audi hit a cement wall and came to an abrupt stop.

The driver hit the brakes hard and the van stopped in the middle of the road about one hundred and fifty feet from the crashed Audi. The van was immediately rammed by another vehicle and thrown sideways, rotating one hundred and eighty degrees.

Davari looked behind him to assess the damage. Raham was holding his stomach. Blood came out from between his fingers.

"Can you fight?" Davari asked him.

Raham's skin had turned pale but he nodded. He fumbled with his seatbelt, allowing Davari to take a closer look at his wound.

"Stay in the van, Raham," Davari ordered.

He ejected the spent magazine and inserted a fresh one. "You two, come with me. We'll make sure there are no survivors," he said to the two remaining Quds Force soldiers.

They climbed out of the van with their weapons aimed in the general direction of the Audi. Unfortunately, the vehicle was shielded by another car that had stopped to render assistance.

Davari was halfway out of the van when he said to his driver, "Find us another vehicle. I want to be out of here in sixty seconds."

"Yes, sir," the driver said.

Davari turned his attention to the remaining two Quds Force soldiers who were advancing toward the Audi. His men were well trained and had seen combat before, but they were too close to each other.

"Spread out," Davari yelled at them as they cornered the Good Samaritan's vehicle. He was a quarter of a second too late.

. . . .

Mike opened his eyes. What had happened? He was between Zima and General Adbullahi. He had been thrown backward when the car crashed. The air bags had deployed on impact and had apparently done their job. At least for Zima. She seemed all right albeit with a bloody nose. She was cutting at her seat belt with her combat knife. He turned his head. The general wasn't moving and his legs were stuck under the dashboard.

Not good.

Eitan was sprawled with half his body on the rear seat and the other half on the floor. He was breathing and appeared to be regaining consciousness. The few windows that had survived the gunfight had all shattered when the Audi hit the wall.

Mike was still assessing his own condition when Zima started shooting.

"They're coming, Mike," she warned him.

Mike frantically looked for his pistol. When he couldn't immediately locate it, he filched Eitan's. It had strangely remained in his hand. Mike got in position and saw that Zima's fire had been accurate. One man was down clutching his leg while the other was doing his best to drag him out of the line of fire. Mike aimed at the man's center of mass and fired. His round hit the man on his right side and spun him around. Another round fired by Zima struck him in the back a millisecond later.

. . . .

Davari watched in horror as his two men fell. They were still alive and one of them stretched his hand toward him.

Shit! Davari rushed to their assistance as rounds continued to hit the pavement close by. He took cover behind the rear left wheel of a car. His men were less than fifty feet away. He crawled to the front of the car, hoping to get some cover from the engine block. Police sirens were wailing close by. Davari was almost out of time. He had to make a move. He got up, but small arms fire forced him to seek refuge once again.

One of his men had stopped moving while the other was using his good leg to push himself to safety. He was less than twenty feet from Davari's position when he was struck again.

No!

For the next three seconds, the enemy fire seemed to intensify, forcing him to stay under cover. There was only one reason this was happening. They were covering their withdrawal. The moment the shooting stopped, Davari got up and brought his rifle to bear. A man had taken position behind the crashed Audi and was in the process of reloading his firearm. Another one was running away, carrying someone on his shoulder. *General Adbullahi?* A dark hair woman followed a few steps behind.

Davari fired two rounds at the man behind the Audi before switching his fire at the escaping trio.

. . . .

"Eitan, Eitan," Mike screamed, shaking the Israeli back to his senses. "We need to go."

"Where's my gun?" Eitan uttered, spitting blood as he spoke.

Mike firmly placed the pistol in Eitan's hand and said, "Keep their heads down. I'll get the general. We'll leapfrog out of here."

Mike tried to open the door, but it was jammed. He kicked away the few pieces of window still in place and crawled out of the car. He landed on his hands with pieces of glass cutting his skin. He ignored the pain and reached inside the passenger seat as Zima and Eitan continued to shoot at the Iranians. He grabbed the general by the shoulders and pulled him out of the car. He hoisted him up in a fireman's carry and was already a good forty feet away when he heard a rifle opening up.

The next second, Mike was propelled to the ground. He fell face first and felt the general's body roll over his neck and head. Zima had placed herself between him and the shooter and was returning fire with her pistol while Eitan—in a half-crouch—sprinted toward them. The general moaned. Mike examined him and found an entry wound in his lower back. Mike flipped him around. The general grimaced.

"Get . . . Get . . ." he mumbled.

"We'll get your family," Mike told him, even though he had no idea how. "Did you tell me the truth about the Canadian assassin being yours?"

The general's face had grown pale, his eyes red and unfocused. His mouth was distorted and twitching. The man was dying. Mike grabbed his hair.

"You want us to take care of your family? Talk."

"It's all . . . It's all . . . the briefcase," Adbullahi managed to say before he took his last breath.

Damn it! The briefcase had stayed in the car.

"We need the briefcase," he said to Eitan who had just taken a knee next to him.

Without waiting for a reply, Mike dashed back to the car.

. . . .

Davari watched in satisfaction as the man carrying the general fell. But before he could pump more rounds at him, he started taking fire from the female operative and ducked back behind cover. Two Hellenic police cars came to an abrupt stop next to the van. They were immediately engaged by Raham and the driver. One more police car arrived, and its two occupants joined their colleagues in the fight. Seeing that his men were about to be overrun, Davari took aim at the closest officer and fired. The officer was hit in the chest and dropped on the spot. Davari moved his sights to the next officer and dropped him with a double tap in his center of mass. It didn't matter that the officers were wearing bulletproof vests; the C8 rounds easily punched through their Kevlar.

Raham succeeded in taking another of the officers down before being hit again. He stumbled backward as more rounds hit him. Davari found the shooter, adjusted his aim, and then fired once. The cop's head split in two as the bullet struck him right below his left eye. Seeing the carnage around them, the other officers took cover and Davari seized the moment to glance back toward the Audi.

They had all vanished. His only solace was the sight of General Adbullahi's corpse.

CHAPTER 37

Athens, Greece

Mike led the way through the small alley. They had holstered their weapons. They needed to get out sight. The odds that someone saw them run away from the battleground were high. Mike had no choice but to consider that a police report with their descriptions had already been issued. And it was hard to blend in when one had blood all over his clothes.

They were the only ones outside. The gunfight's cacophony had forced the shopkeepers to close their doors and the citizens to seek refuge anywhere they could. He gave Zima the briefcase he had risked his life to retrieve from the Audi.

"I need to call James."

Mike punched James Cooper's number on the SAT phone.

"I'm listening, Mike," the Support Six leader said.

"Can you locate me with the SAT phone's signal?"

"It's gonna take a minute but yes, I can. What do you need?"

"Another safe house. And we need it now, James."

"Anything else?"

"No."

"I'll call you back in two minutes."

Three police cars sped past them with sirens blaring. They needed to put some distance between them and the crime scene. The moment the police had the scene secured, they would start asking questions. They had to be gone by then. Mike spotted a small white Fiat Punto parked between two larger vans.

"We'll take the Fiat," Mike said. "You guys cover me while I hot-wire it."

There were still no other pedestrians in sight. Mike tried the door but it was locked. He was about to smash it with the butt of his pistol when he noticed the door-lock pull pin on the passenger door was up. He crossed to the other side and opened the door.

It had been a while since he had hotwired a car, but this was why he had chosen an older model vehicle. They were much easier to steal—when you didn't have the proper equipment—than the newer ones. If you tried to hotwire one of the newer models without being familiar with its quirks, you were likely to end up not only setting off the alarm but also the lock attached to the starter.

Mike removed the plastic cover under the steering column. A coil of electrical wires appeared. The trick was to recognize the right bundle. He took half a minute to differentiate the wires leading to the lights and other dashboard indicators from those leading to the ignition and starter. Mike used his knife to strip about an inch of insulation from all the wires. He twisted the battery wire to the ignition wire. The dash lights came on and the radio started blasting dance music. Mike jumped and knocked the back of his head on the steering.

He turned off the radio but it was too late. Alerted by the music, the car owner walked out of the restaurant to investigate. He became alarmed when he noticed his car door was opened. His eyes then moved to Eitan. The man must have spotted the blood on Eitan's shirt and realized he had walked in on something he shouldn't have because he immediately raised his hands.

Mike let Eitan handle the situation and got back to work. He grabbed the starter wire he had stripped earlier and touched its end with the battery wires. The engine started and Mike used his right hand to rev the engine a few times. Once he was sure it wouldn't stall, he cranked the wheel hard left and right until the steering lock broke.

He rolled the driver side window down and yelled at Zima and Eitan to jump in. The car owner was nowhere to be found.

"What did you do with the car owner?" Mike asked Eitan once he had taken his seat in the back of the car.

"I gave him seven hundred euros," Eitan said.

"You did what?"

"It wasn't worth that much, in my opinion. Please let me know what forms I need to fill in to get reimbursed," Eitan joked.

Before Mike could reply, the SAT phone rang. It was James Cooper. Mike threw the phone into Zima's lap.

"Talk to him and tell me where to go."

CHAPTER 38

Athens, Greece

Colonel Davari was running for his life. The police had killed the embassy driver and were now after him. He had no idea where he was but he felt trapped. He needed a place to hide. He had left his rifle at the scene. It was too cumbersome to carry while trying to blend in. He thanked Allah for not getting shot in the back as he jumped the cement wall bordering the road where the firefight took place. He sprinted across the road and ran as fast as he could for nearly three minutes before he was nearly hit by a speeding car. Fortunately for Davari, the drive managed to brake and swerve out of the way at the last second but lost control and bumped into a parked car, nicking its side mirror in the process. He climbed out of his vehicle, throwing a bunch of insults at Davari.

It was obvious the man wanted a fight and Davari was glad to oblige. He let the man throw the first punch. Davari bent his knees and lowered his body just as the driver threw a left-hand jab. Davari counter-jabbed him straight into the solar plexus and followed it up with a hard left cross to the chin. The man fell to his knees and Davari finished him with a savage elbow strike to the head.

Davari looked in the man's pockets for the key before realizing the car was still running. A couple of bystanders had seen what had happened but Davari didn't care.

He accelerated away and called Musa.

"I tried to call you numerous times, sir—" started the Quds Force soldier.

"Are you at the safe house?" interrupted Davari.

"Yes, sir."

"We ran into problems. I'm on my own. We'll regroup at the safe house and figure a way out of here."

"The others?"

"All dead. I'll be there in less than fifteen minutes."

"I'll be ready."

Davari entered the address in his smartphone and followed the directions to the safe house. Had they been successful? Had they killed General Adbullahi before he passed along the intelligence to their enemies? Davari had no way to know. With most of his team dead, he sure hoped they had succeeded. But one way or the other, he'd find out who had helped Adbullahi. His gut feeling was that it was the damned Israelis.

Again.

He would track them and he would kill them. Just as he had done so many times in the past. He didn't care where his quest led him. People were going to die.

But for now, he had a call to make.

CHAPTER 39

Tehran, Iran

General Kharazi, commanding officer of the Quds Force, feared only one man. And that man had just summoned him. The supreme leader Ayatollah Bhansali wasn't someone you said no to. The debacle in Greece was on every Europeans news channel. This and the assassination of the Canadian prime minister seemed to be the only things worth reporting. The ayatollah had seen it too. Officially, the authorities had no suspect. General Kharazi had called the Iranian ambassador to Greece to let him know what to do. It was imperative that the local news channel didn't mention any Iranian involvement, and the ambassador was given permission to blackmail prominent Greek journalists and politicians to ensure it stayed that way.

A knock on his door told him the car the ayatollah had sent for him had arrived. He didn't look forward to his meeting with the supreme leader. His numerous attempts to reach Colonel Davari had failed, and he feared that his new deputy had been killed in action. His death was better than the alternative. Capture would have been worse.

Much worse.

Another knock at the door angered him. "I'll be there in a minute," he yelled.

He was surprised to see a lieutenant enter his office without being invited. The young officer looked terrified as he stood at attention twenty steps away from Kharazi's desk.

"What is it?" Kharazi barked at him.

"Colonel Davari has made contact, General," the lieutenant said, looking straight ahead.

Kharazi jumped to his feet. "Lead the way."

. . . .

General Kharazi followed the lieutenant into the elevator that would take them to the sub-basement communication room. He didn't like to keep Ayatollah Bhansali waiting but talking to Davari had to be his priority. It took less than a minute for the elevator to descend. The door opened automatically, and Kharazi entered the room where most of Iran's secret communications took place. There were over one hundred communication and intelligence specialists seated in front of their screens.

Colonel Mirzaei, the senior Quds Force duty officer, welcomed General Kharazi.

"Sergeant Musa Mariwala contacted us via secure email a few minutes ago, sir," Mirzaei said. "He said Colonel Davari was on his way to his location. It seems that Sergeant Mariwala is the only one left with Colonel Davari."

"They're the only ones left?"

"Yes, General. The others were killed, including the embassy's driver."

At least Davari hadn't been captured. "I want to talk to him."

"He wanted to talk to you too. That's why I've asked Sergeant Mariwala to contact us again in exactly—" the colonel looked at his watch "—eight minutes. Even though he's using a secured network, I prefer to keep all communications short."

"What do we know so far?" Kharazi asked.

"We know that General Adbullahi had split his forces in two once he got to Athens. Colonel Davari did the same and sent Captain Yavari and two other men after the beacon while he and the rest of his team went on to the King George."

General Kharazi accepted a cup of coffee from one of Colonel Mirzaei's staff. He nodded his thanks. "What else," he asked after taking a sip of the hot liquid.

"For a yet unknown reason, General Adbullahi came out of the King George accompanied by people we've never seen before."

"How many were they?"

"You'll have to ask Colonel Davari, sir. I don't know."

"What happened next?"

"They followed the general for a while and decided to strike once they were on the highway—"

"What I really want to know, Colonel, is this: Is General Adbullahi dead?"

"Yes, sir, he is."

At last something that will please the ayatollah.

"What about the general's protective detail?" Kharazi inquired, thinking about his son-in-law.

"Colonel Davari confirmed that at least one of them was killed by his men. A third one, Sergeant Sanjar Behak, was already dead upon the arrival of Sergeant Musa Mariwala, the only other survivor of Colonel Davari's team."

That meant that whoever had captured Adbullahi had also taken care of the rest of his protective detail. Kharazi didn't think *captured* was the right word to describe what had happened as that would mean the general had fought back. Which was obviously not the case here. An unknown enemy had *rescued* Adbullahi. That was more like it.

"Colonel," the lieutenant said, holding a phone in his hand," it's Colonel Davari."

CHAPTER 40

Athens, Greece

Colonel Davari ditched the stolen car six blocks away from the safe house. He thought about setting it on fire but it would only draw attention. Instead, he left the doors unlocked and the ignition key on the dash. He had briefed Sergeant Mariwala on what to say to General Kharazi in case he didn't make it to the safe house. He had asked him to send him a preliminary report.

The safe house was a second-floor apartment located in Kolonaki, an Athenian neighborhood close to the city center. Once regarded as one of Athens swankiest places, it had become an area filled with artists and wannabe writers once too much traffic and polluted air began to tarnish its high-class image. But its restaurants and small cafes were full and the nice boutiques that had taken over the ground-floor apartments were attracting many shoppers, which was great news for Davari who was trying to disappear in the crowd.

The door to the apartment opened before Davari even reached it. Sergeant Musa Mariwala was waiting for him, a Sig Sauer in his right hand.

"Glad you made it, Colonel," Musa said. "Come in."

The apartment was small but adequate. A large window faced Xenokratous Street from which plenty of sunlight entered the living room.

"I've prepared a small meal for you, sir," Musa said.

Davari followed his subordinate to the kitchen where a plate of miniature pita breads, humus and fresh vegetables was waiting for him on the counter with a bottle of water.

“Thanks, Musa,” Davari said, tapping the younger man on the shoulder. He drank half the bottle of water in one gulp.

“Do we have comms with headquarters?” Davari asked between two bites of bread.

“Yes, I was able to send an email out. But I’m not sure how secure it is.”

“It doesn’t matter. We needed to give General Kharazi a situation report.”

“Give me your phone, sir,” Musa said.

Davari did and Musa plugged it into a laptop.

“The risk of electronic eavesdropping is lower if we go through the computer’s secure network.”

Musa handed the phone back to Davari with the USB cord still attached to the laptop.

“Any way we can use the laptop to send photographs to headquarters?”

“That’s easy. Do you have a memory card?”

Davari fetched it from his pocket and showed it to Musa.

“I need to know who the man in these pictures is,” Davari said.

“They’ll have the pictures within two minutes, sir,” Musa replied. “You’re on speaker and patched through to headquarters.”

. . . .

Davari spent the next four minutes explaining to General Kharazi what had happened.

“I’m sorry for the loss of your men, Colonel,” Kharazi said. “But they didn’t die in vain. Mission accomplished.”

“That is only true if the general didn’t transmit the intelligence to whoever helped him.”

“Right. Who do you think helped Adbullahi?”

“If I had to guess, sir, I’d say the Israelis.”

Kharazi cursed. Then the general said, “I had a feeling it was them. These damn Jews need to be taught a lesson, and I think I know how to do it.”

Davari was curious but Kharazi wouldn’t share anything with him until he was back in Tehran, so he said, “I’d like to be part of any mission against Israeli interests.”

When Kharazi didn't reply, Davari asked, "Sir?"

"Stand by one second," Kharazi said.

Davari looked in Musa's direction. He shrugged. He didn't know what was going on with the general either.

"It was the Israelis."

"Sir?" Davari repeated.

"It didn't take long. We've identified the man on the pictures you forwarded to us as an Israeli agent. We don't know his name, but he works for Meir Yatom."

Davari clenched his fists. He knew who Meir Yatom was. He was head of the Special Operations Division of the MOSSAD. He was a legend within his organization. The Quds Force had tried numerous times to assassinate him using Hezbollah thugs but to no avail.

"We need to find out what Adbullahi told him," Kharazi said.

"I couldn't agree more."

"I've instructed our ambassador to facilitate your transport out of Greece, Colonel. Your services are needed elsewhere."

CHAPTER 41

Mossad Headquarters, Israel

Meir Yatom drummed his fingers on his desk. He had been in this business for more than thirty years but the anxiety remained. Every time he had agents in the field, he couldn't sleep. That meant he didn't sleep much. His wife had left him a long time ago and he hadn't talked to his daughter since she had called him two years ago to announce the birth of his first grandchild. He had promised her he'd visit soon but never did. He devoted his life to the security of Israel. It had cost him dearly. His health, his mood and his family had suffered too. But he believed in his work, and in his team. That's why he was eager to hear back from Eitan.

Mapother had told him his team and Eitan were still in Greece. Yatom didn't like this at all. He wouldn't close an eye until Eitan was back safely in Israel.

Ari Friedman walked through the open door of Yatom's office. Yatom loved Ari like his own son. Ari used to be his most trusted team leader but had been injured helping Charles Mapother's outfit in the attempt to rescue Mike Walton's father in Mykonos earlier that year. A bullet had destroyed his right bicep but surgery had repaired most of the damage. Ari had wanted to go back in the field but, unknown to him, his wife had called Yatom to beg him to give her husband a desk job. She loved her husband, and his last injury had scared her. In his early forties, Ari could have been deployed for a few more years but at what cost? Yatom didn't want him to end up alone too.

When he told Ari his days in the field were over, Ari threatened to quit. Yatom didn't miss a beat and told him to go ahead. It never crossed his mind to tell Ari that it was his wife's phone call that had convinced him to end his career as a field operator. It would have ruined his marriage. Instead, Yatom accepted the onslaught of foul language Ari directed at him. Once Ari was done with his tantrum, Yatom gave him the choice to either leave the building, or serve as his bodyguard and personal assistant. Ari had stayed.

"What is it, Ari?"

"We recovered this in one of your emergency dead drops." Ari held a piece of paper in his hand.

Yatom sat straighter in his seat. He had set up a dozen emergency dead drops in Jerusalem and in areas controlled by the Palestinian Authority when he left the field ten years ago. He had made sure agents were still monitoring the dead drops. All of them were in easily accessible public spaces where the person accessing the drop could be momentarily shielded from view. They were all coupled with another site where agents left signals telling the other party that material had been left or picked up. The risk of being compromised was small since each dead drop was to be used only once.

"Can I see it?"

Ari handed it to him.

The message was coded. Yatom had been out of touch for too long to remember the significance of each letter and number but he recognized the message for what it was. An emergency.

Yatom got up from behind his desk and opened a hidden safe concealed behind a map of Israel. He retrieved a small booklet. It took him less than a minute to find exactly what he was looking for. He compared the series of letters and numbers with the codes he had in his booklet. The message came from an asset codenamed KORZEN. Yatom had recruited him a dozen years ago. Because of the intelligence provided by KORZEN, the security services of Israel had been able to stop countless terror attacks and save hundreds of innocent lives.

KORZEN wanted a meeting at Site Sixteen. He said he had intelligence vital to the security of the Israeli prime minister. That was it. Yatom wished KORZEN had included more info and wondered why he didn't. Site Sixteen was a restaurant in Bethlehem. Meetings at Site Sixteen were always on Mondays at five thirty in the afternoon. Yatom looked at his watch.

That's three hours from now. That's not enough time. Yatom felt he was being forced to do something he didn't want to. Plus, all his field teams were out on missions or on leave. But what if the PM was really in danger? Could he afford to miss a meeting with KORZEN, an asset that had served him well in the past? With the assassination of the Canadian prime minister by a member of his close protection detail, he couldn't. What if the Israeli prime minister was next on the list?

"I need to talk to the prime minister," Yatom said to Ari. "You and I might go on a little op, my friend. What do you say?"

Ari flashed him a smile. "I'm ready."

Yatom nodded, and then picked up his phone and dialed the private number of the Israeli prime minister.

CHAPTER 42

Bethlehem, Palestine

The Ewaan Restaurant was a thing of beauty. The cobbled white-stone walls with elegant arches accompanied by a rich and ornate interior décor made the Ewaan a remarkable place to enjoy dinner. The cool Bethlehem evening convinced Meir Yatom to eat inside instead of enjoying the garden area. Also, an attempt on his life would be much harder if he was inside than outside, where a sniper could take a shot from a quarter mile away.

Ari was seated at another table not far from him, keeping a watchful eye on the door and on the other patrons. His call to the prime minister had been short. With the Canadian prime minister dead, most heads of state were in panic mode, unsure if they could trust they own security service. The prime minister's tone of voice told Yatom he wasn't ecstatic about the idea of sending his most senior intelligence officer to Bethlehem, but he'd allow it if a proper security detail could be organized in time. Yatom had assured him it wouldn't be a problem and had tasked Ari to prepare for immediate deployment.

What made this operation challenging was the fact that Israelis weren't allowed into areas controlled by the Palestinian Authority unless they had received prior approval from the Israeli Civil Administration. That wasn't an issue for Yatom and his security team, but it would have been counterproductive for them to enter with their real names. Instead, they used MOSSAD-issued Canadian passports and went through "Rachel's Crossing" as tourists by hiring two taxis with Arab drivers equipped with yellow license plates. They paid an extra two hundred shekels to each driver to linger in the area while they dined. Yatom had brought an extra Canadian passport in case KORZEN needed to be extracted.

They arrived at the restaurant twenty minutes in advance. With Ari close by and three other MOSSAD agents outside the restaurant, Yatom was conscious this wasn't the "security" the prime minister had agreed to, but it was the best they could do at such short notice. They were all carrying pistols, but that was it.

"Are you ready to order?" the waiter asked.

"I'm waiting for someone." Yatom looked at his watch. KORZEN was now ten minutes late. "But I'd like a tall bottle of sparkling water if you have some."

"Right away, sir," the waiter said.

Yatom would wait another twenty minutes. There was no point staying longer. But something told him he wouldn't have to wait that long.

CHAPTER 43

Bethlehem, Palestine

Colonel Davari looked at the ten Hamas fighters around the table. They were all dressed in civilian clothes. It wouldn't do them any good to wear tactical gear. Bethlehem was to some extent a safe city with a mix of Christians and Muslims cohabiting in relative peace. They needed this operation to go down quietly.

"Any questions so far?" Davari asked.

"What if he doesn't come?" asked one of the Hamas fighters. His name was Nazmi Salama and he was the leader of the group. He was clean-shaven, which was rare for someone belonging to Hamas, and over six feet tall. He had previously been one of Yasser Arafat's bodyguards.

Before Davari could respond, Sergeant Musa Mariwala whispered in his ear, "It's been confirmed, sir. Yatom and a small security team have been spotted."

Davari thanked him.

"My friends," he said to the Hamas fighters, "Meir Yatom is on location."

The men clapped each other on the back, and there were a few "Allahu Akbars" thrown in.

To get a man like Meir Yatom at a known location at a specific time was a great accomplishment. They had to thank General Kharazi for this. The traitor known as KORZEN, a mid-level Iranian agent from the Ministry of Intelligence and Security—MOIS—had been caught selling classified intelligence to the French Secret Service five years ago. In retaliation for his treachery, General Kharazi had killed his wife and had the rest of his family imprisoned with a promise that every two months, one of his child would die of torture. KORZEN, whose real name was Arash Nekoo, pleaded with Kharazi to spare the lives of his children. In exchange, he'd give up the names of his French and Israeli handlers.

Within months, Kharazi had orchestrated a counter-intelligence operation that disrupted the French's intelligence gathering capabilities within Iran so much that they were forced to withdraw the two other agents they had within the MOIS. They never made it. The two traitors and the six French DGSE—Directorate-General for External Security—agents trying to help them cross the Iraqi border were killed in an ambush.

As for the Israelis, Kharazi decided to reinstate KORZEN and to continue feeding him mid-grade intelligence to take back to his former masters in Tel-Aviv. Kharazi sacrificed a few Hezbollah and Hamas fighters in the process but didn't mind doing so. He was playing the long game.

"KORZEN must suspect we're about to move. His usefulness has come to an end and he's to be considered an enemy combatant," Davari said, giving each man a piece of paper on which were printed the faces of their targets. "Memorize what he and Meir Yatom look like."

"What about the other customers?" asked Salama.

"Acceptable collateral damage," Davari said. "We need Meir Yatom alive, whatever the cost. It would be nice to capture his security team too, but I doubt that will be possible."

Salama nodded gravely. Davari knew they wouldn't kill fellow Muslims intentionally, but they would do what was necessary to complete their mission.

"We have to expect that Meir Yatom will be wearing some kind of tracker," Davari said. "The moment we have him in custody, and before we bring him back here to be interrogated, he'll need to be stripped of all his clothes. We can't take any chances.

"And one more thing," he added. "Do not underestimate the Israelis, because that will be the last thing you do."

CHAPTER 44

Bethlehem, Palestine

Meir Yatom got up from his table. He had waited long enough. KORZEN not showing up was bad news. Either it had been a trap all along or KORZEN had been picked up and was about to spill the beans. One way or the other, Yatom and his team needed to get out of Bethlehem. He was about to signal Ari to join him when a heavyset man entered the dining room. Yatom recognized him right away.

KORZEN.

He was dressed in a cheap black suit over a white shirt. His longish, dark-gray hair was combed back with the help of too much pomade. He saw Yatom and made a beeline to his table. The two men shook hands.

"I was about to leave," Yatom said, pouring a glass of sparkling water for his asset.

"I wish you had."

Alarm bells started ringing in Yatom's head. "You called this—"

"That's all the time I could buy. I've been made years ago."

What? Yatom stiffened and his heart rate jumped. All his senses were now on alert. How much false intel did he provide? And why call this meeting?

"So there's no threat against our prime minister?"

"Not that I'm aware of, but I could be wrong."

At least that's that.

"What about the Canadian prime minister? Did you hear anything?"

But KORZEN wasn't listening anymore; his head was swiveling left and right. "This is a trap. I'm sure of it!"

Yatom's heart sank. "Why did you tell me?"

Tears ran freely down KORZEN's eyes. "They murdered my wife, and I've lost contact with my children. A cousin working in the prison system told me they were slaughtered earlier this week."

This is on me. Yatom knew the risks but did KORZEN really understand them when he signed up?

"How long do I have?" Yatom asked.

"Two minutes, maybe less."

"What are you going to do?"

"Kill as many as I can," KORZEN replied, opening his jacket. He had a pistol in a shoulder holster. "Then I'll join my wife."

CHAPTER 45

Bethlehem, Palestine

Colonel Davari and half the assault force were in two separate vans one block away from the restaurant while the remaining Hamas soldiers under the command of Sergeant Musa Mariwala were on foot, keeping an eye on the restaurant and Yatom's protective detail.

"Alpha-two from Alpha-niner," Davari said over the two-way radio the Hamas had provided.

"Go ahead for Alpha-two," Mariwala replied.

"SITREP, over."

"We have eyes on four men we believe are with the target's protective detail. No exit vehicles in sight. Over."

Davari guessed they had hired taxis to enter the city. It was the only way to get in incognito. He knew the local police wouldn't give them any trouble. Hamas had paid them handsomely to remain in their station. The foot traffic was heavy but it would clear away rapidly once the shooting started.

It always did.

CHAPTER 46

Bethlehem, Palestine

"Come with us," Yatom said to his asset. "I have a passport for you."

"I don't want to go with you, but thanks anyway."

Ari's chair scraped against the floor.

"We need to get out, sir," Ari told him. "The men are getting anxious."

Yatom looked at KORZEN. The poor man had lost everything he cared about. And for what? His treachery had saved many Israeli lives, but Yatom would have no choice but to comb through everything KORZEN had given him. But first, they needed to get out of this jam alive.

"I can't reach our men," Ari said, his voice higher than usual. Yatom felt Ari's powerful grip on his arm.

"Follow me."

Yatom had no time to get out before the metallic clunks of stun grenades hitting the tile floor resonated throughout the dining room. Ari reacted immediately and threw Yatom on the ground, covering him with his body. Yatom closed his eyes but the force of the successive explosions disoriented him. Flashes of red had him wondering if his eyes were really closed.

Then Ari opened fire. Yatom got to his knees and Ari pushed him back to the floor, shielding him once again with his body. "Stay down. They're coming in."

Then the bullets started flying.

. . . .

The first phase of the operation was a complete success. Sergeant Mariwali's team had killed the four Israelis agents without them even returning fire thanks to their suppressed Ak-47s. Davari walked into the restaurant and shot the maître d' with a short three-round burst of his silenced MP5 while Nazmi Salama and his men rushed passed him and threw a multitude of stun grenades into the two dining rooms.

That was an overkill that served no purpose whatsoever. A single stun grenade in each dining room would have done the trick. Davari shook his head as he closed his eyes and covered his ears. The explosions shook the entire building and, for a moment, Davari feared the ceiling would cave in. By the time Salama and his men regained their senses and were ready to go in, too much time had elapsed. Davari warned them not to go in but it was too late. Salama led the charge and was shot the moment he set foot in the dining room. The others returned fire but didn't care to aim as they sprayed the entire dining room with lead.

Davari yelled, "I need him alive."

But after seeing their leader get shot, the men were scared and continued to fire their weapon until their magazines were empty. Davari swore he'd kill them all himself if Yatom was dead.

"Stay here, count to one hundred, then go into the dining room. I'll be in the kitchen. It's sandwiched between the two dining rooms."

Nobody replied. "Hey!" he shouted. "Did you understand what I said?"

The Hamas fighters looked in his direction and some of them nodded their heads. *Idiots.*

Davari shouldered the MP5 and rushed into the other dining room, clearing his right corner first. His eyes darted from one person to the other, looking for threats. No one dared to move. The two dining rooms were connected by the kitchen. He wanted to block anyone from escaping. He cleared the dining room in no time. He pushed the kitchen door open with his left hand. The moment he set foot inside he felt movement to his right. A cook wielding a butcher's knife slashed at him. Davari ducked just in time and the large blade missed the top of his head. He was so close to his attacker that he had to shoot him in the legs, as he couldn't bring his muzzle higher than the man's thigh. The man crumbled and Davari shot him in the head. He pivoted quickly to make sure no other brave souls took a swing at him. The remaining cooks had their hands in the air. Davari motioned them to exit the kitchen, which they did.

Ten seconds later, he heard gunfire. It didn't last long. The cooks were dead, cut down my Salama's men.

. . . .

Yatom saw Ari clutching his side. He had been hit shortly after the firefight started. Next to him rested KORZEN's body.

"Can you move?" Yatom asked.

Ari was shaking badly and needed medical attention. Things weren't looking good. Yatom concluded that if the assaulters had managed to gain entry into the restaurant, his team members standing guard outside were either dead or incapacitated. He couldn't count on them.

Yatom picked up Ari's pistol and helped him to his feet. There was a door at the end of the dining room leading into the kitchen. In the kitchen was another exit. It was their only chance.

Another volley of fire forced Yatom and Ari to get back down. By the time Yatom realized the bullets weren't meant for them, he had lost precious seconds. They were getting up again when Yatom heard voices yelling in Arabic. He remained immobile as a group of Arabic men armed with AK-47s entered the dining room. In theory, they should have seen him. But since he was motionless, their eyes, not picking up any movements, continued to scan the room. It gave him the half second he needed to bring up his pistol and start shooting. Outgunned three to one, he couldn't miss. If he did, he'd be cut down immediately.

Yatom squeezed the trigger three times in just over a second. Two bullets found their marks, hitting their targets' center of mass. The third Hamas soldier dropped to the floor and, in his haste to return fire, jerked the trigger. His rounds went wide and Yatom finished him off with a single bullet to the head. One of the soldiers was moaning. Yatom walked to him and shot him again. He did the same with the others. He felt no remorse. None whatsoever.

"Meir Yatom," a voice behind him called. "At last."

A chill went through Yatom's veins. He turned around, aware his pistol's action was opened, and recognized the man instantly. *Colonel Asad Davari. Quds Force.*

"You're a hard man to find, Meir. But here we are."

In his peripheral vision, Yatom saw that Ari was slowly reaching for his ankle hostler where he kept a small revolver. He forced himself to look straight at Davari, not wanting to betray Ari's attempt at saving them both.

"You've been busy, Meir, and I think we're long overdue for a small conversation. Wouldn't you agree?"

"Whatever you say, Asad," Yatom replied.

Davari smiled. "Glad to know there are no secrets between us."

Ari had his hand on the butt of his revolver. If Yatom could only keep Davari focused on him for another second or two there was a chance they could get out of there alive.

"Oh, c'mon, Meir," Davari said. In a lightning-fast move, the colonel swung his rifle to his right, fired a three-round burst into Ari, and shifted his aim back to Yatom's torso before he could attempt anything.

Ari! No. No. No!

The bullets had torn through Ari's head and torso, leaving a bloody mess of flesh and brain matter on the tiled floor of the restaurant. Ari's death sent Yatom into a fit of rage. He surprised Davari by throwing his pistol in his direction. Davari ducked but Yatom was already on the move. For a man over sixty years of age, he was traveling fast and was almost on Davari when he heard the shot. It had come from behind him. The non-lethal round hit him between the shoulder blades.

The pain was immediate and severe. For a moment, Yatom was convinced a 7.62 round had hit him. He fell forward, and, with his momentum, landed less than two feet away from Davari. The colonel didn't waste any time and jumped on him. Davari's knee landed in the middle of his back, and Yatom shouted in frustration and pain. He felt the cold steel of the handcuffs as they closed around his wrists.

"Good shot, Sergeant," Davari said.

Yatom craned his neck to see who had shot him, but Davari smacked him behind the head with the butt of his rifle.

And everything went black.

CHAPTER 47

Over Europe

For the first time in the last seventy-two hours, Mike allowed himself to relax. They had successfully escaped the Greek authorities and the Gulfstream was now safely outside Greek airspace. Thanks to James Cooper, Mike and his team were able to keep their heads down in Athens and let things blow over in relative security. Mike couldn't wait to get back to New York. Not only did he miss his wife like crazy, he wanted to go through the intelligence General Adbullahi had left them. The death of the Canadian prime minister had shaken him and he wanted to know how someone so close to the prime minister could be turned. Plus, there was the flash drive they had retrieved from Zaid al-Menhali. They could have tried opening its content from one of their laptops but James Cooper recommended they didn't. He thought it would be more prudent to wait until they were back at the IMSI headquarters where they had the technology to sniff out Trojan horse programs and similar applications.

"Hey," Zima said, throwing him two sandwiches wrapped in cellophane. "Ham and cheese," she added before taking a seat next to Eitan who had fallen asleep a while ago.

Mike ate ravenously and washed the sandwiches down with a can of pink grapefruit Perrier. By the time he was done, Zima was snoring. Mike was too tired to think straight. They still had a good two hours of flight time before reaching London where they would stop to refuel before heading home to New York City. A couple of hours of sleep would do him a lot of good.

He closed his eyes.

. . . .

"Mike, Mike, wake up, buddy," Martin St-Onge said, gently shaking his shoulder.

Mike opened his eyes. "Yeah, what's up?"

"It's Mapother," the pilot said. "He wants to speak with you."

"Do you have coffee?" Mike asked.

"Give me a minute."

Mike grabbed the SAT phone. "I'm here, Charles."

"Is Eitan with you?"

"He's sleeping, and so was I."

"I don't care, Mike. Wake him up. And Zima too."

Mike didn't like where this was going. *What now?*

Zima and Eitan must have slept lightly because they were both looking at him.

"All right, Charles," Mike said once Zima and Eitan had sat next to him. "You're on speaker."

What Mapother said next shocked them all. "MOSSAD thinks Meir Yatom has been taken."

Mike and Zima turned their attention to Eitan who looked perplexed.

"Care to give us more details?" Eitan asked.

"I don't have many of them, unfortunately," Mapother replied. "All I know is what your colleagues back in Tel-Aviv were kind enough to share with me. I'm sure they'll be more forthcoming with you than they were with me."

"Still, what do we know so far?"

"It seems that Meir was on an operation in Bethlehem—"

"What the hell was he doing in Bethlehem?" Eitan interrupted Mapother.

"I can't answer that," Mapother said. "His protective detail was wiped out. Including Ari. I'm sorry."

Shit! Mike and Ari had fought together in Mykonos only a few months ago. Ari was a true warrior and had played a big part in stopping the terrorist mastermind known as The Sheik from launching a bioterrorism attack on the United States. Without Ari and his team of Israeli assaulters—including Eitan—there was a big chance the Sheik would be prepping his next terror move instead of being debriefed by American interrogators in a black site somewhere in the continental United States. Mike wasn't privy to the Sheik's location. Mapother had repeatedly refused to tell him where he was, and with good reasons. The Sheik had altered Mike's life from the inside out. First there was the kidnapping of Ray Powell—Mike's father and the Canadian ambassador to Algeria—four years ago. He had psychologically tortured Celina Powell, Mike's mother, by sending her pictures of her beaten-up husband and then by orchestrating devastating, multiple-front terror attacks that had killed hundreds, including Mike and Lisa's daughter Melissa. In Mykonos, Ray Powell had sacrificed his life to save a badly injured Lisa and had died at the hands of the Sheik before Mike, Eitan and Ari could save him. And now this?

Mike doubted the Sheik had anything to do with Meir Yatom's capture and Ari's death but he still wanted the chance to conduct a one-on-one enhanced interrogation session with the terrorist.

"They didn't find Meir's body?" Eitan asked.

"No, they haven't found his body. That doesn't mean—"

"You don't need to spell it out, Charles. I know he might be dead."

"Again, I'm sorry."

"I can't go to New York," Eitan said, visibly shaken.

Zima took her boyfriend's hand. Ari and Eitan were close. Best friends. Brothers, really.

"I know," Mapother said. "I've asked Martin to stop by Ben Gurion. Do what you have to do, Eitan."

"Thank you," Eitan murmured.

Mike knew Zima was about say something so he raised his hand, stopping her before she could open her mouth.

"We'll see you in a few hours, Charles," Mike said, before hanging up.

The moment the SAT phone was off, Zima shouted at Mike, "What the hell?"

"There was no point in arguing with Mapother. He'd never say yes."

"You don't even know what I was about to ask," she said, her eyes on fire.

"You want to go with Eitan," Mike said matter-of-factly. "And like I said, Mapother would have never allowed it. You would have ignored him and he would have cut you loose for it. It's often much easier to ask for forgiveness than permission, Zima, you know that."

"And you don't mind? You'll let me go?"

"I do mind, but yes, I'll let you go."

Martin St-Onge returned with three cups of coffee.

"How long till we get to Tel-Aviv," Eitan asked.

"Less than an hour," St-Onge replied.

Without another word, St-Onge walked back to the cockpit.

"Meir doesn't get out in the field much nowadays, and when he does it's with an entourage. For our enemies to successfully abduct him and kill his whole protective detail, it was a trap. Ari was no amateur."

"What could push Meir to take such a risk?" Zima asked. "He must have known he was too valuable to go into Palestine."

Eitan took a while to respond but when he did, his answer made sense. "A direct threat to our prime minister would."

"And with the attack against the Canadian prime minister, Meir would have to take any threat seriously," Mike added.

"I guess I'll know for sure soon enough," Eitan said.

. . . .

An hour later, the plane landed at Ben Gurion without incident. It rolled to a private hangar owned by a MOSSAD shell company. A four-door sedan was waiting.

Mike shook hands with Eitan.

"Good luck, my friend," he said. "Thanks for all your help. I'll pray for your success."

Eitan slapped him on the shoulder. "Thanks, and don't worry, Mike. I'll take care of her."

Mike looked at Zima. "Stay safe," he said to her. "Or Mapother will kill me."

"I really appreciate you doing this for me, Mike," Zima said.

Mike nodded. "See you soon."

Five minutes later, the Gulfstream took off, Mike its only passenger.

CHAPTER 48

New York City, New York

New York Police Department Sergeant Tracy Sassani opened the door of the large black SUV the moment she saw Mayor Anthony Church and his wife step out of Gracie Mansion, the official residence of the mayor of New York.

"Morning, Tracy," Mayor Church said, letting his wife slip past him.

"Good morning to you too, Mr. Mayor," Sassani replied.

"Make sure you guys follow the speed limit, will you?"

"Of course, Mr. Mayor."

"I don't need more bad press. These assholes will do anything to bring me down."

The mayor didn't need to specify who the assholes were; Sergeant Sassani was aware who they were. At the morning briefing, the officer in charge of Mayor Church's protective detail had chewed their asses about a video that had appeared on YouTube the night before showing Church's motorcade going over the speed limit and burning red lights. The fact that Church was about to unveil a 62-point safe street initiative wasn't lost on Sassani, or on the reporters that had run the story. The relationship between the mayor and the press was at an all-time low and both sides were taking swings at each other. New Yorkers were due to the polls in six months, and the stakes were high. Church's position on gun control had turned most of the liberal press against him. They had supported him in the last election but now they felt betrayed and were going to do everything in their power to bury him, even if that meant spending a fortune to keep him under surveillance twenty-four seven to catch a single slipup.

Conscious the motorcade was being followed by at least two vehicles filled with reporters, the motorcade commander took his time to get to One Police Plaza. In fact, it took twice the regular time. But Tracy Sassani couldn't have cared less about the reporters. She was the only one on the protective detail who knew the reporters weren't the real threat today. They wouldn't be the ones taking the mayor down.

She was.

CHAPTER 49

IMSI Headquarters

"Are you out of your goddamned mind?" Mapother roared. "What went through your head?"

It had been quite a while since Mike had seen Mapother get so worked up.

"Do you really think she would have been an effective team member knowing Eitan was in harm's way?"

"It wasn't your call to make, Mike, and you know it," Mapother replied, his voice somewhat calmer.

"That's where she'll do the most good," Mike argued. Mapother was a good boss. A fair one. He hated to disappoint the man who had given a new purpose to his life. A second chance, really.

Mapother sat down behind his desk and pinched his nose. When he spoke again, his voice was flat, devoid of any emotion.

"I've never questioned your judgment in the field. You've always had the full support of this organization, but do this to me again and your status, and Lisa's status, will change. Do I make myself clear?"

Mike knew better than to continue the debate. All in all, Mapother was letting him off easy.

"Understood. It won't happen again."

Mapother nodded. "Follow me. We'll join the techies and try to find out what's on those drives you brought back.

. . . .

Mike entered the control room and spotted Sanchez and Lisa right away. They were hunched over the shoulders of Anna Caprini,

Charles Mapother's assistant and one of the best and brightest analysts the IMSI had on its payroll.

"Anything yet?" Mike asked.

Anna was typing vigorously on her cordless keyboard. She didn't even acknowledge Mapother.

Sanchez shrugged. "We don't know. She isn't talking to us."

"Almost there," she said, her eyes fixed on her screen.

"That the first thing she's said in the last ten minutes," Lisa chimed in.

Mike wasn't an expert in computer science. In fact, he had difficulty keeping up with new technologies. What the IMSI analysts and hackers could do with a simple computer blew his mind. His friend Jonathan Sanchez, and even his wife to a certain extent, never missed an importunity to tease him about it.

"This drive is loaded with naked pictures of our friend Anja Skov," Caprini announced. "Every one of them is a Trojan horse."

"You caught them all, right?" Mapother asked.

"Hard to say. These buggers are difficult to find," Caprini said. "This computer is off the grid, though. It isn't hooked to our mainframe or the Internet. But just to be on the safe side, I'll fry it once I'm done.

"So Anja isn't who we thought she was," Mike stated. "Any clues who she's working for?"

"I can't say for sure," Caprini said, "but these programs are backdoor Trojans. It gives the users remote control of the infected computer. It allows them to do anything they wish."

"Like what?" Mike asked.

"Like sending, receiving and deleting files. They also steal your logins and passwords for messaging and banking programs."

Caprini's hands left her keyboard. She swiveled her chair to face Mapother and said, "If I had to guess, I'd say Anja Skov is Danish intelligence."

Mapother turned to Mike. "Good thing we didn't take her out."

There was a moment of uncomfortable silence.

"So, Charles," Lisa said, breaking it, "any way we can link with the Danes and see what they had on Zaid al-Menhali?"

"Not a good idea, honey," Mike said. "We caught too much heat in Athens already. I suggest we move on."

Mapother seemed to think about it for a moment. "I agree with Mike. Al-Menhali's dead. The Danes won't be happy we took him out, especially if they've been running an op on him. Better to leave this alone and focus on trying to find out what the hell happened in Canada."

"I still can't believe it." Mike shook his head. "I can't even start to imagine what kind of repercussions it will have on the RCMP."

"This is a messed-up situation," Sanchez said. "Even in Delta we never trained for a situation like this. You don't just expect your colleague to turn on you."

"What we need to ask ourselves is where did this attack come from," Mapother said.

"Agreed," Mike said. "I don't believe for one second that al-Fadhi woke up that morning and said, "I'm gonna kill the PM today." In my opinion, al-Fadhi had known for a long time he'd be asked to do something dramatic."

"So should I start working on Adbullahi's stuff?" Caprini asked. "That might provide some answers."

"Yeah, start digging, Anna," Mapother said. "I want to know why he left Iran in such in hurry. If more attacks are headed our way, and the Iranians are behind it, the intel Adbullahi wanted to share might help us understand what's going on."

CHAPTER 50

New York City, New York

Sergeant Sassani stepped out of the SUV and scanned the crowd that had gathered around One Police Plaza. It was smaller than she had hoped but enough media were in attendance to guarantee a wide audience. Her dad, she knew, was in attendance. It would be the end of the road for him too.

Leading the way slowly to the podium, with the mayor stopping every few steps to shake hands, anxiety and doubt crept up within her. Again.

Was she on the right side of this? She had been with the NYPD long enough to know and understand all the good the Americans were capable of. Wasn't she an American too?

No.

Her father had always insisted she was Iranian first. *We're deep into enemy territory,* he had told her countless times. She trusted him. Her father had taught her everything. Showed her what American policies did to her family back home.

But a home I've never visited. Never been to.

She forced herself to think about all the suffering happening at this moment in Iran. All of it at the hands of the United States. There was a lot of good in America, but a lot of hate too. It wasn't right that politicians hundreds of miles away decided of the fate of the Iranian people. It was time for a change. It was time for Iran to take its rightful place in the Middle East, free from the clutches of the American government.

I'm a weapon. I'm the tip of the spear. Behind me, thousands will follow. America will crumble.

They reached the podium and half the crowd cheered the mayor while the other half did its best to bury him by booing louder. The mayor lifted his hands to calm the attendees; he wore a big smile. Somebody threw a plastic cup on the stage. Then another. The smile disappeared. Sassani moved closer to the mayor.

"Crowd is hostile," Sassani heard her team leader say via their communication system. "We might have to leave in a hurry. Make sure the motorcade is ready to go."

Sassani's eyes found the camera crew. They were already filming, unwilling to miss a single thing that could go wrong. The agitated crowd excited them.

Now would be the perfect time. It would be over in seconds.

Why am I still standing here? Do it, Tracy. Do it!

The voice in her ear, loud and insistent, brought her back to reality.

"Sassani? Sassani? What the hell are you doing? We're moving."

Sassani looked to her right. The mayor and his wife had left the stage. They were getting away. The crowd had become too antagonistic. She had to do it now while the cameras were still rolling.

Move! But she didn't. Heart pounding in her ears, she was frozen in place, unable to move.

. . . .

What is she doing?

Razin Sassani watched in horror as his daughter—his own flesh and blood—let the mayor and his wife walk away from the stage. He had spent his life teaching her the true facts about life in America and the ravaging effects of their policies. He thought she understood.

How could she betray him now? How could she betray herself, her country? Everything she believed in? Didn't she understand the sacrifices he had made? He had entrusted her with his most precious secrets. If she was unable to complete her mission, what would stop her from exposing what she knew? He couldn't take that risk.

What a waste. He wouldn't let her spit on his name. He was still an Iranian soldier. He would do his duty, even if it broke his heart.

. . . .

Sergeant Sassani caught sight of a tall man elbowing his way toward the podium, his white hair contrasting with his dark skin.

Father. Her heart skipped a beat. *He knows.*

A gun materialized in his hands.

She hesitated. He didn't.

The bullet entered her abdomen, a quarter of an inch below the light body armor she wore under her shirt. The bullet passed through her stomach and left kidney before lodging in the muscles in her back.

She collapsed on the stage, her body writhing in pain.

. . . .

Razin Sassani knew his daughter wasn't dead but he didn't have the luxury of firing at her one more time. A headshot would have been better, but his skills weren't what they used to be and he couldn't afford to miss.

He had to engage the mayor before his protective detail shoved him in the waiting SUV. He jumped on the stage next to his fallen daughter and scanned the crowd for any sign of the mayor.

There he was.

He and his wife were sandwiched between three officers who were fighting against the frantic crowd. One of the officers did a back check and locked eyes with Razin.

Razin's pistol was already up and he fired eight rounds in quick succession. The officer went down, and so did two bystanders. Razin reassessed and was about to fire again when he was struck in the back.

He turned to face his attacker. A uniformed cop was yelling something at him. Razin raised his weapon, but not toward the officer. He aimed for his daughter. She couldn't be allowed to live to tell her story.

The cop fired again before Razin could pull the trigger. Struck high in the chest, Razin fell to his knees. Blood filled his mouth and he lost his grip on his gun. In his mind, he cursed his daughter. The officer's next round took out the top of his head.

. . . .

Sergeant Sassani still had her earpiece. She heard one of her colleagues yell a warning to the others. Then someone—her father?—fired eight shots. A uniformed officer appeared at the edge of the crowd.

"Police, drop the gun!" he shouted before he too fired.

"Drop the gun!" he repeated, and then he fired again. Twice.

A body dropped next to her with a thud. She used the last of her energy to turn her head. Her father, the man she had loved, the man who had ultimately betrayed her, lay dead next to her.

CHAPTER 51

New York City, New York

Radman Divecha was mesmerized by what he had just witnessed on television. He couldn't believe this was happening.

Just shoot him! Shoot him!

When Sgt. Sassani collapsed on the stage, Divecha understood that he'd have to get involved. His spirits momentarily lifted when her father jumped next to her and pumped a few rounds toward the retreating mayor, but his mood once again hit rock bottom when the old colonel fell next to his daughter, struck by the bullets of a police officer.

Divecha screamed in anger. He grabbed the remote control and hurled it toward the flat screen. He missed and the remote hit the urn containing his wife's remains. Even though his religion forbidden him to cremate his non-Muslim wife, he'd decided to make an exception. She was his first kill after all. Allah would understand. The urn tipped forward and Divecha dashed across the room to stop the inevitable. Going around the coffee table cost him half a second. The urn fell, grazing his hands outstretched in front of him. The urn shattered on impact, sending ashes all over the tiled floor of his living room. Divecha coughed as particles found their way into his lungs.

Stupid bitch.

Why couldn't she kill the mayor?

He had met Sassani only once and he hadn't been impressed. She didn't have the determination the others had. There was something missing. She said all the right things, but, deep down, Divecha had always believed she'd fail. Voicing his concerns had led to absolutely nothing.

PERIWINKLE's third phase was a failure because of her. Mayor Church was a bigger, more important mark than his: the governor of the state of New York. Would he have to go to New York City to take care of this mess? He'd know soon enough.

Divecha climbed the stairs and headed to his bedroom. His walk-in closet was bigger than it needed to be. Dark suits and white shirts claimed the entire space. And the ties. He owned over two hundred of them. His colleagues at the New York State Police Protective Services Unit swore he wore a new one every day. It wasn't true, but it certainly looked like it. He meticulously rotated through them, making sure never to wear the same one in a six-month span.

Did he buy all these ties to fill the void left by his wife? Divecha missed her very much, but she had been a bit too curious and he had to do what was necessary. He always did.

Mission first. His father had taught him well.

He pushed away a couple of police dress uniforms he had just picked up from the cleaner and grabbed the cordless vacuum he kept next to his polished shoes.

Back in the living room, he vacuumed his wife's remains and then emptied the vacuum in the trashcan next to his kitchen sink. He cleaned the vacuum's dirt canister thoroughly with dishwashing detergent and hot water before drying it with a clean towel.

He had just replaced the vacuum in the closet when his cellphone vibrated in his jeans pocket.

He was needed in New York City. There was another mess to clean up.

CHAPTER 52

IMSI Headquarters, New York

News of the One Police Plaza attack reached the IMSI immediately after the first shot was fired. There was always one analyst on duty whose sole responsibility was to monitor the US news channels. When the attack happened, he was watching the mayor's conference live. He pressed a button on his keyboard and the live feed jumped to the control room's two main screens.

Mike, who was at the gym when it happened, stormed to the control room where he found Mapother pacing back and forth behind Anna Caprini.

"What do we know?" he asked.

"The mayor has been shot," Mapother replied.

"What? When did you hear that?"

When Mike had left the gym less than two minutes ago, the media were reporting that the mayor and his wife were safe.

"It just hit the wire," Lisa said from the opposite desk. "The motorcade is on its way to the Presbyterian Hospital on William Street."

The Presbyterian was one of the few hospitals south of Greenwich Village. It was a not-for-profit and they had an emergency room.

"You're thinking what I'm thinking, Charles?" Mike asked.

Mapother shook his head. "I'm not yet ready to go there. Let's wait a bit longer."

Mike didn't think it was necessary. His gut told him this was a replica of what had happened in Ottawa. Deep cover cells were being activated. General Adbullahi had warned him there were more.

The Canadian agent that killed the prime minister is one of ours. And there are many more like him.

"Sir," Anna Caprini said, "Mike's right. Look at this."

Mike was stunned. On Caprini's computer screen, the face of the man—albeit a much younger version of him—who had shot at Mayor Church appeared. A name was written under his picture.

Colonel Razin Sassani. SAVAK.

"How did you get this information?" Mike asked.

Mapother looked incredulous too. All eyes were on Caprini.

"General Adbullahi gave it to us."

"You gained access to the drive already?" Mapother asked.

"It wasn't even protected," Caprini said, rolling her chair to the next working station. "I checked it for viruses but it was clean. The intelligence was in plain sight."

"What was on it?" Mike asked.

Mike stepped aside to leave room for Lisa who had walked over to look at the intelligence Caprini had downloaded.

"What are we looking at?" Mapother inquired.

"There's only one file," Caprini said. "Of course, I'll keep looking for hidden ones, but this seems to be it. This a Word document on which are pasted the pictures and names of seven SAVAK officers."

"The former Iranian intelligence service?" Mike asked. "Wasn't that abolished in 1979?"

"Indeed," Mapother said. "Prime Minister Bakhtiar ordered its dissolution only four years after its creation. Since the CIA helped to establish the organization, we felt compelled to take in high-ranking SAVAK officers when they fled Iran right before Ayatollah Khomeini took control of the country. And I know the Canadians welcomed a few too."

"Were these seven officers amongst those we took in?" Mike asked.

"I'd be surprised if they weren't."

"That's why the Iranians sent a team to kill Adbullahi," Lisa said. "They didn't want us to find out who these guys were."

Sanchez barged into the control room and called out to Mapother. "Sir, we have a problem."

CHAPTER 53

Tehran, Iran

Major General Kharazi was still stunned by his meeting with Ayatollah Bhansali when he sat down behind his desk. He removed a handkerchief from his breast pocket and wiped his forehead. He didn't remember the last time he had received such a long and thorough tongue-lashing. The ayatollah was furious because of the outcome of the Greece debacle and became almost violent when Kharazi told him about the abduction of Meir Yatom—a mission the ayatollah hadn't personally approved. But what had pushed him over the edge was the fact that New York City's mayor was still alive.

Kharazi promised he still had complete control over PERIWINKLE and that even though Mayor Church survived, the effects were almost the same.

Almost. The ayatollah made it clear whose head would roll if there was another *almost.* Kharazi hadn't volunteered the information that he had activated two more single cells to take care of Church and the traitor Tracy Sassani.

Maybe I should do like Adbullahi and run, he thought. *While I still have the chance.*

One of his phones rang, putting an end to his fantasy.

"What is it?"

"This is Colonel Mizraei, sir. Someone accessed one of the documents General Adbullahi downloaded before he left."

"I'll be right down," Kharazi said, a knot forming in his stomach.

. . . .

Kharazi's heart rate jumped when Colonel Mizraei told him someone had opened at least one of the pictures associated with PERIWINKLE.

"They probably have access to all of them," Mizraei confessed.

Kharazi pictured himself in front of a firing squad with Ayatollah Bhansali giving the crowd the "thumbs down." Kharazi forced the image out of his head and concentrated on the task at hand.

"You will not share this information with anyone else, Colonel. Is that understood?"

"Of course, sir," Mizraei replied, shaking his head left to right. "I only answer to you."

"How do you know the file was opened?"

Kharazi was a strategist, not a computer engineer. He didn't need to know the details, but he wanted to at least understand the basics.

"The file from which General Adbullahi downloaded the information came from a source code my department created for all Level Ten accounts. That code signifies that at least one word, graphic or image per page contains a hidden malicious steganographic code."

"An image within an image?"

"Exactly, sir. In this case, it's a file concealed within an image."

"I would have thought a virus scan would find such a thing."

"It is often the case but not with ours. You want to know why?"

Colonel Mirzaei was clearly in his element. His pitch had moved up a notch and he was moving nonstop from his left foot to his right and vice versa.

"Please continue."

"You can download the actual image without risk, but if you run any exec files on it, like facial recognition software for example, the files will find the hidden code within the image and inform themselves what to do next. So the actual virus, or program, arrives in two parts. That's why it doesn't set off the antivirus. The image isn't doing anything malicious. It's dormant! You understand?"

Kharazi didn't but nodded nonetheless.

"Okay, good."

When Marzaei didn't add anything, Kharazi asked, "That's it?"

Marzaei frowned. “Yes. You want to know something else?”

“How do we know someone opened it?” Kharazi said, exasperated.

“Because we embedded a code whose sole purpose is to let us know the exact location of the user who opens it.”

“Show me.”

Kharazi followed Mirzaei to his office, a large cubicle with three different computer screens. Mirzaei pointed to a red dot. “Here.”

Kharazi’s spirits sank to a new low. *New York City.*

Were the Americans working with the Israelis? A joint operation between the CIA and the MOSSAD could mean trouble. But would the person who opened the file understand what he was seeing? Would he act on it immediately? With the second phase of PERIWINKLE completed, he had some leverage, notwithstanding the problems encountered during the third phase. The Americans were scared. They had to be. It was time to press his advantage.

CHAPTER 54

IMSI Headquarters, New York

"What is it, Jonathan?" Mike asked once they were all in the bubble.

Sanchez pointed to his computer screen. "Look who else is on the list?"

A name was blinking on the computer screen.

Colonel Farrokh al-Fadhi. SAVAK.

"That's Khalid al-Fadhi's father," Mike said, anger creeping in at the thought of former colleagues being killed by a traitor. "The RCMP officer who turned against his teammates and killed the Canadian prime minister."

Mike hoped that any leftover doubts Mapother had about who orchestrated the attack on the mayor were now gone. What Sanchez had been able to put together regarding the links between the attacks on the Canadian prime minister and Mayor Church gave the IMSI a leg up. But how long would it take for the other agencies to add it all up?

"Don't tell me you're not seeing it, Charles?" Mike said. "That can't be a coincidence."

"I see it all right, Mike, but I don't want to believe it."

News was coming in fast. The major networks were all covering the shootout at One Police Plaza. The cop who'd been shot had been identified as thirty-two-year-old New York Police Department Sergeant Tracy Sassani. What the news networks didn't know yet—but Mike was sure they'd make the connection fast enough—was that her father was the man who had not only shot her but also tried to assassinate the mayor of the largest city in the United States.

"We can't sit on this," Sanchez said. "Who's next?"

Who's next?

That was the question they needed answered.

"We must find a way to get our hands on Tracy Sassani," Lisa said. "She knows something."

"Play it again, Anna," Mapother said.

Mike moved closer to the screen and watched the playback of the attempt on Mayor Church's life. It was easy to see that Sergeant Sassani was distracted. She looked nervous and her body language indicated she was preoccupied.

"She knew what was coming," Lisa said. "She seems hesitant."

"But why?" Sanchez asked.

"Because when it was time to pull the trigger, she couldn't do it," Mapother said with finality. "She was the one who was supposed to kill the mayor. Not her father. He was the backup."

"So her father shot her because she wouldn't do it?" Lisa asked.

Mike nodded. "I think Charles is right. The list we got from General Adbullahi contains the names of seven colonels belonging to the SAVAK. What if we were facing off not only against them, but also against their offspring?"

"That would mean there are at least five more cells waiting to strike," Mapother said. "We need to find these colonels and their children."

Mike was about to add something when Mapother's phone rang.

"Charles Mapother."

Mike watched as Mapother's face turned pale.

CHAPTER 55

Ramallah, Palestine

There was no denying it now. It would serve no purpose. A cold, naked fear wrenched his gut. Meir Yatom had fought. Hard. He had resisted as long as he could. But he wasn't a young man anymore. He knew that.

His tormentor knew it too.

He was sitting upright on a wooden chair positioned in the middle of what used to be the basement of a medium-sized factory. His hands and feet were securely bound to the chair. His bindings were tight enough to severely restrict the blood circulation. Sweat and blood dripped down his chin onto his naked chest. Barring a miracle, there was no way to escape this hell. And even if he was able to free himself from the restraints that were cutting through his ankles and wrists, he was too weak to offer more than a token resistance against a well-trained soldier like Asad Davari.

Yatom had lost track of time after the second time he'd fallen unconscious but Colonel Davari seemed to work in patterns of ten minutes. Ten minutes of torture, ten minutes of rest, ten minutes of traditional beating and then ten minutes of rest. Repeat.

His eyes were swollen to such an extent his vision was limited and blurry at best. He could barely make out Davari standing in front of him. It was agonizing to breathe, and he deduced he had a couple of broken ribs. Prolonged beatings from someone who knew what he was doing tended to do that.

"You . . . You don't have to do this," Yatom managed to say, panting.

"But I do, Meir, I do," Davari said, approaching one step closer. In his hand was a power drill he had picked up from the rusted toolbox behind him. Yatom wondered how big was that damn toolbox. How many objects of torture could it hold?

"You see, Meir, you've done much worse to my people," Davari continued, "so your words, your pleas, they mean nothing to me."

Davari pressed the drill against Yatom's right knee hard enough for the bit to break the skin.

"I get no pleasure from this," the Iranian colonel said. "These kind of methods are beneath me, to be honest. But you're a tough bastard, and I'm short on time."

In anticipation of the pain to come, Yatom's pulse was faster than ever. He prayed for a heart attack but knew that was wishful thinking. His heart was too strong.

Davari's index finger moved to the power drill's trigger. "Don't let me do this, Meir. We both know you'll break. Everybody breaks."

Davari moved the bit away from Yatom's knee and pressed the trigger. The screech of the power drill filled the air. Davari released the trigger and the whine died slowly as the bit came to a halt.

"What—"

"What do I want?" Davari asked. "You know what I want. But I'll tell you again. I need to know what your man was doing in Athens, and I want to know who the other operators were. Simple enough, yes?"

It was time to give Davari a little something. There was no way he didn't already know why Eitan had traveled to Athens.

"My agent was—"

"What's your agent's name?" cut in Davari.

Was Davari bluffing, or had he really no idea?

"His name's Ely Loewe—"

The pain was sudden and seared through every single nerve in Yatom's body. He screamed as Davari drilled into his left kneecap. Yatom jerked and bucked in his chair as new waves of pain washed through him. The smell of his burning flesh and bones reached his nose.

Davari extracted the bit from his knee. Yatom screamed, a guttural, anguished cry of sorrow. Never had he felt such intense agony.

"What's his name," Davari asked again, moving the bit to Yatom's right knee.

"Eitan David!" yelled Yatom. "His name is Eitan David!"

"Thank you. We didn't know his name."

Tears of pain and rage ran down Yatom's cheeks. He had been played and he had just betrayed his man.

"Shall we continue?" Davari asked. "Why did Eitan travel to Athens?"

Before Yatom could reply, Davari raised a hand and said, "Hold that thought for a second, will you?"

. . . .

Davari wanted to throw up. What he had said to Yatom about not enjoying any of this was the truth. It disgusted him to have to torture the Israeli spy. The phone chirping in his pocket was a break he welcomed.

"Yes?"

"New developments have come to my attention, Colonel."

"I'm listening."

"It's been confirmed. The Americans are working with the Jews and they've gained access to the intelligence General Adbullahi carried with him out of Iran."

"That's inconvenient."

"Yes, it is, but it's unclear if the Americans understand what the intelligence truly means."

"They'll figure it out soon enough, General."

"I need you to buy us some time, Asad. You understand?"

Davari understood. General Kharazi wanted him to do whatever was necessary to interfere with the Americans. He didn't want them to grasp and act upon the intelligence they'd stumbled across. How the general wanted him to achieve that, he had no idea. There wasn't much he could do from Ramallah.

"Do we know which organization gained access to our secrets?"

"Maybe you could help me find out, Asad? I think your guest might know the answer to that question."

Davari turned to face the Israeli spy. His face was so bruised and bloody he was almost unrecognizable. His chest was bare and crisscrossed with lacerations. Still, his eyes were open and looking straight at him. Was it defiance? The old man had balls. Davari gave him that.

"We'll see," Davari said to the general.

"Do whatever you feel necessary to loosen him up, Colonel. You have another hour or so until you're relieved."

"Relieved?"

"Yes, we've pretty much pinpointed where the breach took place. It's in New York City, and I'm sending you and Sergeant Mariwala to take care of it. Our Palestinian friends will babysit Yatom while you're away."

CHAPTER 56

Ramallah, Palestine

Meir Yatom wanted the pain to end. He had spent his whole life protecting the national interests of Israel.

At any cost.

There were some things he wasn't proud of, but he had no regrets. He had never taken a life in vain. The targeted violence he used was for the greater good of his people. In over forty years of service, he had not once betrayed the trust of his superior officers, but, more importantly, he had never let his subordinates down.

Until now.

Yatom was a beaten man. He'd led many successful operations against his nation's enemies. He had a few failures too, but that was to be expected. Still, every time he had lost a member of his team, a little part of him had died. Even now, with his battered body tied up to a chair, he could remember the names of all the operatives he'd lost in his quest to rid Israel of its adversaries.

Jamian, Mate, Eleazar, Shoshana, Ari . . .

The shock of searing pain brought him back to reality. He opened his eyes, only to see Davari's fist connecting with his jaw one more time.

"Wake up, Meir, I have one more thing to ask you."

On principle, Yatom wanted to defy the Iranian, but at what cost? Davari was going to kill him anyway. Why suffer even more?

"We know you're working with the Americans," Davari said, picking up the power drill. "I'd like you to tell me which agency they're working for."

The IMSI was as covert as they come. Even Yatom wasn't one hundred percent certain how they were financed and how they were able to access the raw intelligence they had. Following the failed mission he had run in tandem with Charles Mapother in Mykonos to rescue Ray Powell, Mapother had shared his concerns regarding the potential political repercussions if IMSI's existence was ever uncovered. President Muller's involvement with the IMSI could be enough to get him impeached. Yatom did not want to be responsible for that, but what choice did he have? Davari had shown he wouldn't hesitate to inflict pain.

"Meir, what agency are they working for?" Davari said, once again pressing the bit against his good knee.

"What difference does it make?"

"Don't do this to yourself. Tell me, and I promise you a death with dignity."

"You already took that away from me," Yatom spat. "And you're a bad liar, Davari."

Davari was lying through his teeth. There was no way a high-value target like him would be allowed to die without a thorough debriefing. His brain was worth much more than the quick gratification his death could give the Iranians. No, if he was in General Kharazi's shoes—Yatom had no doubt he was the one pulling the strings—he'd insist Yatom be brought back to Tehran for further questioning. Incapable of walking, even less of defending himself, Yatom's hopes of escaping were gone. But could he push Davari far enough for the colonel to kill him by mistake? That would be the best-case scenario.

Davari smiled. "Well, it was worth a try."

Davari moved the bit from Yatom's knee to his left thumb, just below his knuckle. Yatom had never been so afraid in his life, never felt so powerless. His body began to shake with such intensity that when Davari started drilling into his thumb, he had already passed out.

. . . .

Davari stopped drilling the moment he realized Yatom's eyes had rolled over, but he was already halfway through his thumb.

"Is he dead?" Sergent Mariwala asked.

Davari shook his head. “No, he’s unconscious. He has endured a lot. Honestly, I’m surprised he’s still alive. I don’t think we should continue. A medical team will need to fix him up before we start again.”

“What do you want to do, sir?”

Davari watched the old Israeli spy shiver in his chair, his head slumped on his chest. Yatom deserved a quick death, and Davari wished he could give it to him, but he feared General Kharazi wouldn’t allow it. As the second-in-command of the Quds Force, Davari understood why Meir Yatom couldn’t be killed. But, as a soldier, he wished he could simply put a bullet in the Israeli’s head.

“We’re done for now, Sergeant. We’ll give it a rest. The general needs us somewhere else.”

Mariwala looked surprised. “Tell me we haven’t been ordered to leave him to the Hamas, sir?”

Mariwala wasn’t an officer, but he was sharp. He understood the value of a man like Yatom. Davari was glad the sergeant would join him in New York City.

“General Kharazi is sending a team to transport him back to Tehran where he’ll undergo further interrogation. The Hamas will babysit him until our colleagues’ arrival.”

“What about us, sir?”

“We’re going to visit New York City.”

CHAPTER 57

Tehran, Iran

General Kharazi sat back in his chair, smiling. He had regained most of the self-confidence the ayatollah had sucked out of him. He was moving his pieces across the chessboard. He had the Americans on their heels. His conversation with DNI Richard Phillips—President Muller's Director of National Intelligence—went better than he had expected. His men from the intelligence division had gotten their hands on the DNI's private number a while ago, but Kharazi never needed it before today.

At first, Phillips was resistant, not believing the man he was speaking to was indeed the commanding general of the Quds Force. A few accurate details of the attack on Mayor Church quickly changed his attitude.

Kharazi's demands, which came directly from the ayatollah, were simple. President Muller had seventy-two hours to sign all the sanction waivers he had canceled the prior month due to Iran's unwillingness to fully comply with the nuclear deal Muller had himself brokered with them.

Publicly, that was the only demand.

Behind the scenes, the ayatollah was also asking for payments of fifty million dollars per day for the next three years. And that wasn't negotiable. At first, Kharazi was staggered by the amount, but when the ayatollah told him the United States federal government spent more than ten billion dollars per day, he realized fifty million wouldn't make a dent in their budget. It would, however, jumpstart the Iranian economy. In Kharazi's mind, the allocation of the lion's share of the past budgets to current expenditures rather than to infrastructure spending explained why his country's economy wasn't moving toward its sought destination. He was also aware that for the last two decades, less than seventy percent of the budget allocated for infrastructure spending was actually funded. Iran's economy was crumbling. In a shambles really. Another couple of years—maybe less if the current economic sanctions weren't lifted—and the ayatollah's vision for the country would be reduced to a mirage. The central government wouldn't have the means to pay public servants or the military. If that became public knowledge, Iran's regional position and international reputation would take a giant hit and a military coup couldn't be ignored. This could lead to a gory civil war.

Now was the time for a bold move. The first supreme leader had certainly not envisioned using PERIWINKLE in this fashion, but the built-in mechanism of the operation could work. If PERIWINKLE could give the ayatollah a way to steer the United States' foreign policy to his advantage, it was worth a shot.

Iran's reluctance to fulfill its obligation on the nuclear deal was a masquerade orchestrated by the ayatollah to force Vienamin Simonich—Russia's president—to offer his assistance. Kharazi thought the nuclear deal treachery was a superb example of realpolitik. With Muller announcing he intended to sell half of the United States' strategic oil supply on the open market two days after the Russians and the Saudis—the top two oil producers—agreed to extend output cuts for another year, the ayatollah had seen the opportunity of a lifetime to rally an annoyed Russia to its cause by exploiting Simonich's frustration toward the Americans. After all, Simonich had tried to bring a deadly virus into the United States less than a year ago. In bed with the Sheik, he had almost succeeded.

For a second, Kharazi wondered if the rumors were true: was the Sheik really dead? Even though he once was touted as the most elusive and dangerous man on the planet, the Americans had ultimately defeated him, and his complex terror network had soon after imploded. As brilliant as he had been in his prime, the Sheik had underestimated his enemies. Kharazi wouldn't commit the same deadly sin.

Nor would the ayatollah.

The economic sanctions imposed on his country by the United States could become quite expensive for the Russians, who had already started to build eight nuclear power reactors in Iran. And that wasn't counting the S-300 air-defense system Russia had agreed to sell to Tehran.

For Moscow, the sanctions had to go. They had too much capital already invested in Iran. And with their own not-so-flourishing economy, they were committed. If the Americans had had the stomach to start a war against Russia, they would have done it the moment they learned about the botched biological attack.

Kharazi expected to hear from Richard Phillips very soon. Part of him wished the Americans would say no. He'd love to see what number "8" could do if activated. Russian involvement or not, if number "8" was given the green light, Kharazi doubted war could be avoided. The supreme leader might disagree with his assessment, but Kharazi didn't believe war was such a bad thing. The Americans and their allies had much more to lose.

Truth was, if Radman Divecha succeeded in shutting up the traitorous bitch Sassani, and Davari and his men were able to seize or destroy the data General Adbullahi had smuggled out, there'd be no need to activate number "8." He could be saved for later use.

There was also the capture of Meir Yatom to consider. It had put him in a good mood. The ayatollah might have given him a thorough tongue-lashing about it, but that was the supreme leader playing politics. With nothing connecting Meir Yatom's kidnapping to Iran, there was even a possibility that Kharazi could exploit the whole thing to his advantage. If he could repatriate Yatom to Tehran, extract the secrets he had in his head, he'd not only consolidate his power as the commanding general of the Quds Force, he could blackmail his way to the very top and coerce the Assembly of Experts to select him as the new deputy supreme leader of Iran. Even though the Assembly of Experts hadn't elected a deputy supreme leader since the deposition of Hussein Montazeri in the late eighties, there were rumors they'd be open to doing so if the right candidate came through. He'd make sure the Assembly of Experts would see *him* as the right candidate.

CHAPTER 58

The White House

Charles Mapother stood in front of President Muller. DNI Richard Phillips sat on one of the couches behind him. Mapother could hear him typing angrily on his smartphone. Mapother wasn't sure where he stood with Phillips. Phillips had recently advocated for terminating the IMSI. The existence of the IMSI alone was enough grounds for Congress to call an impeachment hearing, but with the IMSI's recent successes, it was a tough sale. The president was a strategic man and he'd cut the IMSI loose the moment he felt it caused more harm than good to the country. That was a risk Mapother was ready to accept.

"Richard told me about your outfit's involvement in Greece," Muller said. "Well done."

"Thank you, Mr. President," Mapother replied.

"He also brought me up to speed regarding the intelligence you fumbled upon."

Mapother didn't feel the need to correct the president but he wasn't convinced *fumbled* was the right choice of word.

"Do you know who General Kharazi is, Charles?" Muller asked but caught himself. "Don't answer that. Of course you do. Can I presume Richard shared Kharazi's demands with you?" Muller continued.

"He did."

And they're outrageous.

President Muller seemed lost in thought for a moment. Then he said, "My next meeting is with the members of the Joint Chiefs of Staff. I'll ask them to come up with viable military options against Iran."

"I'm not sure there are any, sir," Mapother said. "Unless you want to face the Russians too."

"That's exactly what I told him," DNI Phillips said from his couch. He got up and took a few steps until he stood next to Mapother.

"I didn't think you two agreed on anything," Muller said.

"I do when he's right, Mr. President," Mapother said.

Phillips flashed him a dirty look.

"Kharazi made it clear he had Simonich in his corner," Phillips finally added.

"That sonofabitch!" Muller slammed an open palm on his desk. "I was naïve to think he'd lie low after we captured the Sheik."

"It's not like him to lie low, sir, but it was worth a try," Mapother conceded.

"Now what? We can't let Ayatollah Bhansali and Simonich bully us like this. They want fifty million *a day*, gentlemen. *A day*."

"Maybe the Security Council—" started Phillips but Muller stopped him by raising both his hands.

"Don't even start with the Security Council."

President Muller wasn't the United Nations' biggest fan. As far as Mapother knew, Muller had no respect left for the organization.

A knock at the door and Yash Najjar—the senior supervisory Secret Service agent on duty—took a couple steps toward the president.

"The Joint Chiefs are waiting for you, Mr. President," Najjar said.

"Please let them know I'll be right there." Muller rose from behind his desk, walked to Mapother and placed his hands on his shoulders. He looked him straight in the eyes.

"With what happened to Prime Minister Ducharme, we can't afford not to take the Iranians seriously. Somehow, they found a way to harm us. They've been at it for decades, or so it seems. I don't want to go to war with them, or the damned Russians." Muller paused for effect and then asked the questions Mapother expected all along. "With the intel you've got, can you find these Iranians within the next sixty hours?"

Mapother knew what was at stake here. With all the pressing domestic issues Muller had to deal with, the last thing he wanted was to get the country into another war the nation couldn't afford. So far, the intelligence acquired from General Adbullahi had been spot on. The IMSI had the names of seven SAVAK colonels. That was a good start.

But the clock was ticking. Fast.

"Yes, Mr. President, I can."

An immense weight seemed to lift off the president's shoulders. Muller's gaze switched to his director of National Intelligence. "You give him everything he needs, Richard. I want the IMSI to take the lead on it. But if they need support from another agency, you'll make it happen."

To Mapother's pleasure, Phillips replied without any hint of hesitation. "Yes, sir."

There might have been friction between him and Phillips, but Mapother knew he could count on the DNI when it was crunch time.

"What are your orders, sir?" Mapother asked.

"Kill them all. This is war."

PART TWO
No Mercy!

CHAPTER 59

Washington DC.

Exhausted, Yash Najjar entered the breakroom and slumped into the largest available sofa. He hadn't gone home to his wife and four children since the assassination of the Canadian prime minister. The attack against Mayor Church had further guaranteed he'd be sleeping at the White House for a while. It didn't matter if Church was still alive; the fact that a lone wolf had almost succeeded in killing him live on television had resuscitated the fear that an attempt on President Muller was imminent.

Najjar's request to get more men was approved and a fresh contingent of Secret Service agents, who'd previously served on the presidential protective detail, was on its way. Najjar would assign these men to the existing teams to allow some agents to rotate off-duty for thirty-six hours or so. Of course, Najjar would stay in position at the White House. As an American Muslim, he always felt at a disadvantage, that he had to do more to keep his friends' and peers' trust. His first four years with the Secret Service hadn't been easy. He tried to fit in but 9/11 had left a mark in the minds of many of his colleagues. Najjar didn't blame them. At first, Najjar doubted the wisdom of proclaiming his devotion to Islam. His father, a former US ambassador to the United Arab Emirates, told him to listen to his heart, and to do what he thought was right for him, his family and his country. After a period of reflection, Najjar became one of the strongest advocates of Islam within the United States Secret Service, proving there was a way to serve his country proudly while practicing the faith of his choice. His volunteer positions within many American-Muslim civil rights groups all around Washington made him popular amongst the fellow Muslims at the White House.

Appreciated by his colleagues and trusted by President Muller, Najjar was exactly where he wanted to be spiritually and professionally.

"Sir? Sir?" Someone's voice intruded into his reverie.

Najjar jerked awake on the sofa, taking short fish gulps of air. Alan Laurence, a young agent on his detail, was shaking his shoulder. "Sir, the new agents are here. What do you want me to tell them?"

Shaking his head to clear the cobwebs, Najjar stretched to release the tension in his neck and back. He got up, walked to the closest mirror and fixed his tie.

He needed coffee, a fresh suit, and a toothbrush.

"Sir?" Alan repeated.

"Bring them to the briefing room, Alan. I'll brief them personally."

"Of course. I'll take care of it."

"And Alan," Najjar added, "make sure there's a fresh pot of coffee. I'll be there in five minutes."

Once Alan was gone, Najjar called home.

"Hey, it's me," he said to his wife.

"Everything okay, Yash?" Her voice sounded sleepy. She must have been napping, cuddled next to their newest child, a beautiful nine-month baby girl.

"I miss you guys, that's all," he replied truthfully.

"When will we see you?"

Najjar sighed. He had no idea.

"Not sure, hon. It's kinda busy around here."

"I had to turn off the television. I can't watch it anymore. So many lies."

Najjar couldn't fault her for that.

"Just be careful, okay?" his wife added, clearly worried. He could hear his baby girl fuss in the background.

"Always."

"We love you."

"Kiss everyone for me, will you? I'll see you guys soon. I promise."

CHAPTER 60

Tel-Aviv, Israel

Zima Bernbaum took a moment to admire the men and women working in the small, windowless office housing the command center of the MOSSAD Special Operations Division. They had lost many of their own in Bethlehem less than twenty-four hours ago, but the atmosphere wasn't one of loss and despair but of resolve and determination. A few nodded at her, but most kept their eyes glued to their screen.

A small but bulky man stood in the middle of the room, his hands crossed behind his back. He turned to Eitan.

"Thanks for coming," he said.

"Zima, please meet the legendary Matthias Sachar," Eitan said, making the introduction.

Sachar took a small bow and kissed the top of Zima's hand, the one with the missing finger.

"And Matthias," Eitan continued, "this is Zima Bernbaum. Formerly from the Canadian Security Intelligence Service—"

"Now working for the International Market Stabilization Institute, and the first woman to win our Eitan's heart."

"Happy to meet you, Mr. Sachar—"

"Matthias, please."

"Matthias, I just wish it was under other circumstances."

"So do I. At your wedding maybe?"

Zima involuntarily took a deep breath. She blushed, just a little. How nice would it be to get away from all this with Eitan? Maybe one day. The mere contemplation of Meir Yatom being tortured right at this moment made her feel guilty about entertaining such delightful thoughts. But, for a moment, her eyes met Eitan's and a warm feeling enveloped her.

One day.

"So what do we know?" Eitan asked, breaking the spell.

"We were able to repatriate the bodies of our fallen," Sachar said.

"That's something."

"But wait until you see this." Sachar led them toward a map with a bird's-eye view of Ramallah.

Located about six miles north of Jerusalem, Ramallah was the biggest city in Palestine. The hilltop city was home to the headquarters of the Palestinian Authority, a couple of beautiful parks, some of the most chaotic markets in the world and the tomb of Palestinian leader Yasser Arafat. It could also become, in a heartbeat, the most dangerous place on Earth.

On the interactive map, a small orange dot was visible.

"What is it?" Zima asked.

"This is the last known location of Meir Yatom," Sachar informed her, using his fingers to zoom in.

"So he's alive?" There was nothing Zima desired more.

"He was two hours ago when one of our sources sent us this," Sachar said. He swept the interactive map away with his fingers. A grainy picture of man being carried on a stretcher appeared. "I presume the picture isn't as clear as we'd like it to be because it was taken while our source was on the move."

"Are we sure it's him?" The picture quality was such that Zima didn't recognize the man being carried away.

"Ninety-three percent sure."

"I want in," Eitan said. "Whatever you're planning, I want in."

"Me too," Zima added. "That's why I'm here. I owe Meir my life."

Sachar smiled, squeezed himself between Eitan and Zima and wrapped his arms around their shoulders. "I'm glad you said this, because you two are the key players in our strategy to get Meir back."

CHAPTER 61

New York City, New York

Lara Firouzgari took the sim card out of her smartphone and dropped it in the kitchen sink. She pushed it into the garburator with her finger. She added a couple of pieces of cucumber and opened the water faucet. She turned on the garburator and kept it running until she was sure the sim card was no more. She was a deep-cover asset for the Iranian government and her direct contact was none other than the Quds Force commanding officer, General Jalal Kharazi.

Her father, Colonel Forood Firouzgari, had trained her from a very young age. Home schooled, she'd never had the opportunity to develop friendships with other children her age. Her father had taken the roles of mentor, friend and superior officer. He had taught her everything she needed to know to one day fulfill the mission he knew he couldn't do himself. His sickness had been brief. And for that, she thanked Allah every day. Before passing away, he had introduced her to another single cell, a man named Radman Divecha, who worked for the New York State Police. She had met him only once, but he had seemed capable enough. Radman's father had entered the United States the same way her own father did decades ago. She wasn't sure why Radman seemed to think he was in charge, but Lara suspected it had to do with the fact she was a woman. Muslim or not, she sometimes wondered why women weren't treated equally in Iran. It was true the Americans lived a degenerate lifestyle, but at least their women weren't mistreated.

Lara went to her bedroom and lifted her mattress. She pushed it off the box spring and opened the compartment hidden beneath it. She picked a few items and crammed them into her purse. She wouldn't need much for this job. If everything went well, she'd be back in time to watch her favorite television show.

CHAPTER 62

Presbyterian Hospital, New York City

Radman Divecha parked his unmarked Crown Victoria in one of the numerous spots reserved for police vehicles. With Mayor Church still in intensive care and the number of police vehicles already parked at the hospital, it was a small miracle he had found a parking space so close to the main entrance.

Divecha was still debating if he'd follow the orders he had received from Kharazi or go with his guts. His orders were simple enough. Go in, kill Mayor Church, and take down as many NYPD officers as he could.

But he didn't like that plan. In fact, he hated it. Why? Because he wasn't yet ready to die. Of course, taking down a few cops and the mayor would be easy. Like any terror attack, if the perpetrator was ready to give his life in exchange for mission success, triumph was almost guaranteed. But he wasn't a terrorist. He was a soldier, just like his father. His gut told him to take an entirely different path.

Kill the bitch that had betrayed them, get out, and wait for another opportunity to kill the mayor. Since Sassani had failed so miserably, he didn't see why the other woman would be any different. He had met Lara Firouzgari only once, but her attitude hadn't impressed him. Just like Sassani, she had been in America too long and he feared her commitment would falter at the critical moment. If she failed to kill Sassani as he had ordered her to, they were in trouble.

Damn it! It was bad luck two out of the three SAVAK colonels assigned to New York had daughters instead of sons. If he'd been dealing with male agents instead of these worthless bitches, Mayor

Church would already be six feet underground and the New York governor would be next.

But no, here I am cleaning up Sassani's mess.

Flustered, he entered the hospital by the emergency room and headed directly to the information desk. He flipped his wallet open and showed his badge to one of the two receptionists. She gave him a practiced smile and a look that said, *I couldn't care less about your badge.*

"What can I do for you?"

"Staff Sergeant Divecha, New York State Police," he said, replacing his wallet in his back pocket.

"Again, what can I do for you?"

"I'm looking for Sergeant Tracy Sassani."

"So are many others."

"Can you tell me where she is?"

"No."

"Why?" Divecha was getting frustrated. "This is official police business."

"If you're not with the NYPD or a close family member, I don't care who you are. You're not seeing her."

"Can you at least tell me if she's all right? I'm a friend, too," he said, throwing a bit of compassion into the mix.

The receptionist let out a sigh. She hit a few keys on a keyboard and said, "She's in surgery."

"She's still in surgery?" he asked.

Another sigh. "That's what I just said."

Sassani had been shot six hours ago. How long did it take to remove a bullet?

"Thanks for all your help," Divecha said before walking away. He hadn't yet made ten steps when someone put a hand on his shoulder from behind.

Divecha automatically pivoted one hundred and eighty degrees on his right heel and deflected the wrist by sweeping his right arm from left to write. His knees were bent and his left hand coiled to strike when his would-be assailant backed off, his hands in the air. Divecha saw an NYPD badge attached to his belt. The man was a plainclothes officer. Mid-fifties with a generous waistline.

"Whoa there, partner," the officer said. "Relax."

Divecha hadn't realized he was so on edge. A quick look around him confirmed only a few people had noticed the altercation.

"I'm sorry."

The officer frowned. "Anyway, I heard you talking to Val here," the officer said, his eyes toward the receptionist. "She's just doing her job, you know."

"Of course."

"So you want to see Tracy?"

"You know her?"

"We work together. Well, we used to before she joined Church's protective detail."

"I wanted to ask her a few questions," Divecha said. "It can wait. I'm Radman by the way."

"Daniel," the officer replied. He was tearing up and used the sleeve of his shirt to wipe what might have been a tear.

"You guys were close?"

"I guess you could say that," Daniel said. "Like father-to-daughter kind of thing. So you knew her too?"

"We met a few times. I'm with the governor's protective detail, so we crossed paths at special events and such, you know?"

Daniel nodded. "You want a coffee?"

"Sure, lead the way," Divechia replied, having found his ticket to Sassani.

CHAPTER 63

Presbyterian Hospital, New York City

Seated in the passenger seat of the IMSI's newest ride—a Volvo XC90—Lisa Walton felt the adrenaline run through her veins. It was a pleasant feeling. One she didn't experience often enough anymore. Truth was, it was hard to get excited behind a computer screen. She understood Mapother's decision to keep her out of the field, but it didn't mean she didn't long to go back out.

For the first time since the events in Greece and Russia—where she was severely beaten and tortured by Sheik al-Assad—Mapother had agreed to let her out of headquarters to conduct a mission, albeit with a chaperone; her husband, which made the pill a little easier to swallow.

She looked at Mike and placed her hand on his lap. Their eyes met. She smiled.

"How do you feel?" Mike asked as he turned into an underground parking lot two blocks away from the Presbyterian Hospital.

"Happy to be out and about."

"I told Mapother you were ready for light field work."

"I'm surprised he granted your request," Lisa said, scanning for a parking space. "Even if it's only for *light field work*."

"I think the exact words I used were *super-light field work*," Mike said, chuckling.

Lisa retracted her hand and punched him in the shoulder. It was fun to be back in the field with her husband. They were a good team. They had gone through so much together.

"Are you up to it?" he asked her.

She didn't bother to reply. Instead, she asked, "What if she doesn't want to talk to us?"

"Then we'll change tactics."

Sergeant Sassani not wanting to talk to them was indeed a possibility. Charles Mapother had wanted to use his newfound presidential sanction to move in quickly, take Sergeant Sassani into custody and interrogate her at the IMSI's headquarters. Mike had agreed but Lisa had voiced her objection. She argued that since Sassani had clearly made the choice not to kill Mayor Church in cold blood, there was a chance she'd willingly give them the intelligence they so badly needed. If they moved on her too aggressively, she may revert to being the person her father wanted her to be. Mapother had granted her request but had nevertheless given Mike the authority to do what was necessary to extract everything she knew if Lisa's gentle approach didn't bear fruit.

They entered the hospital by the emergency room and went directly to the third floor using the stairs, bypassing two men talking to each other next to the information desk.

"We're in," Lisa said into her throat microphone. "Status update on our target?"

"She just got out of surgery. They're moving her to the recovery room now," replied Jonathan Sanchez from his desk at the IMSI headquarters. "But it might take a while before she wakes up."

"Copy that."

"How long before we can speak with her, Lisa?" Mike asked her.

In another life, before the Sheik stole her children and shattered the nice life she and Mike had built for themselves, Lisa had been a trauma surgeon. If anyone could guess how long it would take Sassani to wake up, she could.

"Depends what they used to keep her down during surgery. I'd say thirty to forty-five minutes," Lisa said. "Then they'll give her opioids like morphine or dilaudid. That will keep her drowsy."

"What do want to do? There's no point trying to get into the recovery room if she can't talk."

"You're right. There's nothing for you to do until she wakes up, so why not get a coffee or something? Civilians aren't allowed in the recovery room."

"What about you?"

"I'll go check on our patient."

CHAPTER 64

Presbyterian Hospital, New York City

Lisa had to climb two more stories to reach the locker rooms. Some hospitals—like the one she used to work for in Ottawa—had beautifully appointed locker and shower rooms for their doctors. The Presbyterian Hospital's weren't as quaint but Lisa found what she was looking for. After a quick stop at the restroom, she took a minute to look at her reflection while she washed her hands. Her strawberry blond hair was in a ponytail behind her back. The white lab coat she had grabbed from an unlocked locker fit her frame perfectly. For a moment, the sight of the stethoscope around her neck transported her back in time. A time when her life was marvelous, when her only worry was whether her husband would make it in time for dinner or not. A time when she tried to save lives, not take them. The last two years had transformed her soul. Gone was her limitless compassion. Gone was her willingness to help others. So much had been taken from her, she had nothing to give back. If it wasn't for Mapother and Mike, she wasn't sure she'd have the strength to continue. Bleeding to death on that dirty floor in Russia had taught her something; death wasn't something she feared anymore. With the Sheik rotting somewhere in a black site, her vengeance was complete. Or was it? Mike had found a higher purpose, something to live for, but, deep down, she wasn't there yet.

The door of the locker room opened, startling Lisa and bringing her back to the present. She turned around to greet the young woman who had just walked in.

About my height, slim build, blond hair and radiant blue eyes. Dressed in a pink summer dress and yellow flat shoes. A young doctor.

"Good morning," Lisa said, leaning back against the counter. The locker room's entrance wasn't large and the space between the door and the row of sinks wasn't big enough for two people to stand side by side.

"Good morning," the newcomer said. "I don't think we've met. Are you new here?"

"Just visiting for the week," Lisa said without missing a beat. "I'm Dr. Lisa Walton."

"I'm Dr. Christine Simpson."

Lisa shook hands with Christine. "Nice to meet you."

"Same here. You been here long?" Christine pulled a longer than usual toothbrush from her handbag.

"A couple days."

"I haven't seen you before, that's why I'm asking." Christine was now carefully applying a generous quantity of toothpaste to her toothbrush. "Where are you from, Lisa?"

"I'm from Canada—"

"I love Canada. I'm told you guys have the best healthcare in the world. And it's free, isn't?" she said before she started brushing her teeth with a vigor Lisa had rarely seen.

Lisa didn't feel like getting into a discussion about the politics of Canadian health care, but it never ceased to amaze her how little the Americans really knew about the publicly funded Canadian health care system. The single-payer system consisted of thirteen provincial and territorial socialized health insurance plans that provided universal health care to all Canadian citizens. It basically worked like the United States' Medicare, but for everyone. It covered almost everything, with the exceptions of dental care, prescription glasses and prescription drugs, but most people had private insurance to cover these exclusions. In theory, Lisa had to admit it looked great. But practically, it was a nightmare.

"Kind of, but it's more complicated than that. Anyhow, nice to meet you, and have a wonderful day, Dr. Simpson." Lisa tried to squeeze between the wall and Christine.

The moment she was behind her, and with a speed and agility that left Lisa momentarily paralyzed, Christine used her hip to shove her against the wall and used her left elbow to strike Lisa behind the head.

. . . .

Lara Firouzgari—AKA Christine Simpson—was pretty sure the woman wasn't who she said she was. Her eyes had betrayed her inner self. Her smile was genuine, her voice graciously soft, but the deep sadness in her blue eyes was easy to detect by anyone knowing what to look for. By hacking into the hospital's database, Lara had memorized the names of all the doctors and nurses who were scheduled to work in the recovery room and the two adjacent floors today. It was easy to figure out which lockers she could pry open without fear of getting caught by its owner. There had been no mention of a Dr. Lisa Walton visiting from Canada. It could have been a slipup by the administrator in charge of logging in the doctors' hours, but Lara didn't feel like taking the chance. It would be naïve to think they were the only ones after Sassani.

Lara used her hip to pin Walton against the wall and delivered a powerful elbow strike to her head. Walton ducked at the last second and parried with her left arm, confirming Lara's thought that the good doctor from Canada wasn't who she said she was. If her elbow strike had landed as intended, it would have knocked Walton out, or at least incapacitated her until she finished her off. But now Lara was at a disadvantage. With Walton behind her and her back exposed, she had to do something or she'd be the one found stuffed in a locker with a broken neck.

. . . .

Lisa's heart was racing. What had just happened? She punched Simpson in the ribs with her right fist but without much strength. Still flattened against the wall, she didn't have the room to make it more powerful. She wrapped her right arm against Simpson's neck, locked it tight with the other one and kicked the back of her knees with her left foot. In a few seconds, it would be all over.

. . . .

Lara's breath was knocked out of her. She clawed at the skin wrapped around her neck but the pressure only intensified. Her face was contorted in rage. How could she have underestimated her opponent like that? Dizziness enveloped her. There was not enough air coming through to fill her lungs. In a last effort to save herself, and knowing she had only a couple seconds left before passing out, Lara let go of the arm around her neck and grabbed with two hands the toothbrush she was still clutching in her right hand. She twisted it and pulled it apart in the middle. A small knife, about two inches long and half an inch wide and as sharp as a scalpel, was embedded within the lower end of the toothbrush.

She didn't have much strength left, but, fortunately, stabbing someone's thigh with a sharp object didn't require much.

. . . .

Catching a glimpse of the blade in the large mirror above the sinks, Lisa just had time to angle her body away from its trajectory before it sliced through her jeans and embedded itself in the drywall next to her thigh. A gurgle escaped Simpson's mouth. She was about to suffocate. Lisa tightened her hold. Simpson tried to kick at her but Lisa didn't let go. As much as she wanted to keep Simpson alive, Simpson's preemptive attack meant she didn't share the feeling toward her. Simpson went limp, and Lisa made the decision to hold the choke for another minute. When it was done, Lisa called Mike.

"Join me in the doctors' locker room. Bring a wheelchair with you," Lisa said, out of breath.

"What happened?"

"I was attacked by someone claiming to be a doctor."

"Damn it! We're not the only ones after Sassani. Stay put. I'm on my way."

Before replacing the phone in her back pocket, Lisa snapped a few pictures of the dead woman and sent them to Sanchez at the IMSI headquarters.

CHAPTER 65

Presbyterian Hospital, New York City

S*assani*. Did someone say Sassani? Radman Divecha searched his surroundings. People sipping coffees and playing with their phones occupied most of the hospital cafeteria's tables. A man seated two tables away bolted from his chair. He had his phone glued his ear. The man left his coffee behind and headed straight for the exit. Maybe Divecha wouldn't need to befriend Daniel after all. Divecha was sure this was the man he had heard say *Sassani*. If this was indeed the case, it was worth pursuing.

"Daniel, would you excuse me for a minute?" Divecha said to the NYPD detective.

"Of course," Daniel said, without knowing his life had been saved *in extremis*.

Divecha got up and patted Daniel on the shoulder. "Hang in there, brother. She'll be fine."

Daniel grabbed his forearm. "Thanks for the support, Radman. Means a lot."

Divecha nodded and walked away. He had lost a few precious seconds. Who was the man who had said Sassani? Had he heard correctly? He checked his watch. If Lara Firouzgari had done what was asked of her, Sassani should be dead by now. Or just about to be. Why did he have the feeling she had failed? Outside the cafeteria, Divecha looked right and left. Where had the man gone?

Damn!

Should he go straight to the mayor and have done with it, or listen to his gut and check on Sassani? There was no point in killing Church if Sassani was still alive.

His eyes caught movement to his right. A man was entering the elevator, pushing an empty wheelchair. Black hair, medium build but fit, a few inches short of six feet. This was the same man who had left the cafeteria in a hurry, but he was now wearing a white lab coat.

Divecha sprinted to the elevator and inserted his arm just as the doors were about to close. The doors opened and the man looked at him. For a millisecond, the man looked perplexed but he recuperated quickly.

"Which floor?"

. . . .

Mike borrowed the wheelchair from the emergency room. A lab coat was neatly folded on its seat. He put it on. It was without a name but it was better than nothing. He rushed back to the elevators and was glad to see one had just arrived. Three nurses dressed in blue scrubs exited the elevator and turned to their left. Mike entered the elevator alone and pressed the button for the fourth floor.

For the love of God, what had Lisa got herself into? It was her first mission since Russia. It was supposed to be a simple interrogation, or abduction if everything else failed. They were in the United States, not a third-world country. It should have been an easy operation. Lisa was a superb operator—even gifted some people said—but attracted more than her fair share of bad luck. What worried Mike more, though, was that they weren't the only ones after Sassani. And if Sassani was in danger, so was Mayor Church.

The elevator doors were almost shut when someone forced his right arm between them. The doors bumped against it and reopened. A man walked in. He was taller than Mike and at least forty pounds heavier than his one hundred and eighty. A New York State Police badge was clipped to his belt. His eyes were dark and menacing, betraying the fake smile on his lips.

"Which floor?" Mike asked.

The man looked at the panel. "Same as yours."

Mike remembered seeing this man when he had first entered the hospital. He had been standing by the information desk speaking to another individual. And if his memory served him well, hadn't the man been in the cafeteria sipping coffee with that same person?

This was a bad situation, especially now that he had seen the badge clipped to the man's belt. Mike couldn't subdue the man simply because he had a fake smile.

"Here to see someone?" Mike said, keeping a hand on the wheelchair and slipping the other behind his back where his Glock 19 was secured.

"Yeah," the officer replied, turning toward Mike. His suit jacked was open and his hand rested on the butt of his service pistol. "NYPD Sergeant Sassani."

Mike's heart jumped. Had he heard Mike say her name? He had definitely slipped up in the cafeteria; Lisa's distress call had taken him by surprise. If the New York State Police officer had overheard his conversation, there was no point lying.

"Me too. I just got a call. She's out of surgery. You guys work together?"

"I'm with the governor's protective detail. We've met a couple times."

Mike allowed himself to relax ever so slightly. With the events of the last few days, from the assassination of the Canadian prime minister to the attempted killing of Mayor Church, it made sense that police officers—particularly those working the protection details—were a bit edgy.

The elevator came to a halt. Mike looked at the display. They were on the second floor. The doors opened and a couple of doctors joined them in the elevator. Mike was glad to see them position themselves between him and the state trooper. The doctors never acknowledged them but kept talking about a patient who'd been diagnosed with stage-four pancreatic cancer. When the elevator stopped on the third floor, the doctors exited the elevator without giving the two other men a second glance.

Once the doors were closed and nobody else boarded the elevator, the trooper pivoted one hundred and eighty degrees on his right foot and at the same time pulled a knife from its nylon sheath on his duty belt. In a flash, he was on Mike.

CHAPTER 66

IMSI Headquarters, New York

Jonathan Sanchez didn't lose any time. The moment the pictures Lisa sent him popped up on his screen, he shared them with Anna Caprini who in turned advised Charles Mapother of the developing situation at the Presbyterian Hospital.

In less than a minute, Sanchez had a hit.

"Who is she?" Mapother asked.

"Her name is Lara Firouzgari. She was one of them," Sanchez told him.

"Her father was one of the colonels?"

This time it was Caprini who replied. "Yes, sir. Colonel Yavar Firouzgari. He was on the list provided by General Adbullahi."

"What do we know about him?"

"So far, not much, I'm afraid," Caprini admitted. "We've just started to canvass our systems. What we do know came from the intel Adbullahi gave us."

Sanchez could see Mapother was getting impatient. He gestured Caprini to keep going but her mind was fully occupied by her screen. Caprini had the tendency to withhold information until she had a clear understanding of what was going on. She didn't do it on purpose; she just wasn't comfortable sharing incomplete intelligence with her boss. Sanchez had no such problems. Being a former Delta operator, he understood more than most how important every bit of intel really was.

"He entered the United States with the help of the CIA in nineteen seventy-nine, had one daughter and worked in a shoe factory," he said to Mapother.

"What about his daughter?"

"We know absolutely nothing about her."

"And yet, she went to the hospital and tried to kill Lisa," replied Mapother. "Call her back, Jonathan. Let her know who the woman was and tell her I'm sending Support Team One to help her and Mike out."

"Right away."

"In the meantime, I'll make sure the NYPD double-up on Mayor Church's security."

CHAPTER 67

Presbyterian Hospital, New York City

Lisa wanted to lock the door of the locker room but realized that Simpson had already done so. She texted Mike to let him know she was still there and that he should contact her prior to entering the locker room.

Her phone chirped twice. It was the IMSI getting back to her.

"Who is she?" she asked.

"Her name is Lara Firouzgari. She's by all accounts an Iranian agent. Her father was on the list," Sanchez told her.

"She was after Sassani too," Lisa said.

"That's what we think. And if the Iranians are after Sassani, it means—"

"That they're after the mayor too. Yes, I know, Jonathan."

There was a pause, and then Jonathan said, "You're okay there, Lisa?"

"Just send a support team to take care of her. Mike and I will go check on Sassani. I guess a quiet talk with her at the hospital is now out of the question, right?"

"It's probably best we take her in."

"If the Iranians were ready to waste an asset on Sassani, she must know something they don't want us to learn."

"Maybe."

"What do you mean maybe? Am I missing something?"

"*Maybe* they just want her to keep quiet. If she voluntary failed in what was asked of her—in this case the assassination of Mayor Church—there's a possibility she'd be willing to go public with what she knows."

That hadn't yet crossed Lisa's mind. Sanchez was right.

Her phone vibrated in her hand, indicating receipt of a text message.

I'm here. Door is locked.

"I'll call you back. Mike's here."

Lisa unlocked the door and opened it.

She gasped.

The man in front of her wasn't Mike.

CHAPTER 68

Ramallah, Palestine

Less than a year ago, while conducting a rescue mission for Mike's father in Syria, Zima Bernbaum had lost a finger to a sniper. The pain, intense as it had been, was nothing compare to the agony she was now experiencing. For the last ninety minutes, Eitan and Zima had been trapped in a tiny secret compartment hidden under the back seat of the medical supply van they were using to enter the West Bank. Within ten minutes her legs began to tingle and cramp up. After thirty minutes, she couldn't feel her legs anymore. After an hour, she wanted to die. The only thing keeping her from screaming was the thought of Meir Yatom. To his credit, Eitan, who was much taller than her, hadn't complained at all. In fact, he snored straight through the last half hour.

The van belonged to Ungava Bay International Medicine—a genuine international pharmaceutical company headquartered in Canada. UBIM operated schools in impoverished neighborhoods around the world, donated tons of medicine to underprivileged elderlies and children, and, above all, it remained apolitical in all conflicts by never publicly endorsing an organization or a political party. Their reputation allowed them to travel anywhere on the globe without interference from local governments.

The MOSSAD, aware of UBIM's flawless reputation, had decided a long time ago it needed a stake in the company. Since UBIM was a non-profit organization, the only way it could somewhat control, or at least know, what was really going on within the walls of UBIM's offices in Tel-Aviv was to have its own people working there. There were now a dozen MOSSAD agents embedded within UBIM in Israel. One of them was Eugene Zaret, a delivery truck driver.

Zaret had been employed by UBIM for five years. In that time, he had safely and successfully infiltrated and exfiltrated over a dozen MOSSAD agents from the West Bank. Zima was told Zaret was the best. If you needed to get in and out of the West Bank unnoticed, Zaret was the guy.

The van slowed down. The brakes squealed, and the van came to a stop before backing up.

"We're there," Eitan whispered.

"About time you woke up."

"What? I didn't even sleep."

"Liar."

A door opened and closed. Someone yelled something in Arabic that Zima couldn't understand. This was Zaret's first and final stop today. He had briefed them on how to exit the compartment. It wasn't a difficult or dangerous process, as long as they didn't do it while the vehicle was running. There were two levers to pull. One was above Zima's head and the other next to Eitan's right hip. Both needed to be pull at the same time or it wouldn't open

"I need to get out of here," Zima whispered. "I can't feel my legs."

"And you think I can feel mine? Toughen up, buttercup," Eitan replied. "We can't exit now."

"What? Don't fuck with me, Eitan. I'm not joking. I need to get out of this box." Zima fought to keep her voice low. Panic was slowly taking over.

"The warehouse we're in isn't friendly to MOSSAD agents. If we get out before they close shop, we're done."

Shit.

CHAPTER 69

Presbyterian Hospital, New York

Mike shoved the wheelchair toward the trooper. He easily sidestepped it, but it gave Mike the second he needed to assess the situation. The trooper held the knife in a reverse grip with its edge out. That was bad news, especially at close quarters. This trooper was no ordinary cop and he knew how to fight. Mike had no time to grab his gun. This type of reverse grip had many advantages. Since the blade's cutting edge faced Mike no matter where the trooper's hand was located, even a punch-like motion was dangerous. Because the trooper held the knife how one would hold an ice pick, he could bring tremendous force to bear on the tip, not only when oriented downward, but also behind or beside him. By using this grip, the trooper gave himself an enhanced defensive position too. The only thing in Mike's favor was the limited reach of this grip technique. The point and the edge couldn't be extended like a forward grip.

Not that it's gonna make a huge difference in this elevator.

The trooper's knees were slightly bent and so were his elbows. Whatever the outcome, everything would be over in less than five seconds. Knife fights were very fast. In the first half-second of every fight, deceptions were involved to distract you. The chances of getting cut were high, and it was important to seize a window of opportunity. Mike had learned the hard way that, in a knife fight against a skilled opponent, you might have one or perhaps two openings at most. For Mike there was only option, and it wasn't defense.

He attacked.

. . . .

Divecha was caught off guard. The kill should have been easy, but the man reacted immediately by shoving the wheelchair forward. He then took one step forward and used his right leg to kick Divecha's left knee. Divecha countered instinctively by trying to slash at the man's foot. He realized his fatal mistake too late.

. . . .

Mike's foot missed the knee and hit the trooper three inches lower. The kick hadn't much force in it but it served his purpose. In a natural attempt to deflect the upcoming blow, the trooper brought his knife down, leaving himself open. The tip pierced Mike's pants but missed the flesh. Mike threw a powerful right hook that caught the trooper's unprotected chin and followed immediately with a left uppercut. The trooper arched back, and Mike's fist missed his mark. He quickly stepped back and ducked as the trooper's knife sliced from left to right. Mike drove his fist up and hard into the trooper's kidney. The trooper groaned and tried to bring the knife back from right to left. Mike ducked again and used his knees to power another uppercut. This time, it connected right under the trooper's chin. The trooper flew backward and into the elevator's doors. His head hit the doors at a weird angle and his body slipped sideways.

The fight had last less than five seconds.

Mike disarmed the trooper, pocketed the knife and the holstered pistol. He handcuffed him and grabbed him under his armpits. He lifted the trooper and sat him in the wheelchair. Mike removed his lab coat and placed it on the trooper's torso to hide the fact that he was handcuffed. Two seconds later, the elevator's doors opened and Mike pushed the wheelchair out.

CHAPTER 70

Presbyterian Hospital

Lisa's eyes moved from the man in the wheelchair to her husband.

"What happened?" she asked Mike as she moved away from the door to let him and the wheelchair in.

"I have no idea. He's a New York State trooper; or at least he says he is."

"You talked to him?"

"We exchanged a few words in the elevator, then he pulled a knife on me."

"You think they worked as a team?" Lisa showed her husband the body of the woman who had tried to kill her. "Name's Lara Firouzgari. Another second-generation Iranian agent."

"Until we know for sure who the trooper is, I don't know what to think, but I wouldn't be surprised if they were both after Sassani."

"What do we do with them?"

"Did you call this in?"

"Charles is sending a support team."

"This guy," Mike said, tapping the trooper on the shoulder, "might wake up before the support team makes it here."

Lisa looked at the trooper. His head was tilted to the side. Blood flowed out of his right ear. Lisa checked for a pulse.

"There's no danger of that happening now."

"What do you mean?"

"You killed him."

. . . .

Mike's knees buckled but he held on to the wheelchair's handles. Killing the man had never been his intention. Not only did he want to know why a New York State trooper would assault him, he needed to chat with him regarding his connection with Sassani.

"He was alive when I pulled him up from the elevator's floor," he said, light-headed.

"How hard did you hit him?"

"Too hard, I guess," Mike said.

Mike searched the man and located his credentials inside the trooper's suit jacket. He took a photo with his smartphone and sent it to the IMSI for verification.

"There's no doubt in my mind he wasn't a good guy, Mike," his wife said. "A regular cop would never have attacked you with a knife."

Lisa had a valid point. "We'll know soon enough."

"We need to check on Sassani," Lisa said. "But first, we need to hide the bodies until the support team shows up."

Mike looked around. "Why don't we put them in the handicap stall?" he offered.

Mike pushed the wheelchair into the bathroom and helped Lisa carry the body of the dead woman. He positioned her on the toilet with her back tilted backward. Once he was sure she wouldn't fall, he locked the door from the inside and crawled out of the stall.

"Time for our chat with Sergeant Sassani."

He and Lisa were still in the locker room when his phone beeped. It was Charles Mapother calling from the IMSI headquarters. Mike's heart skipped a couple beats. He took a deep breath before answering. More than anything, he hoped Mapother was going to confirm the trooper wasn't a real police officer.

"Yes, Charles?"

"I'm sorry to say this, Mike, but the man you killed was indeed a New York State trooper," Mapother told him. Mike's chest tightened and he dropped his phone. He fell to his knees, his heart beating much faster than it should have. He was aware of what was happening to him. It wasn't the first time.

A panic attack. Just like the one that had nearly cost him his life in Russia. Suddenly he couldn't breathe, couldn't talk, and his eyes couldn't focus. He felt like throwing up, but darkness enveloped him. Mapother's next words were lost on him.

I killed a cop.

He sensed Lisa kneeling next to him, forcing him to sit down with his back resting against the wall. She pressed a cold-water paper towel against his forehead while explaining to Mapother what just happened.

"Mike, Mike," his wife said, squeezing his shoulder. "Focus, baby, focus. The trooper was an Iranian asset. His father was one of the colonels."

Somehow the words made it through to Mike. He forced himself to inhale and exhale deeply, just as the doctor told him to do in situations like this. After a few seconds, the fog around his mind started to clear.

"Are we sure?" he finally asked.

"One hundred percent. His name is Radman Divecha. That confirms he and Firouzgari were working together."

Mike used the countertop to help himself back to his feet. "Sassani must be important if the Iranians sent two assets to take her out," he said, regaining control over his mental state.

"They're afraid she'll talk to us," Lisa said, handing Mike his phone. "Mapother is sending more people to take care of the bodies. You're good?"

"Yeah," Mike replied, reaching into his front pocket. He grabbed a couple of tablets and popped two in his mouth. He washed them down by drinking directly from the tap. He never understood how people were able to swallow tablets without any liquid intake. He splashed water on his face and dried it with paper towel.

"Let's go." He led the way out of the locker room. He opened the door for her, but Lisa didn't move. "What?"

"Wait for me downstairs, Mike, and link with the support team. I'll get Sassani."

Mike was about to protest but Lisa's expression told him it wouldn't be a good idea.

CHAPTER 71

Presbyterian Hospital, New York

Not for the first time Lisa wondered if it was time for her and Mike to pull the plug after this mission. With the Sheik in prison and the people responsible for the death of Melissa and their unborn child now six feet underground, wasn't their revenge complete? Being back in the field felt like a breath of fresh air, but how long before she was shot again? How long before Mike's emotional state brought him to a dark place he'd never get away from. The last years—and Lisa's near-death experience in Russia had accelerated the process—had chipped away at Mike's mental health. In Lisa's professional opinion, Mike's bi-weekly appointments with Dr. Howe, the IMSI psychologist, and the tablets he kept popping more and more frequently, weren't enough anymore. She should talk with Charles Mapother and tell him how bad it really was. She doubted Mike was totally honest with Dr. Howe. Of course, he'd say just enough to show he was trying, but Lisa knew her husband. He had a hard time admitting he needed help.

Once this was all over, that's what she was going to do. Enough was enough. She needed Mike. They had given enough, more than their fair share. Mapother would understand. He had to.

But first, there was a mission to complete. The recovery room was located at the end of the corridor. Lisa walked the hallway as if she belonged and avoided eye contact with fellow medical personnel. Four uniformed NYPD officers stood in front of the recovery room but they seemed relaxed compared to those positioned a floor below where Mayor Church was being treated for his injuries. The officers chatted among themselves and didn't even look at the doctors and nurses going in and out of the recovery room where

Sergeant Sassani was resting. Lisa concluded the NYPD didn't yet know what was really going on.

Lisa entered the recovery room and spotted Sassani right away. There were only five other patients. But the good news stopped there.

Two men stood next to Sassani. Their hair was cut short and it was easy to see the demarcations of their bulletproof vests under their dark suits.

Detectives.

Their presence worried Lisa and she wondered if she had been wrong about the NYPD not knowing Sassani's role in Mayor Church's assassination attempt. She walked to the next female patient and feigned reading her chart while eavesdropping on the conversation between the detectives and Sassani.

"I need protection, Chuck," Sassani said, clutching the hand of the taller of the two detectives.

"Why would you need protection, Tracy?" Chuck asked. "You took a bullet for Mayor Church, for God's sake."

"You're a hero," added the other detective.

Lisa noticed Chuck hadn't withdrawn his hand.

Sassani closed her eyes. "I'm no hero, Shawn."

The detectives exchanged a glance. They looked puzzled.

"I'm in danger. Call Assistant Chief Thomas, please," Sassani pleaded.

"The boss of the Intelligence Division? That Chief Thomas?" Chuck asked. "Why would I—"

"Just do it, Chuck," Sassani said.

"What have you got yourself into?" Chuck asked before adding, "Whatever it is, I'm here, okay?"

"I know," Sassani said, her voice cracking.

"I love you, Tracy. I'll do it. I'll call Chief Thomas. Everything's gonna be all right. I promise." Chuck headed toward the exit. He hadn't made it halfway when he stopped and looked straight at Lisa.

"Hey you," he said with the tone of a cop directing traffic before he realized to whom he was speaking. "Take care of her, doctor, will you?" he added more gently.

"I certainly will."

. . . .

It was clear to Lisa that Sassani was willing to cooperate. Sassani knew she was in danger and wanted protection. That was a good sign. Time was of the essence here. Lisa had to move fast.

She approached Sassani and asked, "How do you feel, Sergeant?"

"Not too bad, doctor, considering I've been shot."

"Trust me, I know exactly what you mean."

Sassani raised her eyebrows. "You've been shot before?"

Lisa smiled and gently touched Sassani's forearm. "I'm one of the good guys, Tracy. The organization I work for will offer you protection. If you cooperate, that is."

Sassani's eyes opened wide and she withdrew her arm. "Who are you?" she said, a bit too loud for Lisa's taste.

"Keep your voice down," Lisa warned her. "Less than fifteen minutes ago I killed a female Iranian agent who was probably on her way here to finish what your father started."

Sassani shivered. "So you know," she finally said.

"I do. And so does my organization. We're ready to help, but you'll have to come with us."

"I . . . I can't. I need medical attention. I—"

"We'll provide you with the best medical services," Lisa said, "but we need to go now."

"You're not with the FBI. I'd be chained to my bed if you were."

"I'm not with the Bureau," Lisa confirmed.

"How do I know you're not working with the Iranians?"

"Valid question," Lisa replied. She dug her phone out of her pocket and showed Sassani Lara Firouzgari's picture. Then she said, "Her name was Lara. She's dead now. She was supposed to kill you."

Tears rolled from Sassani's eyes. "I'm not a terrorist. I love this country . . . It's home."

"Now's your chance to prove it."

CHAPTER 72

Montreal, Canada

Colonel Asad Davari sat in the third row of the Airbus A330's first-class cabin, a cup of coffee in hand. A flight attendant pushed a sweets trolley down the aisle and Davari wondered why Air Canada insisted on serving ice cream for dessert. It made no sense to him. By the time the flight attendant reached his seat, the vanilla ice cream the flight attendant had scooped in the bowl was half melted. She offered one to Davari.

"Thank you, but no," he said. "Do you have anything else?"

She didn't roll her eyes, but Davari sensed this was exactly what she wanted to do. It seemed to take all her energy to ask him what he had in mind.

"A candy bar would be nice, if you have one."

The flight attendant returned to the galley and came back a minute later with a Coffee Crisp.

"Will that do?" she said, handing it to him without a hint of a smile. She didn't wait for him to reply and rolled her trolley to the next passenger.

"Ice cream?" she asked the traveler seated in front of him, a heavyset man dressed in a dark business suit.

"You have another Coffee Crisp?" the man said. "I usually like my ice cream frozen, you know."

The flight attendant looked annoyed, and Davari couldn't help it; he smiled. It didn't matter where he was in the world or which airline he used, flight attendants, male or female, didn't seem to like their jobs. Davari didn't blame them. He hated dealing with the public too. He'd be a poor flight attendant.

Davari wished Mariwala had been with him in first class. It would have allowed him to rest in anticipation of their next mission.

But the only seat left was in economy. Halfway through their flight from Heathrow to Montreal, Davari had taken a walk down the aisle. Mariwala was squeezed between a breastfeeding woman and her young child, and a gigantic man who must have weighed north of three hundred and fifty pounds.

The landing was a non-event, but the line to go through Canadian customs was longer than expected. The last time Davari had entered Canada, it had been through Toronto. It was his first time in Montreal. The Quds Force had only one full-time safe house in Canada and it was located in Montreal. It would have been easier to fly directly to one of New York City's three main airports, but the enhanced security measures in all American airports heightened the chance of exposure. Entering the United States through Mexico used to be the safest and easiest route. Not so much anymore. Entering through Canada was now deemed the most secure path for clandestine operatives. The assassination of the Canadian prime minister by a member of his own protection detail had not only created an international outrage, it had also triggered a tightening in security across the country, but General Kharazi had judged Canada was still the path of least resistance.

Davari hoped he was right.

He kept an eye on Sergeant Mariwala, who was now six persons in front of him and waiting for his turn to be questioned by the young Canada Border Services Agency—CBSA—officer sitting in his glass booth. So many things could go wrong, but Davari tried not to think about them. He reminded himself that the Canadian passport in his possession wasn't a forgery. It was part of a batch the Iranian government had bought from a corrupt Canadian official. Davari had brokered the deal. That was why he had traveled to Toronto.

Davari watched as Mariwala approached the booth. The young agent was Caucasian. That was good news. Out of fear of being pilloried as racists or Islamophobics, white police officers and CBSA agents across Canada and the United States were now walking on eggshells because of how they were treated by the media. This meant he was less likely to be sent to secondary inspection. Davari was too far away to hear the exchange between Mariwala and the CBSA agent, but it lasted less than a minute.

Mariwala was in the clear.

Davari's pulse was a tad faster than usual but he kept it in check. Still, a single bead of sweat trickled down his back as he advanced toward the glass booth.

"Good evening, sir," the agent said.

Davari looked at his nametag. *Davidson.*

Davari smiled and handed over his passport and declaration card. "Good evening, Officer Davidson."

Davidson scanned the passport and inserted it into the reader.

"What were you doing in England?" Davidson asked, his eyes on his computer screen.

"I was doing business research," Davari replied.

"How long were you there for? You wrote two days in your declaration card."

"Yes, that's correct. I stayed for only a couple nights."

"Where did you stay?"

"I stayed at the Marriott Grosvenor Square in Mayfair."

That got Davidson's attention. "Really?"

Davari was momentarily caught off guard. He hadn't expected to be challenged about where he had stayed. The unit in charge of creating backstops had fabricated proofs of his stay, but the officer's retort had surprised him.

"I—"

"That's where my wife and I stayed on our honeymoon," Davidson explained. "I love that place."

"Yeah, it's great," Davari managed to say. "I'll make sure to stay there again on my next visit."

"You travel to London often?"

"Yes, more often—" Davari stopped mid-sentence, realizing his mistake. There was only one immigration stamp from Heathrow in his passport.

Davidson removed the passport from the reader. "You were saying?"

Maybe Davidson hadn't noticed his slip-up?

"Oh, I was just saying that I wish I could go more often."

Davidson gave him back his passport and said, "You and me the same."

"All right, thanks officer," Davari said, glad the interview was coming to an end.

"What kind of business are you in?" Davidson asked.

"I do commercial real estate."

"Is that why you were in London?"

"One of my clients is looking into expanding his business overseas and he sent me to scout a building he was interested in near London."

"Any luck?"

"Not really. You wouldn't believe how expensive London has become. I'm not sure it would make financial sense for my client. But, hey, I'm just the messenger, right? He'll make his own decision."

"Do you have a business card?"

Davari's heartbeat quickened. He didn't have one. He made a show of searching his pockets. "I think I'm out," Davari apologized. "I gave them all away."

"Why would you give them away in London? Aren't you a Canadian realtor?"

The duration of the interview was getting worrisome. "I'm always looking for new clients. You know what I mean?"

"Of course, Mr. Yazdanian, but what would be the best number to reach you at?" Davidson asked, a pen in hand.

Tehran had prepared a number for such an eventuality. Davari gave him the ten-digit number he had memorized on the plane.

"Thanks. My in-laws are looking at purchasing a Subway franchise," Davidson explained. "So I'll give them your number in case they need the help of a commercial real estate agent."

"I appreciate this. Thanks."

"Nice chatting with you," Davidson said, dismissing him. "Have a great day."

Davari grabbed his carry-on bag and made his way to the conveyor belt where Mariwala was supposed to wait for him.

. . . .

CBSA officer Nicholas Davidson took one last look at the real estate agent. *Sheldon Yazdanian.* The name didn't ring a bell, but something wasn't quite right, and, on second thought, he should have sent him to secondary inspection.

The next passenger walked to his booth, but Davidson sent him back to wait behind the red line. He spun his chair around and brought his computer screen back to life by left clicking on his mouse. He searched the real estate agent's name on Google and then on the CBSA main database.

Nothing.

Sheldon Yazdanian loved his privacy. There was no Instagram account, no Facebook account and no website.

Rather unusual for a real estate agent.

Davidson did the only thing he could: he flagged the name and phone number. Next time Mr. Yazdanian entered Canada, by air, land or sea, he'd be sent to secondary inspection.

. . . .

Davari spotted Mariwala. He was making conversation with the mother he had sat next to on the flight. They made eye contact and Mariwala subtly nodded. He got up, kissed the baby's forehead and shook the mother's hand before walking to the exit. Davari followed him a minute later. He had the nagging feeling he was missing something. Was it something he had said? Something Davidson asked?

He spotted the white Chevrolet minivan parked curbside. The windows were tinted but he recognized the license plate. Mariwala slid the door open for him and grabbed his carry-on.

"I'm Captain Piran Mondegari," the driver said once the sliding door was shut.

"Thanks for coming, Captain."

"Everything is ready for you."

"I appreciate it."

The van sped away to the highway. Traffic was slow and orange traffic cones pushed the cars into one lane. Davari didn't like it.

"Is this normal?"

Mondegari actually smiled. "First time in Montreal?"

"It is."

"That explains your question. Yes, this is normal. Montreal is an absolute nightmare when it comes to traffic."

"How far are we from the safe house?"

"We'll be there in about thirty minutes. Maybe less."

Davari allowed himself to relax. Sergeant Mariwala touched his shoulder.

"I was worried, sir," Mariwala said. "At the airport."

"Officer Davidson was nosy," Davari replied. Since the plan called for them to stay in Canada for less than twenty-four hours, Davari decided he'd let it be. He wouldn't take any drastic measures to silence Davidson. But it wouldn't come as a surprise if his identity had been flagged.

"I'll need a new passport," Davari said to Mondegari.

"When do you need it for, sir?"

"Now."

"I'm not sure this will be possible," the captain replied. "We don't have the capacity to generate one on such short notice. Even if I contacted Tehran right away, it would take at least seventy-two hours for a new set of identity papers to arrive by diplomatic pouch."

That wouldn't work. General Kharazi wanted them in New York City in the morning.

"Then we won't be able to drive to New York," Davari said. "Do you know someone who could smuggled us across the border."

Mondegari was silent for a minute and Davari was about to repeat the question when he got his answer.

"I know someone who could get you across the border. But he works for the highest bidder. I wouldn't trust him with too many details."

That wasn't an issue. Davari could make sure the man remained silent.

"Is the rest of the team ready?"

"Yes, sir. There's only one more guy. That's all we could get at such short notice. He's waiting for you at the safe house."

As soon as he reached the safe house, he ordered one of the men to immediately travel to New York and conduct a reconnaissance of the objective. Since being smuggled across the border would take more time than if they had simply driven, Davari wanted a detail assessment of the tactical situation the moment he got to New York.

The driver had the radio tuned in to the local news station.

"Can you turn the volume up?"

"The mayor of New York City is presently resting at an undisclosed hospital in Manhattan . . ."

So the mayor was still alive. Not the news Davari expected to hear. Something had gone terribly wrong.

What kind of mess am I getting myself into?

CHAPTER 73

Presbyterian Hospital, New York

Because of the traffic, Mike spotted Mapother's black Yukon when it was still half a block away. It parked in one of the spots reserved for emergency vehicles. Mike hadn't expected Mapother to show up.

"What are you doing here?" Mike asked the moment Mapother stepped out of the vehicle. "The support team hasn't arrived yet."

"I was in the area when Lisa called. Where is she?" Mapother asked as both men walked toward the main entrance of the hospital.

"They're waiting inside," Mike replied. Did Mapother hear him? The support team was yet to arrive. That meant the two dead bodies were still hidden in the locker room.

"So she'll cooperate with us?"

"It looks like she will."

"But she wants protection," Mapother said matter-of-factly.

"I would want that too if my former employer had sent two people to take me out."

. . . .

Lisa was scanning the waiting room for additional threats when Mike and Mapother walked in. *What was Mapother doing here?*

"These two gentlemen work with me," Lisa quietly informed Sassani.

Rustling Sassani out of the recovery room had been easier than she had anticipated. Lisa had brought in a wheelchair from another room on the same floor and simply mentioned to the police officers that they'd be back in a few minutes. One of the officers offered to go with them but Sassani brushed him off by saying she needed privacy.

Lisa pushed Sassani's wheelchair toward Mike and Mapother. "We need to go before they figure out what's going on."

"I have two support teams less than five minutes away," Mapother said. "One will take care of the situation in the locker room and the other is bringing the medical van."

"I'm not sure we have five minutes, Charles," Lisa said.

"We can use the Yukon," Mike offered. "We'll help her in if she needs it."

Mapother turned on his heels and headed back to the Yukon. The others followed. They assisted Sassani to climb into the Yukon before taking their seats.

The Yukon's configuration was custom made. The rear compartment had been modified to fit Mapother's needs. Instead of the regular second- and third-row bench seats, four leather captain's chairs faced each other. In the center was a communication console with two laptops on extendable platforms. There were two twelve-inch screens tuned in to two different news channels.

"Control from Mobile One. We're heading to location Charlie with an ETA of twenty minutes," the driver said over the Yukon's communication system. "We need a medical team on stand-by.

Location Charlie was the IMSI's headquarters. Since the driver had his earpiece plugged into the comms system Lisa didn't hear headquarters' reply but she had no doubt they'd be ready for them. Control—the IMSI's communication center—was on watch twenty-four hours a day, three hundred and sixty-five days a year. They were in charge of monitoring all the IMSI assets around the globe. Since the attempt on Mapother's life at the New York Grand Central Terminal and the death of his bodyguard Sam Turner at the hands of Zakhar Votyakov—one of the Sheik's sons—the two IMSI employees responsible for tracking Mapother's movements had become paranoid. They wanted to know where Mapother was at all times. His new driver's name was Russ Schneider. Lisa had briefly chatted with him in the IMSI cafeteria and had learned that he was a former Naval Criminal Investigative Service special agent who'd seen action in Afghanistan and Iraq. Before Mapother scooped him out,

Schneider had been assigned to the secretary of the navy's protective detail.

"Are you comfortable?" Lisa asked Sassani.

"I'm fine," Sassani replied, her hand on her stomach.

The NYPD sergeant was putting on a brave face but she couldn't completely hide her pain. Sassani grimaced and removed her hand from her abdomen. The scrub was red with blood and pasted the dressing underneath.

"Our people will take care of you upon arrival," Mapother said. "But I need to ask you a few questions, if that's okay with you."

"Where are we going?" Sassani asked. "I'd like to know what's going on before I say anything."

"Understandable," Mapother replied, "but it's paramount that you understand the situation you're in."

"I do."

"I'm not sure you do." Mapother's voice was steel. Sassani was walking a very thin line and the slightest hesitation might cost her her life. Lisa hoped she understood how lucky she was to get a second chance.

Mapother continued, "Your masters sent two killers after you—"

"Two? I thought—"

"It doesn't matter what you think, Sergeant Sassani, you don't have all the facts. I do."

"Where are you taking me?"

"To the only place in New York where you'll be safe."

"Thank you."

"Don't thank me yet because the second I feel you're lying to me or are being less than forthcoming, the Iranians will be the least of your concerns."

Sassani twitched in her seat. Mapother's warning was loud and clear. "As I said earlier to your colleague, I love this country. I won't lie to you."

The rest of the trip was spent mostly in silence. Mapother made a few phone calls and Schneider kept control aware of their progress but that was it. Lisa pondered the implications of Sassani's capture. But was capture the right term? Since two people were killed during the operation, Sassani's capture felt more like a rescue mission.

Nineteen minutes after their departure from the hospital, the Yukon passed under the Brooklyn Bridge and made several quick turns onto small secondary streets before approaching a fenced area.

"What is this? A black site?" Sassani asked. She sounded alarmed.

"Nothing to be worried about," Lisa said.

If she'd been in Sassani's shoes, she'd be worried too. The IMSI headquarters didn't look like a welcoming place. A double gate opened and the Yukon crept forward. The chain-link fence was ten feet high with barbed wire looping around its top. Beyond the double gate, dozens of concrete wall panels were aligned on each side of the single lane road, forcing the driver to follow to the main checkpoint. There was enough space for only one vehicle at a time. The checkpoint was a large guard hut with a nine-foot concrete-and-steel fence behind it. A tall man wearing a nondescript uniform approached the driver-side window Schneider had lowered. Schneider handed the guard his ID card.

"I have the director, Mike and Lisa Walton and one injured NYPD officer riding in the back," Schneider told him.

"Unlock the doors. We'll take a quick look," the guard said. Lisa didn't remember the guard's name but he was a former military police officer who'd served overseas for over a decade. He had kept his military haircut and his suspicious eyes didn't miss much. The automatic locks popped open and the guard opened the rear driver-side door while another guard walked an explosive-sniffing German shepherd to the back of the Yukon.

"Good day, Director," the guard said, his eyes scanning the interior of the Yukon.

"Hello, Peter," Mapother replied.

Peter. That's his name.

"A medical team is waiting for you in the garage," Peter said before closing the SUV's door.

Moments later, the heavy steel door rose and the Yukon smoothly accelerated toward a square-shaped medium-sized concrete building. The structure had no windows and looked more like a storage facility than a state-of-the-art intelligence headquarters.

The Yukon took a slight right before heading downhill to a large, solid-looking garage door that was in the process of opening.

Inside the garage, two women and one man were waiting for the Yukon. Next to them was a gurney. Sassani must have seen them too.

"Thank you," she said, just loud enough for Lisa to hear it.

Sassani was crying. Was it from relief? Lisa thought so. The events of the last twenty-four hours must have shaken Sassani to her core. It wouldn't surprise Lisa if Sassani continued to have nightmares about this day for the rest of her life. Who wouldn't after what she had gone through? Lisa had her own demons to fight every night. Images of her dead daughter and unborn child visited her dreams almost daily. It used to be every single time she closed her eyes, so, in a way, her mental health was getting better. Mike worried her the most. The death of his father had taken its toll. Mike had spent two years looking for his dad, and, in the end, Ray Powell had given his life to save Lisa's. If it hadn't been for Ray's heroic actions, she wouldn't be here today. And that made her feel terrible. What kind of man sacrifices everything to save someone else without thinking about it? There were too few of them, but, luckily, she had married one. Mike was just like his father; he wouldn't hesitate to go through hell to save her, or anyone else for that matter. That was why she thought it might be time to get out of this life, for both of them. At their present pace, it was only a matter of time before one of them caught a bullet in the chest or a knife in the back.

Mapother's voice brought her back to the present.

"You're coming, Lisa?"

Mapother was outside the Yukon, holding the SUV's door open. Mike was already out and with the medical team, ushering Sassani away.

"Are you okay?"

"I'm fine," she said, climbing out of the SUV. "I dozed off for a second."

"More like two minutes, Lisa, and your eyes were wide open."

"I'm tired, that's all."

Mapother closed the reinforced Yukon's door behind her. "I shouldn't have sent you into the field. You weren't ready for something like that."

"I'm—" Lisa started to say, but Mapother interrupted her.

"But you handled yourself like I knew you could. You kept your cool and did all the right things. And so did Mike."

Lisa didn't think it was a good time to mention Mike's small panic attack.

"Thanks, I guess."

"Walk with me to my office. I'll get some caffeine into you."

Mapother swipe his ID card in a black electric keypad and punched in his seven-digit code. The door opened automatically with a soft click to reveal a long hallway with white marble flooring. Mike and the medical team were nowhere in sight. She followed Mapother down the hallway, her mind already searching for ways to move quickly on the intelligence Sassani was about to reveal.

"Did President Muller give you a timeline?" she asked.

"We have just about forty hours left before the Iranians do whatever they're planning to do. We need to know how many Iranian agents are left, and who are their targets."

"What will happen if we don't?"

Mapother stopped and turned toward Lisa. "Failure isn't an option, Lisa. President Muller was adamant. If there's another attempt on the life of a federal or state official, it would be like a declaration of war."

"Against the Iranians?"

"And the Russians, I'm afraid."

Mapother was right, failure wasn't an option. With a North Korean nuclear threat looming in the background, the slightest mistake could ignite a war no one could win.

Lisa wanted to say something, but her mouth had run dry.

CHAPTER 74

Ramallah, Palestine

"Someone's coming," Zima whispered.

"Wait for it," Eitan reply. "Four quick taps followed by two more."

Zima didn't care. The last two and a half hours had been the worst of her life. So much so she would have willingly switched places with Meir Yatom. A few months ago in Syria, during a botched operation to rescue Ray Powell—Mike's father—Zima had lost a finger to a sniper. As painful as that was, it was nothing compared to the last two hours. She couldn't feel anything below her waist and she wondered if this was because her neck was twisted. The little holes, meant to allow oxygen through to the secret compartment, were either clogged or not big enough because she could barely breathe. Her sweat acted as glue between her clothes and her skin. She had long stopped caring how awful she smelled, and Eitan had been kind enough not to say anything when she had to relieve herself.

Zima had never been prone to claustrophobia, but she was beginning to feel the effects. How long she had left before completely losing it was anyone's guess.

Four quick taps to the side of the van followed by two others set her heart pumping and the adrenaline flowing.

"We're good," Eitan said.

They each pulled on their lever and the compartment opened. Zima wriggled out of her plywood prison onto the dirty floor of the building. No lights had been turned on, but Zaret was holding a flashlight to the ceiling, careful not to shine too much light into her eyes. He rolled two bottles of water in her direction.

For a minute, Zima remained on the floor, panting. She tried to move her legs, but a jolt of pain passed through her body. She moaned, afraid something terribly wrong had happened to her body.

"I can't move my legs, Eitan," Zima said, fighting tears. She looked at him. Eitan wasn't in much better shape. His black hair was slick with perspiration, his eyes were red and puffy and he was shivering, despite how warm it was.

"Give it a minute or two, Zima," Eitan said, forcing a smile. "Drink the water."

Zima unscrewed the cap of the first bottle and emptied it in two large gulps. She opened the second and used it to splash her hair, face and neck. The water was lukewarm but it felt divine.

Eitan had his eyes on her. "You look stunning. Will you marry me?"

What? She must have misunderstood. She had to. Or did Eitan just ask her to marry him? No. He couldn't be. Not here. Not now. *I just peed my pants, for God's sake!*

"Did you—"

"Yes, I did."

He crawled toward her, using only his elbows. His legs were useless too.

"This is the worst shape we'll ever be in, Zima. We're exhausted, hurt and dirty like hell, but the only thing I kept thinking about while we were stuck in this cage was kissing you."

His lips were fresh and cool, which surprised her.

"I love you, Zima Bernbaum. Please marry me."

Despite the throbbing pain in her lower back, the pinched nerve in her neck and the fact that there was a man she didn't know standing five feet from them, she laughed.

"You're completely crazy. You've really lost it this time."

"Maybe, but what do you say?"

This wasn't the sweet proposal she had dreamed of since she was a little girl. She had always seen herself being proposed to during a romantic getaway on an exotic island, or in the Alps, halfway down a quiet trail. This wasn't it. But, again, Eitan wasn't the type of man who'd do that. Still, she'd fallen for him. Hard.

"Yes, Eitan, I will marry you."

When their lips touched again, an electric current went through her, from her hair to the tips of her toes. She felt rejuvenated.

"Okay, you two," Zaret said, "that's enough. We have to move."

Zima massaged her legs. The cramps were still there, but at least she could feel them again. Eitan was doing the same, looking at her with a huge grin plastered to his face.

"Where are we going?" Zima asked.

"There's a weapons cache half a mile from here. After that, it's up to you. I don't know what your mission is and I don't want to know."

That made sense. In case of capture, Zaret couldn't betray them if he didn't know what she and Eitan were up to.

"Any other friendlies in the area of operation?"

"Officially, no. But I've heard rumors that an American special operations team—I'm not sure if they're CIA or military—is in or around Ramallah. That's all I know."

Zima took an extra minute to stretch while Zaret and Eitan discussed how they'd get from their current location to the weapons cache. Zima's mind drifted away and she thought about Mike and Lisa. She hoped they were fine. They were good friends who deserved much better than the hand they had been dealt. A few years ago, before the Sheik changed their lives, Zima used to look at them with envy. They were so perfect. A match made in heaven. She too had wanted a partner, someone with whom to share the good or the bad. Her job had made it difficult to find someone. As a Canadian Security Intelligence Service—CSIS—field agent, her life had been compartmentalized, and the handful of men she had let in weren't ready to make the sacrifices required to be with her. Being in love with a spy wasn't the same as being married to a bureaucrat. An abnormal work schedule and broken promises were part of the deal, not the exceptions. When she joined the IMSI, she gave up all hope of finding someone. Then came Eitan, an arrogant, misogynist prick who sacrificed himself to save her.

Her knight in shining armor. Her future husband.

But first, they needed to finish this. They were Meir Yatom's only hope.

CHAPTER 75

Ramallah, Palestine

The city of Ramallah, just north of Jerusalem, wasn't exactly the first place that came to mind as a vacation destination, especially for Israelis. Ramallah used to be a hub of anti-Israel activities during the First Intifada in the late and early nineties and the Second Intifada at the beginning of twenty-first century. Fresh in Zima's mind were the scenes of clashes between Israeli soldiers and protesters she had seen on television. Ramallah was founded in the sixteenth century by Christians from Jordan and had remained a Christian city up until the Six Day War in 1967. The municipality didn't have official figures as to how many Christians still lived in Ramallah, but it was thought to be less than twenty-five percent of the population. Zima had read somewhere that there were more Christians from Ramallah living in Detroit and Jacksonville than in Ramallah itself.

It was well past nine o'clock at night when Zima, Eitan and Zaret left on foot. The local development organization UBIM was doing its best to help. The weapons cache was located close to the central square known as "Manara." Zaret had told her and Eitan that most English-speaking folk in Ramallah called the place "Lions' square" due to the four lion statues gracing the roundabout. Ramallah city officials were trying their best to open the municipality's arms to tourists by marketing it as a hip, energetic destination. But it seemed to Zima their efforts had fallen on deaf ears. Restaurants weren't even a quarter full and there were no queues to get into the clubs. Still, the wider streets they walked on were dotted with a few casual but somewhat trendy cafés that reminded Zima she hadn't eaten in a while.

Zaret must have caught her eyeing the inside of a restaurant because he said, "Let's take ten minutes to find something to eat."

Zima was grateful for the suggestion and glad she wasn't the one who had to admit out loud she was hungry. She wanted a change of clothes too but that could wait. Getting food into her was a priority. She needed the energy.

Half a block down, a street vendor was preparing falafel sandwiches. Her belly growled at the smell of coriander and fresh herbs.

"A falafel sandwich plate with a sugar-cane smoothie," she ordered in Arabic.

"I'll have the same," Eitan added.

The vendor looked at Zaret who shook his head.

Zima loved to cook, and observing this vendor prepare their meal helped her escape reality, if only for a short while. For a minute, she wasn't in Ramallah anymore. She wasn't about to engage an unknown number of enemy fighters in what might be a futile attempt to save Eitan's boss. No, for a moment, she was back in Ottawa, hundreds of miles away from the IMSI and all the violence that came with it, and she was comfortably seated in her futon watching the latest *Master Chef* episode.

"Twelve shekels," the vendor said.

Zima gave him twenty-five. "Keep the change."

The vendor smiled and thanked her profusely. She handed one falafel sandwich to Eitan and took a bit of the other one.

Oh. My. God.

It was crunchy on the outside but warm and moist on the inside. The second bite was even better, with exploding garlic and chickpea flavors. She dipped the rest of the sandwich in hummus and chased it down with the smoothie.

Eitan and Zaret were looking at her with interest. Eitan had only taken one bit out of his falafel.

"What?"

"Did you know twelve shekels was the cost for two falafels?" Zaret asked. "You gave him a huge tip."

"That's cheap. What's the conversion rate these days?"

"About four shekels to every US dollar."

A good falafel would cost more than five times this amount in the United States. At least Ramallah had this going for it.

"We should go," Zaret said. "We're only three minutes away."

Eitan took one last bite of his sandwich and discarded the rest in a trashcan.

The safe house was just off Manara Square and they reached it two minutes later. Zaret knocked six times on a large, gray doublewide garage door and waited fifteen seconds. He then knocked five more times and waited another ten seconds before the door opened automatically.

"Go inside," Zaret ordered. "Quick."

The door only lifted two feet from the ground. When it was clear it wouldn't go up further, Eitan rolled under it and Zima followed him.

The garage closed behind her before she had the time to get up. There were no lights inside the garage.

"What the hell?" Eitan said. Clearly, he wasn't impressed either. The air reeked of motor oil and cigarette smoke. A sour knot formed in Zima's stomach. Why had Zaret not followed them in? Had he been turned?

She placed her hands on the garage door and was about to try to pull it up when a powerful bright light came from the corner of the room, blinding her. She instinctively moved her hands to her eyes but it was too late. She had lost the little night vision she had. Her next move was to go for her weapon, a Beretta Pico.

"Keep your hands where I can see them," someone snapped in English.

Even though she couldn't see them, Zima sensed people moving around the room. By the number of boots trundling the floor, she estimated at least three men. There was no way she could get a shot off before being mowed down. She hoped Eitan had come to the same conclusion.

"I'm Captain Burke, United States Special Forces," said the man holding the spotlight to their eyes. "You're surrounded and you'll be cut to pieces before you reach for your weapons."

Burke, Special Forces. Zima had heard the name before. But where? When?

The Special Forces officer continued, his voice firm but non-threatening. "Keep your hands up, get on your knees and interlock your fingers."

Zima hesitated, but the unmistakable sound of a selector switching from safe to full-auto convinced her to obey the commands.

The moment she was on her knees, another light shone in her face. She involuntarily stared away and saw that Eitan was getting the same treatment. A man was aiming what looked like a modified M4 at Eitan's head while another man patted him down. Hands expertly searched her for hidden weapons and found the small combat knife she kept strapped to the inside of her right calf and the tiny Beretta Pico concealed in her inside-the-waistband holster. The search was a little too thorough for Zima's taste.

"All clear," said the man next to her.

"Same here," the man standing next to Eitan said.

Someone flicked on the lights in the garage. Zima examined her surroundings. The garage was larger than she'd thought but there was no furniture. The walls were painted a dirty shade of beige. A door behind Captain Burke was the only other exit. Her initial estimate of three men was wrong. There were six in total. With the exception of Burke, who was wearing a pair of blue jeans and a black t-shirt, all the others were dressed in civilian khakis.

"Sorry about this," Burke said, turning off the spotlight he had used to temporarily blind them. "We needed to make sure you didn't carry a vest. You wouldn't believe how many guys get blown up because they don't do their due diligence."

"We understand," Eitan said, getting up.

"And you're late," Burke continued, looking at his watch.

"Our drop off spot wasn't secured. We had to wait longer."

"Be that as it may, there's a possibility our mark was moved to another location."

"Let's hope not. What do you have for us?" Eitan asked.

Zima studied Burke's face, searching her memory for hints of where she'd seen him.

"You're coming?" Eitan asked her, following Captain Burke through the door.

She was still on her knees. The man next to her helped her to her feet.

"Here you go," he said, returning her knife and Beretta. "I'm Dean."

Zima replaced her knife in its sheath but checked her pistol before holstering it.

"Zima," she offered, accepting his extended hand.

"I hope I didn't invade your privacy too much," Dean said. It sounded like a genuine apology. He had a wedding ring and sincere eyes.

"Not at all."

She joined Eitan and Burke in the other room. Same ugly paint, same horrid smell, but it had no garage door, only a lonely window so dirty the space would be kept in infinite darkness if it wasn't for the bulb attached to the ceiling. A simple wooden table with four odd-looking chairs provided furniture. A small white fridge was plugged into a wall socket.

Eitan and Burke were busy removing a wide metallic plank from the floor. In a flash, she remembered where she had seen Burke. It was at the IMSI headquarters. She had never spoken to him but Mapother had seemed to know him pretty well. If Mapother trusted him, that was good enough for her.

"Come and look at this, Zima." Eitan pointed to the weapons cache.

The cache held a multitude of rifles, pistols, magazines, ammunition and grenades. It contained more than a dozen tactical vests and an assortment of silencers, flashlights and Meals Ready to Eat—MREs.

Zima was impressed.

"Take what you need and join us in the garage," Burke said. "I'd like your opinion before we finalize our ops plan."

"You're coming with us?" Eitan asked.

Zima was surprised too. Matthias Sachar hadn't mentioned joining forces with another element.

"We are."

"What's your angle, Captain?" Zima asked.

"No angle. Me and my team were ordered here."

"Don't get me wrong, we appreciate the help, but who ordered you here?"

"Someone with enough pull to take me and my team out of our theater of operations," Burke said. He didn't look pleased about his new assignment. "And that's not a small feat."

Burke did an about face and joined the rest of his team in the garage.

"You didn't know about this?" Zima asked, poking Eitan on the shoulder.

"No, but, like you said, I'm grateful for the help."

"I've seen him before."

That caught Eitan's attention. "Really? Where was that?"

"At the IMSI headquarters. I saw him speaking with Charles Mapother."

"Is he with the IMSI?"

"No. Mapother would have told me, I think."

. . . .

There wasn't a single thing Captain Burke liked about this half-assed mission. He and his team were doing good work in Syria. Embedded with the Kurds' forces for the last two years, they had led them on numerous operations against ISIS troops in Syria. One of these missions, the last-minute rescue of three CIA officers—at least that's what he thought at the time—had garnered interest from DNI Phillips himself. A week later, he was ordered to return to Washington to receive new mission directives from Phillips. Since Phillips wasn't in his chain of command, a four-star army general had been present to impress upon him the importance of the meeting. He had left the moment Burke acknowledged that Phillips had all the authority he needed to make Burke's life even more miserable than it already was. Another man, a certain Charles Mapother, had also attended. Mapother explained that he was the director of a small and privately owned intelligence agency and that the three operatives whose lives he had saved in Syria belonged to him. Burke had never heard of the International Market Stabilization Institute, but Mapother seemed to enjoy the DNI's confidence.

Following his fifteen minutes meeting with Phillips and Mapother, his budget had quintupled, which was great. What wasn't so great was his new chain of command. He was to report directly to DNI Phillips. He had no problem dealing with civilians, but they often didn't understand how the army worked and asked for things that weren't even remotely possible. Still, he appreciated the latitude—and the money—the DNI had given him. Burke and Mapother had then flown to New York where Burke was given a small tour of the IMSI building. It had seemed like a waste of time to Burke. So, when he asked Mapother point blank why he'd brought him to New York, Mapother had replied, "This is where some of your orders will come from, Captain. I want to make sure you know that we understand the dynamics of the battlefield you're operating in. The missions won't be half-cocked. I promise."

Before this specific mission, Mapother had kept his promise. The operations the DNI—or did they really come from Mapother?—had assigned to his team had played a major role in helping allied forces break through ISIS lines. There was still a lot of work to do, but Burke was beginning to see more and more cracks within the ISIS elements he was fighting against. His team was just about to embark on a new mission deep down into ISIS territory when the DNI countermanded his own order and asked him and his men to travel to Ramallah for a rescue operation. Burke had protested. Strongly. It made no sense to go from Syria to Ramallah to save a single asset. But there was a limit to how much weight his opinion carried with the Director of National Intelligence. So here they were in Ramallah, with two unknown operatives, on a mission to save a man named Meir Yatom. He had no idea who Yatom was.

Alistair Rousseau, the team's communication specialist, was holding the sat phone.

"For you, boss."

Burke looked at the display to make sure the phone was secured before he spoke.

"This is Caveman."

"Caveman, this is Alpha Zero Six."

Charles Mapother. That was a first. Mapother had never called him during an ongoing operation before. Burke signaled his men to be quiet.

"Go ahead for Caveman, Alpha Zero Six."

"Please confirm my two assets have made it to your location."

"Confirmed. One female and one man."

"That's good news," Mapother said. He sounded relieved. "Both are experienced operators. Follow their lead."

Burke didn't like where this conversation was going. His men wouldn't be pleased either. Burked sighed loud enough. "Alpha Zero Six, I don't—"

"This is an approved Level-One Sierra Whisky Tango operation, Caveman."

What? A Level-One Sierra Whisky Tango designation indicated the president had approved the mission and that its success was deemed vital to the security interest of the United States.

"Caveman copy," Burke replied.

"Good luck."

Burke threw the phone back to Rousseau.

"We're good?" the communication specialist asked.

Burke didn't respond to him directly. Instead, he asked his men to gather up around him. Once he had their attention, he explained the situation to them.

"Who the hell is Meir Yatom?" Albert Manchester asked when he was done. Manchester was the team medic. He had been a second-year medical student at Harvard when the twin towers collapsed. He enlisted a week later.

Before Burke could answer, Eitan walked in and said, "I'll answer that."

CHAPTER 76

IMSI Headquarters, New York City

Mike watched the medical team as they carefully changed Sassani's dressing. The trip from the hospital to the IMSI headquarters had been rougher on her than expected. Sassani had passed out on her way to the medical bay. Mike wasn't sure why she had lost consciousness, but she had some of the best health professionals in the state of New York working on her. Her wellbeing didn't concern him as much as the fact that he couldn't talk to her.

"What happened to her?" Mapother asked.

"I have no idea," Mike said truthfully. "The doctor has been ignoring me for the last fifteen minutes."

"That's problematic."

Mapother knocked on the glass partition dividing the area he and Mike were in from the sterile medical bay. Dr. Doocy looked up and approached the glass when he saw it was Mapother. He was clearly annoyed at being disturbed.

"Dr. Doocy," Mapother said through the glass. "When will we be able to speak with her?"

"Ten to fifteen minutes."

"Did you find out what happened to her?" Mike asked.

Dr. Doocy nodded. "I did. Well, I should say one of the nurses did. The patient suffers from hypoglycemia. We injected her with glucagon. She'll be fine."

Mike had no idea what glucagon was, and Mapother's expression revealed he didn't know either. So, when Lisa walked in a minute later, Mike asked her.

"Why do you need to know?"

"Dr. Doocy told us he injected Sassani with glucagon."

"It's a hormone, Mike," his wife replied. "It causes the liver to release glucose into the blood. We use it on patients who need a quick increase of their blood sugar level."

"The doctor said she'd wake up in a few minutes," Mapother said. "Any side effects we should worry about?"

"Nausea and vomiting are the most common, but I wouldn't worry about it. Ask her what you need to, Charles."

"Mike will handle the interrogation."

As a former police officer, Mike was an experienced interrogator, though the last interrogation he handled had turned deadly for the interviewee. Mike remembered it vividly and was sure Mapother did too since it had taken place at his brother's penthouse in Tversakaya, one of Moscow's most sought-after neighborhoods. He had transformed Frank Mapother's white, marble-tiled hallway into a crimson river when he had severed the jugular of one of the Sheik's Russian thugs.

Mike was confident Sassani's interrogation wouldn't end the same way. Sassani seemed genuinely willing to cooperate.

"How's Sassani's background check going?" Mike asked.

"Jonathan is almost done. You wanna see it now?"

"I'd better. I'll need a few minutes to get ready."

To establish dominance over Sassani, it was important to know when she was lying and when she was telling the truth. To do that, Mike would know the answers to the first twenty questions he was going to ask her. Some questions would be mundane, others more specific. What Jonathan Sanchez had dug up on Sassani would help him achieve that.

CHAPTER 77

The Canada-United States border

By area, Canada was the second largest country in the world while the United States was the fourth. The boundary between the two countries—including the maritime boundaries—was over five thousand five hundred miles long, making it the longest international border in the world. It was also undefended, applying the term in the military sense. Civilian law enforcement agencies were present on both sides of the border and it was illegal to cross the border outside border controls. The low level of security stood in sharp contrast with the Mexican-United States border. Although one third the length of the Canadian border, the Mexico-United States border was much more problematic for the Americans. Tehran estimated illegal entries from Mexico into the United States at more than half a million per year. It was believed that the United States Border Patrol had twenty thousand agents guarding the border with Mexico, a number that impressed Davari. His own Quds Force had less than fifteen thousand members.

It was no secret to both the Canadian and American governments that the border wasn't easy to guard, due to its size. Hidden sensors scattered in the wooded areas near the crossing points and on the roads and paths could detect illegal crossings, but it wasn't adequate. There weren't enough personnel on either side of the border to verify and intercept coordinated incursions like the one Davari and his team used to cross into the United States.

"Here you go, safe and sound like I promised," the smuggler said as they arrived at a junction of two roads. "Welcome to the United States."

The trip had taken a little less than six hours. The walk through the woods hadn't been particularly difficult. No wonder hundreds of illegals were taking the same route every day to reach Canada.

Davari checked his GPS. They were four miles into the United States. Transportation had already been arranged. He just needed to secure it.

"What's your name again?" he asked the smuggler.

"Bertrand."

"Musa, you would mind giving Bertrand his due?"

Mariwala threw a backpack to Bertrand. Even though the only light came from the moon, Bertrand caught the backpack mid-flight. He unzipped it and peeked inside with the help of a small red penlight. When he looked back at Davari, he was smiling.

"That's more than we agreed on," Bertrand said. "Thanks."

"For a job well done."

"It was an easy job. You guys didn't complain at all. People usually moan and bitch the whole way in."

Davari wanted to tell him they were elite soldiers, members of the Quds Force and accustomed to working in harsh conditions. The last six hours had been nothing more than a walk in the park for him and his men. But he kept quiet.

"Will you need anything else?"

"You told me earlier you'd be waiting for someone else before getting back to Canada?"

"Yes, a young family." Bertrand checked his watch. "They should be here momentarily."

As if on cue, Davari heard a vehicle approaching from the west.

"No one drives on this road. It's them," Bertrand said.

"Or border agents," Davari snapped.

"No, it's impossible. All the available agents went after our two decoys fifty miles east of here."

"You sure about that?"

"Look for yourself," Bertrand said, handing his night-vision goggles to Davari.

Sure enough, a single man climbed out of an SUV less than one hundred yards away. The man paused for about a minute. He didn't move, didn't make a sound, as if he was waiting for someone. But

Davari knew better. He was acquiring his night vision and listening for threats.

"I think he's waiting for you," Davari whispered.

"That's right. Believe me now?"

Davari grabbed his knife and spun around. He stabbed Bertrand in the side of his neck three times in less than a second. It was too dark to see the blood gushing out of the wounds but Davari heard it. Bertrand's legs collapsed under him but Mariwala was right behind him and ready to slow his fall.

"Musa, with me. We'll secure the van," Davari ordered. "Variyan, stay back in reserve."

Mariwala already had his sound suppressor screwed on.

"I'll approach from the front," said Davari. "With any luck he'll think I'm Bertrand. You flank him from the right and take down anyone coming out of the van, copy?"

Mariwala moved silently into the woods and Davari gave him a full minute to get in position. Davari doubted Bertrand would have tried to surprise his contact, so he walked toward the minivan without bothering about the noise his boots made on the dry leaves that covered the ground. The night-vision goggles gave Davari an unfair advantage. The smuggler heard Davari when he was still fifty yards from the minivan; his body language gave it away. The man pulled a gun out of his jacket but kept it close to his leg, muzzle toward the ground. Davari raised his own pistol and aimed it center mass. Even with night-vision goggles, fifty yards was a long shot.

The man whistled, a low-pitched whistle that sounded like wind flowing through the branches. Davari knew right away it was a signal; a challenge to which he didn't have the answer. The man whistled again, but this time he had his pistol up. His firing stance was good, but his aim was to Davari's left.

Forty yards. Still too far for a head shot but close enough to hit the man's center of mass. Since the man's pistol didn't have a silencer, Davari couldn't risk the man firing. Not only would this attract unsolicited attention, the man could get lucky.

Davari stopped and took half a second to adjust his aim. He squeezed the trigger gently, not wanting to jerk it. At this distance, the slightest jolt could cause the bullet to go astray. The pistol burped. A neat hole appeared in the man's torso, an inch left of his heart. The nine-millimeter round didn't have remarkable muzzle velocity, and the silencer didn't help either, so Davari fired two more rounds. Crisp, clean trigger pulls. Two more holes. Tight grouping. The man fell to his knees, and then to his side.

The side door of the minivan opened and two other men got out. These had AK-47s. Davari swore under his breath. He was still thirty yards out. The two men hadn't heard the shots but had seen their colleague fall. Davari took a knee. He pulled the trigger four times, two shots on each man. His first target was hit twice in the chest and pushed back into the van. The other man dove away to his left and let loose with this AK-47. Davari ducked behind a tree trunk as bullets flew overhead, shredding tree branches and foliage. The noise was deafening and exactly what he had hoped to avoid.

The man fired again and retreated behind the minivan at the same moment Sergeant Mariwala exited the woods right behind him. The minivan concealed from Davari what happened next but it wasn't hard to imagine Mariwala firing point blank at his target. A moment later, Mariwala emerged from behind the minivan and signaled Davari to join him.

"What do you want to do with them, Colonel?"

Inside the minivan, cramped on the backseat, was a father holding his young son close to his chest. Next to him, the mother. What Davari wanted to do and what he knew he had to do were two completely different things. He wasn't a monster, but the success of this mission was paramount and trumped his feelings about the poor family that had found itself in this situation through no fault of their own. Plus, there was a chance someone had reported the firefight to the police or border agents. They had to move fast.

"Bring them out."

While Mariwala forced the family out at gunpoint, Davari scanned the forest. Sergeant Variyan Malegam jogged toward them with the two duffel bags they had left behind.

Davari turned his attention back to the family. Mariwala had lined them up next to the ditch. Davari estimated the boy to be six or seven years old, about the same age as his own son. The father looked at Davari with pleading eyes. "Plea—"

Davari shot him once in the forehead, spraying the gravel road with blood and brain tissue. He didn't want to listen to the man's pleas. It was hard enough as it was.

The mother screamed. He shot her in the throat. She collapsed next to her son. Only he remained standing, between his dead parents. No speeches, no warning, just killing two unarmed parents.

Murder.

The boy ran at him, yelling at the top of his lungs. Davari, with tears in his eyes, pointed his pistol at him but couldn't bring himself to shoot the kid. Allah would never forgive him. Sergeant Mariwala had no such problem. He grabbed the boy from behind and threw him in the ditch.

"Stop!" Davari yelled.

Mariwala pointed his pistol at the child. "Sir?"

"He can't stop us, Musa," Davari said. "Someone will find him. It will be daylight soon."

Mariwala didn't look convinced, but he was too good a soldier not to obey a direct order.

"Let's go."

Davari climbed into the driver's seat and looked for the keys. They weren't in the ignition. He combed through the glove compartment and the storage box between the two front seats. Nothing.

He exited the minivan and walked to the first man he had killed. He reached into the dead man's jacket pockets. His fingers came out sticky with blood, but he had found the key.

Thirty minutes later, and without encountering a law enforcement vehicle, they reached Route 16.

"I'll drive for the first hour. Change, eat and get some rest, Asad. I'll wake you up in exactly sixty minutes."

Davari's thoughts were of the young orphan he had left behind in the ditch. The world was a cruel place and men like him didn't make it better. They only brought death and sorrow. Look at what he had done to Meir Yatom. He couldn't even imagine what kind of twisted torture methods General Kharazi would inflict on Yatom. Davari wished Yatom would admit defeat and talk, but from what Davari had witnessed, it wouldn't be the case. Yatom would fight tooth and nail every step of the way, and get hurt for it. Once Kharazi had extracted everything from him, cracked every bone and carved pieces of flesh from his body, only then would Yatom be allowed to die.

Davari shook his head in disgust and shame. Maybe he should have become a teacher? He had had enough of the killings. This was going to be his last mission.

The small clock embedded in the dashboard told him it was time to wake up Mariwala. His GPS indicated they'd reach their destination in a little less than five and a half hours and that they were still two hundred and ninety miles away from Manhattan. His rendezvous with Captain Piran Mondegari was in seven hours.

That gave him more than enough time to say a prayer for the souls of the parents he had just killed. And for his own too.

CHAPTER 78

IMSI Headquarters, New York

Mike had insisted on questioning Sassani in one of the IMSI conference rooms. It seemed less dramatic than if he had chosen to do it in one of the cells they kept in the basement. No *enhanced* interrogation techniques would be used, at least for the time being. Mike's objective was to create a partnership between him and Sassani. It didn't mean he wasn't ready to waterboard her if it came to that.

"How do you feel?"

"Have you been shot before?"

"More than once."

His response appeared to surprise her.

"I'm not a desk jockey," he added. "Like you, I belong in the field. In fact, we have a lot in common you and I, Tracy."

"Like what?"

Mike hadn't originally planned to share much about himself but he needed to establish trust first. Then dominance. Besides, Tracy Sassani would never see the light of day again, except from the small window of her prison cell. She didn't know that, of course. But Charles Mapother had made his decision. Cooperating with the IMSI was going to save her life, nothing more.

"I used to be a cop. I know the life, the toll it takes on the family."

"The only true family I ever had was my dad, and he shot me."

"Do you have siblings?" Mike asked. He knew she didn't.

"No. My mother died from a car accident when I was young. My father never remarried."

"Which school did you go to?"

"You really wanna do this?" Sassani exclaimed. It took Mike by surprise.

"Do what?"

"I'm not a rookie, Mike, or whatever your real name is. I've been in your chair before. You're trying to establish the ARC triangle with me," Sassani said, putting her hands together so her index fingers and thumbs formed a triangle. "Affinity, reality and communication."

She was right. This was exactly what Mike was hoping to accomplish. The ARC triangle was a technique used to gain the interviewee's trust. The technique didn't work all the time but, more often than not, especially when a suspect showed legitimate remorse, it brought the interrogator and the interviewee closer.

"Mike's my real name," he said. "What do you suggest?"

"What about I tell you everything I know, right here, right now," Sassani offered.

"What do you want in exchange?"

"I'm not dumb. I know you'll send me to a black site and hope no one will ask questions. It might work with terrorists you scoop out of the Middle East or Africa, but it won't work with me. I'm an NYPD detective, and, in some people's mind, a true hero. Questions will be raised, and answers expected."

"That hero thing, it will stop the moment they learn you conspired against the mayor, the same person you swore an oath to protect."

"And I did!" Sassani shout.

"Bullshit! You didn't protect him at all."

"I'm not the one who pulled the trigger."

"That's right," Mike said, sickened by Sassani's denial and attitude. "Your father did."

"I—"

"Shut your mouth and listen to me," Mike said, getting up. He pointed his finger at Sassani. "This is your chance. Don't miss it."

. . . .

Anger and self-loathing washed through her. It was worse than the physical agony she was in. Her soul was being pulled in two directions. Whichever way she chose to go, there would be no peace of mind, only pain and frustration. Her father had given her everything, but he had also taken everything. He had shot Mayor Church, the man she was supposed to protect, but also the man she had sworn to kill. Her whole life was a lie.

Why wasn't she born into a regular middle-class American family? Why did her life have to be so complicated? And what about Chuck? The news of her betrayal would crush him. They'd been together for two years and he had made it clear that she was *the one*. He was yet to propose to her, but one afternoon, while she was shopping with friends, she had seen him talk to a jeweler at the mall. It didn't take long to figure out what he was shopping for. Of course, she hadn't said a word to him, not wanting to ruin it all.

But she did ruin it all.

She'd always known it would end badly. Her father had warned her not to get too close to anyone. It wasn't as though she had no idea what was coming. She knew she'd be called upon eventually. A few years ago, she'd been proud of who she was. Working hand in hand with her father and being entrusted with his secrets had fueled her desire for revenge. She had been so angry at the world. Her father had made sure of it by feeding her misinformation and fallacious arguments against her adopted country. She could see this now. Yes, injustices had been committed against the Iranian people, but the Americans weren't the guilty ones; the Iranian government was the culprit. She'd been given the chance to rectify her actions, her sins. It was a bit late in the game—definitely too late for her—but there was a chance. Her father had made a mistake by trusting her. She could still save thousands—maybe hundreds of thousands—of lives. She had that power. She had no choice. She had to tell them about PERIWINKLE.

"You're right," she finally said. She had made up her mind. "My life's over. I know this. I understand it."

"Good." Mike's eyes were cold steel, his mouth fixed in a hard line. The muscles in his jaw twitched. "I'm glad you get it."

Sassani didn't mind the sarcasm.

"Are you recording this?"

"We are, yes."

"Bring in a polygraph."

"What?" She knew this would startle him.

"Don't look so surprised. It will make it much easier for all involved. This way you'll know I'm not lying."

Mike locked eyes with her. He was trying to figure out if she was being deceitful. She wasn't, but what else could she do to convince him to play ball with her?

"All right, I'll prepare the polygraph," Mike said.

"Good—" She never completed her sentence. The bitterness in her mouth came first, followed half a second later by the actual bile. She threw up on the table—a few drops making it to Mike—and almost choked on her vomit. She felt the wound in her stomach tear open but there was nothing she could do about it. She continued to retch even though there was nothing left in her stomach. A bitter-tasting, filmy mucous ran down her nostrils. Her whole body shook and the walls began to spin around her. Lisa rushing into the room was the last thing she saw before darkness enveloped her.

CHAPTER 79

New York City, New York

The drive to New York City took a little less time than anticipated. They ditched the minivan at a small airfield close to Waterville—a small town in Maine—and stole a Ford Explorer from the parking lot. They then drove to the supermarket and exchanged the license plate with that of an identical SUV. The only issue after that was a flat tire on I-95 five miles north of Portland, Maine. It took Mariwala and Malegam less than ten minutes to change it while Davari stayed inside the vehicle, weapon ready in case a police officer felt like volunteering his help.

The Manhattan traffic was heavy. Davari had never seen so many taxis in his life. It was pure madness. As much as he hated America, there was something marvelous and free about it.

"We should be close now," Malegam said, checking the SUV's navigation system from the front passenger seat.

"We're still two blocks away, brother," Mariwala said, his two hands on the wheel.

In the last five hours, Captain Piran Mondegari had forwarded Davari hundreds of pictures and a dozen pages of notes. Davari was combing through them with his laptop and he was impressed with the intelligence Mondegari had provided. Mondegari was an urban reconnaissance specialist. There were not too many of those in the Quds Force and Davari was grateful to have him on his team. Davari had tasked Mondegari with conducting reconnaissance and surveillance operations on their target, a medium-sized building with no windows located at the Brooklyn Navy Yard. The building looked like a fortified storage facility, but appearances didn't mean much.

"There he is," Malegam said. "At the corner, to your right."

"He saw us," confirmed Davari, keeping an eye out for the signal that all was clear. When Mondegari put his Mets baseball cap on, Davari breathed a sigh of relief. "Okay, pick him up."

The Explorer stopped in front of the Quds Force Captain and Davari moved over to let him in. Davari noticed right away that Mondegari was pissed off.

"What's on your mind, Captain?" Davari asked, once they were on their way.

"I've been on location for thirty-six hours, sir," Mondegari started, adjusting the rear air vents of the SUV to force the cold air to hit him straight in the face. "And I took over five hundred pictures of the target building. I photographed it from different angles and heights, I constructed—"

"What's your point, Captain?"

"We have a major problem."

"Which is?" Davari asked without missing a beat. He didn't fear problems. He embraced them. He was yet to meet a problem he couldn't solve.

"It's a fortress. There's no way we can get in. Have you looked at the pictures I sent you?"

"I did—"

"Bring them up, sir. I'll show you."

For the next thirty minutes, Mondegari explained why he didn't think they could gain access to the facility.

"Okay, Captain. Good job. Let's head back to the safe house and think this through. We'll find a way in."

. . . .

The safe house was on the first floor of a nondescript apartment building in Brooklyn. It was a small apartment with only one bathroom, but the refrigerator was full. Davari wasn't sure why Mondegari had taken the time to do such a large grocery shop, but he was famished, and so were his men. Davari cooked four vegetable omelets for him and his men while he let them brainstorm new ways to access the facility. While the omelets were cooking in the hot pans, he took a wooden cutting board from under the sink and a long bread knife from one of the kitchen's drawers. He sliced the baguette in thick slices and spread butter on them. Davari was at ease in a kitchen. A fact his wife enjoyed very much. Would he have the chance to cook again for her? It wasn't his first time operating deep inside enemy territory. But this mission, which had started in Greece, was unusual. Operating in the United States wasn't the same as running an operation in Iraq. The mindset was different, the risks greater and the rules of engagement more complex. The time constraint played against them too. And, finally, they were only four for an assignment that needed at least five times this number. That was the biggest drawback of operating so far from home base.

The pictures provided by Mondegari showed how difficult it would be to enter. The only point of entry was through a double-wide garage door. Only one vehicle could drive through the security gate at a time. Davari didn't like the look of the men manning the security post. They were professionals. They had dogs, weapons and they checked the interior of every vehicle, no exceptions.

They had to find a way.

Davari brought the omelets to the dining tables and went back to the kitchen for plates and cutlery. He fetched four cans of coke from the refrigerator and sat at the dining table.

"Did you find a solution to our problem?" he asked between bites of omelet.

Mariwala and Malegam both had their eyes on Captain Mondegari, who was chewing on a piece of bread. He took a sip of coke to wash it down.

"I didn't see any maritime defenses," Mondegari said. "That's option one."

Davari opened his laptop and scoured through the pictures. "Continue."

"Can I?" Mondegari pointed to the laptop.

Davari slid it toward him.

"We could get in from here," Mondegari said, scrolling to a picture that displayed an aerial view of the building and its surroundings. "I took this picture from the Williamsburg Bridge."

Davari examined the picture carefully. There was no visible fence protecting the building from an amphibious attack.

"But the NYPD regularly conduct patrols on the East River," Mondegari added.

"The NYPD?"

"They call it the Harbor Unit."

"What do we know about them?"

"They used to be a small unit but they've grown since 9/11. They're in charge of patrolling the city's one hundred and fifty miles of waterways. The unit has thirty boats ranging from forty-five to seventy feet. Most of them are bulletproof and eight of them have the equipment to detect radioactive material."

"Weapons?"

"Yes, sir. Heavy weapons on all launches and sonar to check the river channels for explosive devices."

"Frequency of the patrols?"

"I wasn't here long enough to gather reliable intelligence about that, but I did notice they tended to escort the ferries a lot."

Davari wasn't trained in maritime warfare. Nor were his men. There were too many unknowns. The odds were that they'd never reach their target.

"The risks are too high," Davari said, his decision made. "We need to find another way."

"What about an air assault?" That came from Mariwala. He had spent the last two minutes looking at the pictures.

"You can't be serious, Sergeant," Mondegari said. "How—"

"Let him speak," Davari snapped. He had come to trust Mariwala's instincts.

"Sir, I think there's an access door on the roof," he said. "Look carefully, a few feet to the left of the antennas."

Davari did see it. The roof was flat but there was definitely something that looked like a trap door. He couldn't commit to a plan unless he was sure an access point existed on the roof. He turned to Mondegari. "Captain, do you have more pictures like this one? With a better resolution?"

Mondegari looked uncomfortable.

"What is it?" Davari asked.

"I flew a drone close by," Mondegari said, his eyes to the floor. "It recorded a short video but—"

"But?"

"But the building was equipped with a DroneShield," Mondegari explained. "I'm sorry, Colonel, I should have seen it. When I realized what it was, I had already lost control of the drone."

Davari had no idea what his subordinate was talking about. Did he say a drone shield?

"What's a drone shield?"

"It's a drone countermeasure, sir. It uses a multi-sensor approach to analyze and identify potential drone threats," Mondegari said, speaking with confidence. "There are three different components. The first is the radar. It tracks a moving object and separates it from the background clutter. The second is the radio frequency sensor. It provides the target's bearing. And finally there's the acoustic sensor that compares the audio it gets from the target to a large database of acoustic signatures."

"I didn't even know this existed," Davari admitted. "So what happened to our drone?"

"I guess I flew it too close to the target location."

"So it crashed in the East River?"

"I'm afraid not, sir. It was confiscated."

"What are you talking about? How can it get *confiscated*?"

"It was actually brought down by a drone gun."

Davari had never heard of this either and gestured Mondegari to continue.

"It is rifle shaped and jams signals between the two point four and five point eight gigahertz frequencies."

"Meaning?"

"They were able to take over the control of the drone. I'll show you."

Mondegari clicked a few keys and spun the laptop around so Davari could see.

"What am I looking at?"

"This is the last thirty seconds of footage I was able to download from the drone."

Davari watched with interest as the drone flew near the target building. "How far were you?"

"I was controlling it from the Williamsburg Bridge, but the drone was flying over the Navy Yard Basin and approximately one hundred and twenty-five yards away from the target."

"Here," Davari said. "The trapdoor."

Someone dressed all in black and holding some kind of long gun emerged from the trapdoor.

"Yes, this is when I realized I was in trouble. I didn't recognize the threat for what it was in time. That's on me."

"I wouldn't have known either, Piran."

The next ten seconds showed the man in black pointing the rifle in the drone's direction. Suddenly the screen became black.

"I'm sorry, sir."

"Don't be. We found our entry point."

CHAPTER 80

Quds Force Safe House, Brooklyn, New York

"Any questions?" Davari asked his men.

The plan was simple. It had to be. But, to make it work, he had to place a call to General Kharazi and asked for a huge favor. Not something a colonel would usually do. But since Kharazi had named him second-in-command, it was worth a shot. And it worked.

After considering all the scenarios, Davari and his team had been unable to come up with a single tactical solution that would see them escape once they had completed their mission. Security was just too tight. Davari had promised mission success to Kharazi, but only if the commanding general of the Quds Force agreed to exchange them for Meir Yatom in the event the enemy captured them.

To the general's credit, he had accepted.

"I still think the four of us should go in," Captain Mondegari said. "What are our chances of getting away with the helicopter? Why waste twenty-five percent of our team babysitting the pilot?"

Davari understood Mondegari's concerns. He respected his commitment, but Davari wasn't the type of officer who sent his men on a suicide mission. It was true the odds were low they'd be able to escape, but his conscience forbad him from throwing in the towel. He needed an out.

"Babysitting the pilot isn't his only duty, Captain. He has to secure the rooftop too," Davari explained. Then he added, his finger touching the laptop's screen, "Do you see this ladder?"

Mondegari nodded.

"There's a chance the guards will try to climb on the rooftop."

"And we need someone to protect our rear," Mondegari concluded. "Understood, Colonel."

Davari could feel the tension in the room. Elite soldiers or not, no one relishes the idea of attacking a well-defended enemy position without proper intelligence. His men didn't need to voice their concerns. Davari had them too. This was going to be an ad-hoc operation with lots of moving parts. They were well armed, well trained and had the element of surprise. If the pilot was able to land the chopper on the rooftop on the first try, and if Mariwala was successful in breaching the trapdoor in less than a minute, they had a chance. There were too many "ifs" to Davari's liking but they had to do this. They had to move forward. His country was counting on them.

He hoped they weren't too late.

CHAPTER 81

IMSI Headquarters, New York

"When can I talk to her?" Mike asked his wife. Lisa had just come back from talking with Dr. Doocy—the IMSI emergency surgeon.

"If we're lucky, maybe in an hour or two," Lisa answered. "It depends how she feels. She's resting now."

"I don't give a shit how she feels," Mike said, exasperated. Things weren't moving fast enough for him. And when they were moving, they were going the wrong way. "We need to get in her head, and we need to do it now."

"Dr. Doocy won't allow it. He won't let anyone talk to her before she's had time to recuperate."

"Bullshit!"

"Talk to Mapother if you wish," Lisa said, touching his arm. "But you'll waste your time. He agrees with Dr. Doocy."

"What the hell happened to her anyway?"

"We're not absolutely sure, to tell the truth. Dr. Doocy thinks it's a combination of different things. Fatigue, stress, pain, you name it."

"This is ridiculous," Mike said, frustration taking over. "I'll talk to Mapother."

Lisa nodded. "I'll keep an eye on her."

. . . .

Mapother's door was open. He was seated behind his desk with Jonathan Sanchez and Anna Caprini standing in front of him. Sanchez held what looked like a medium-sized drone. It was all white except its center, which was black.

"Where did you get this?" Mike asked.

"Security shot it down earlier today."

"Really? With the new laser gun?"

Sanchez shook his head in disbelief, and Anna Caprini rolled her eyes. "How many times do I need to tell you this, Mike?" Sanchez asked. "They're not laser guns, they're—"

"I know, buddy, I'm pulling your leg."

"No you're not," Sanchez replied.

Mike wasn't known for his technological skills. Sanchez and Lisa never missed an opportunity to remind him.

"Why did security shoot it down?"

Mapother answered. "It was lurking a bit too close to our building."

"I'm sure this isn't the first time," Mike said.

"Yes and no," Mapother replied. "No it's not the first drone we've taken down. It's happened twice before. On both occasions, the drones belonged to recreational users. Not this time."

"How do you know?"

Sanchez opened a laptop and plugged its USB cable into the belly of the drone. "Watch this."

The video lasted just over thirty seconds and it was clear that the IMSI headquarters was its target.

"This was taken this afternoon?" Mike asked.

"Yep, and it was launched from the Williamsburg Bridge."

"How do you know that?"

"You just have to—"

"Never mind, Jonathan, I'm kidding. I don't want to know," Mike said before turning his attention to Mapother. He wanted to get back to Sassani as soon as possible. "Charles, I was wondering if you'd authorized me to accelerate the process with Sassani. I'm afraid we won't be—"

Mapother raised his hands, interrupting Mike in the process. "No. Dr. Doocy already warned me you'd come to me. He has my full support."

Goddamnit! Didn't Mapother understand every hour counted?

"Charles, listen—"

"No, you listen, Mike," Mapother said. "I understand we have no time to waste. If I thought for one second that we could extract reliable intel out of her at this moment, I'd tell you to go and do whatever you feel is necessary. But this isn't the case. If we spend our resources on intel we can't verify, and that intel is bad, we're screwed. You get that, right?"

Mapother had a point. Mike didn't agree with him, but he understood Mapother's point of view. "I do."

"Okay, now that we're clear on that, can we focus on what Jonathan learned about the drone?"

Mike saw his friend hadn't appreciated being cut off. "Of course."

"Thank you, Mike, you're very kind," Sanchez said. His sarcasm was evident. "Here's what we know so far. The drone was purchased right here in New York City yesterday afternoon. It flew for nine minutes. Eight of those minutes were for a practice run over Central Park. We all know where it spent its final sixty seconds."

"We need to find who's watching us," Mike said, concerned. It could be nothing, but they had to investigate.

"Already on it," Caprini said, looking at her smartphone. "They know who made the purchase."

CHAPTER 82

IMSI Headquarters, New York

Mike and Sanchez followed Caprini to the control room.

"What do you have for me?" she asked one of the analysts.

"We were able to access the traffic cameras on the Williamsburg Bridge. By using the timing from the drone's hardware, we were able to pinpoint exactly where and when the pilot was. Voilà!"

Mike was impressed. On the analyst's flat screen was the drone's pilot. "Are we sure it's him?"

"One hundred percent, sir," the analyst replied. "The timing matches perfectly. And look at his face when he loses control."

There could be no doubt. This was the pilot. Mike watched the pilot as he tossed his joystick over the bridge's ramp.

"Would we gain anything by getting the joystick back?" Sanchez asked.

"I doubt it," the analyst replied. "And I'm pretty sure it didn't sink right away. It would be impossible to recover."

Caprini tapped the analyst on the shoulder. "Good job, Suzy. Did you get a match on the facial recognition software?"

"Nothing yet. I'll let you know if I do."

CHAPTER 83

Manhattan Heliport, Pier 6, New York City

The sixty-minute, five-thousand-dollar private helicopter tour included a hotel pickup and drop-off and a free Champagne toast. Not wanting to leave anything to chance, Davari insisted the whole team take two cabs to get to the New York Marriott Marquis where the charter company was to send their car to pick them up. They were going to play tourist until they were safely in the air.

Right on time, a black town car stopped outside the Marriott. The driver lowered the window.

"You guys are waiting for your ride to get to the heliport?"

"That's us," Davari said.

The driver—a tall, skinny man who seemed to have one leg shorter than the other—climbed out of the vehicle. Everybody shook hands.

"Who's the groom?"

Since Sergeant Variyan Malegam was the youngest, it made sense he'd play the groom. He raised his hand. "I am."

"Fantastic. And I presume all of you are his groomsmen?"

"We are," Davari replied, making sure to put as much joy as he could behind his words.

"I'm Brian and I'll be your host until we reach the heliport," the driver said. "And when the tour's over, I'll drop you right back here."

"Sounds good," Malegam said.

Brian opened the doors for them. Malegam took the front passenger seat while Davari, Mondegari and Mariwala crammed in the rear.

"If you want, I can take your backpacks and put them in the trunk."

"We're fine, but thanks anyway," Davari said.

Brian shrugged and got behind the wheel.

Davari smiled at the thought of Brian carrying the backpacks in the trunk. He would have found them heftier than normal. Stun grenades, C-4 explosives, combat knives, MP5K sub-machine guns and a few spare magazines weren't the usual items carried by travelers out for a fun day-trip.

It didn't take long for Brian to get on Davari's nerves.

"You guys booked the nicest package we have," Brian said, looking in his rearview mirror. "You know that, right? As long as you stay within your allocated flight time, you can modify your itinerary."

"Only the best for our buddy," Davari said, tapping Malegam's shoulder.

"Seriously, how cool is that? I mean, not everyone gets picked up in a fancy black car. You know what I mean?"

Davari would have liked to slice Brian's throat and be done with it. Like most special forces soldiers, Davari needed some quiet time prior to an operation. This was his time to reflect on the mission, his family and his team. And sometimes, when he felt like it, he prayed to Allah to give him the strength to lead his men in combat without failing them. But today, Brian's nonstop chatter didn't allow him, or his men, to concentrate and focus on the events that were about to unfold.

Mercifully, it was a short ride to the heliport.

"I'll see you in about an hour, guys," Brian said as Davari and his team walked to the terminal.

Waiting for them behind a long white counter was a tall blond lady with huge blue eyes. Married or not, no man could remain indifferent to this natural beauty. She was the most beautiful woman Davari had ever seen.

"Good day, gentlemen, I'm Jennifer," she said. She had a very pleasant, slightly goofy smile. "I'm your pilot for today's tour. I trust my husband Brian took good care of you?"

What? Davari hadn't expected that. *One of the greatest mysteries of the world, if you ask me.*

"He was very nice," Sergeant Malegam replied. "We were fortunate to have him as our chauffeur."

Jennifer looked at him strangely, as if she was wondering if her leg was being pulled.

"When are we leaving?" Davari asked.

"Safety briefing starts in ten minutes," Jennifer replied, still looking at Malegam. "It's only eight minutes long, then we'll be on our way."

"Fantastic."

CHAPTER 84

IMSI Headquarters, New York

Mike was on his way back to see Lisa in the medical bay when his smartphone vibrated in his pocket. It was a text from Sanchez.

We've IDed the pilot.

If the IMSI had identified the pilot using their database, it wasn't a good sign. Good guys usually didn't end up in the database. Mike hurried back to the control room.

"Who is he?" he asked Sanchez.

Sanchez handed him a printout. "Meet Captain Piran Mondegari from the Quds Force."

Mike studied the picture. It was hard to say how tall the man was, but he was medium-built with thinning black hair combed to the back. He was dressed in a dark business suit over a white shirt with no tie.

"Where was this taken?"

Sanchez hit a few keys on his keyboard. "This is a recent photo, Mike. The DIA took it six months ago."

"Why?"

"Gimme a sec. I need to read the transcript."

The DIA—Defense Intelligence Agency—was one of the external intelligence services of the United States. It specialized in the collection—overt and clandestine—of human-source intelligence. The organization didn't belong to a single military element but answered directly to the secretary of defense. Most of the employees were civilians, although half of them had past military service. Its main objective was to inform policymakers about the military intentions and capabilities of foreign governments, friendly or not.

“Got it,” Sanchez said. “The short report that came with the photo says, I quote, “DIA Counter-Surveillance Unit, Congress Heights Metro Station. Believed to be Captain Piran Mondegari. Quds Force. Iran. Entered the continental US with a Canadian passport.”

“Why wasn’t he arrested? Ain’t the Quds Force a terror organization?”

“I have no idea, buddy. I’m sure the guys over at the DIA had their reasons.”

Mike remembered that the DIA didn’t have law enforcement authority. So it was entirely possible that they had passed along the intelligence they’d gathered on Mondegari to the FBI.

Quds Force. Mike had never dealt with them before this week. He didn’t believe that Captain Mondegari’s presence near the IMSI was a coincidence. Very few people knew of their existence. Somehow the Iranians knew. It was almost impossible to comprehend. How?

Shit! Meir Yatom.

“Come with me, Jonathan,” Mike said. “I have a feeling we’re being played.”

CHAPTER 85

Manhattan Heliport, New York

The AS350 was a single-engine light utility helicopter, perfect for chartering tourists around New York City. This specific configuration offered space for six passengers, all of them with their own cushy leather seat. Everyone wore a noise-reduction headset that also facilitated communication with the pilot.

"Where are you guys from?" Jennifer asked.

"We're from Canada, and it's our first time in New York City."

"How do you like it so far?"

"It's fabulous. I didn't expect it to be so special," Davari said truthfully.

"There's no other place in the world like New York City," Jennifer said. She turned around and flashed him a warm smile.

Davari responded in kind.

"You guys okay if we start with the Statue of Liberty?"

"Absolutely," Malegam replied. "Let's go."

. . . .

FBI Special Agent Jennifer Jordan's heart was beating so fast she couldn't count the beats.

Calm down. You got this.

It was her first undercover operation. Last week, to congratulate her for surviving her first twelve months with the FBI, her colleagues had thrown a party in her honor at a small local pub. A lot of wine and too many chicken wings had given her heartburn, but it had been worth it. Her father, a thirty-two-years veteran of the

FBI, had always told her how important it was to bond with your teammates.

One day, baby girl, you might need them to risk their lives for yours, and yours for theirs.

She had learned to fly choppers in the air force. She'd served one tour in Iraq flying VIPs around. One tour was enough for her. She wasn't built for a career in the military. But she'd learned to trust her gut and to recognize the threats. And, right now, her threat meter was in overdrive.

The initial intelligence report had come from the DIA. Their counter-surveillance unit had come in contact with a possible foreign operative. When they ran his photo in their powerful facial-recognition software, they realized they were dealing with an officer of the elite Iranian Quds Force. This had been confirmed by one of the DIA contacts within the INIS—the Iraqi National Intelligence Service. The DIA dug deeper and successfully retrieved his credit card information from a ticket booth located in a subway station.

His name was Captain Piran Mondegari.

And he was seated right behind her.

Six hours ago, Mondegari had used his credit card to book a last-minute private helicopter tour for four adults. All kinds of alarms had gone off within the FBI field office. The SAC—Special Agent in Charge—had ordered her and agent Brian Olson to keep an eye on them. Since a chopper couldn't do the damage an airliner was capable of, the SAC was confident this was a reconnaissance mission with very little risk. And, so far, he'd been right. Brian had done a fantastic job boring them to death in the car, allowing the surveillance team to remain undetected. Numerous pictures were taken and were presently being analyzed. Her job was to keep them happy and to listen to what they were saying since her Farsi was excellent.

So far, she hadn't much to report. They were polite and didn't ask any questions. In fact, they were very quiet.

Maybe too quiet.

CHAPTER 86

IMSI Headquarters, New York

"I have a bad feeling about this," Mike said to Mapother. Mike and Sanchez were in the director's office to share with him what they had found out about Captain Piran Mondegari. Mike continued, "I know you're against me talking to Sassani, but, frankly, sir, I don't think we can wait any longer."

Mapother raised his eyes from the report he was reading and said, "Mike, I have four ongoing operations. Be specific. What changed in the last thirty minutes?"

"The drone pilot, he's Quds Force."

That got Mapother's attention. "Show me what you've got."

Sanchez handed him all the intelligence he'd gathered about Mondegari. "I know this isn't much, Charles, but Mike's right. We need to talk with Sassani. Now."

Mapother read the sheet. "Shit."

"My thoughts exactly," Mike said.

Mapother slammed his fist on his desk, spilling hot coffee all over his files. Then, in a calm voice, he said to Mike and Sanchez. "I don't know how long we have, gentlemen, but we're not safe here anymore. Our organization has been compromised."

"Could Meir Yatom be the source?"

Mapother shook his head. "If he is, I don't blame him. I can't imagine what these savages have done to him."

"Zima and Eitan will get him back," Mike said. Zima and Eitan were two of the finest operators he knew. If anyone could rescue the Israeli spy, it was these two.

"I took the liberty of sending them extra help," Mapother said. "You remember Captain Burke?"

"Of course. He saved our lives in Syria. You sent him and his team to back her and Eitan up?"

"I couldn't do otherwise. Zima's family."

Mike nodded. Mapother was a good man.

"I'm sorry, Charles," Mike said. He knew the IMSI was Mapother's baby. If there was one thing that could shut down the IMSI almost instantly, it was its discovery by a foreign power.

"Go talk to Sassani. See what you can extract from her. In the meantime, I'll call DNI Phillips to share our concerns about the IMSI."

"Can't you wait a bit longer? At least until we figure out exactly what's going on?"

"I appreciate your thoughts, Mike, but waiting isn't an option. There's too much at risk. It wouldn't be fair for those whose necks are hanging by a thread because of us."

"You know as well as I do that Phillips will go to Muller and ask that we be shut down," Mike said,

"There's no doubt about it, but, ultimately, and like it should be, it will be the president who'll decide if we close shop or not."

Mike had heard enough. There was nothing else he could do. If Mapother wanted to commit hara-kiri, so be it. But, until then, he had a job to do.

. . . .

Charles Mapother knew this day would come. The IMSI had done a lot of good since its inception. Stopping the Sheik had been Mapother's crowning achievement. They had saved countless lives. Because of the IMSI, the world was a bit safer.

He looked at Sanchez. "Go help him, Jonathan. I'll handle the DNI."

Sanchez walked out of his office without another word.

Mapother dialed Phillips's number. The DNI answered on the first ring.

"Charles?"

"Where are you, Richard?"

"In my office. I'm meeting with the president in two hours. What can I do for you?"

Mapother thought about his options. Maybe he could give Mike and the rest of his team a few hours to figure out exactly how much they were compromised? If he could meet with President Muller, he'd be able to control the narrative.

"Can you wait for me?" Mapother asked. "I need to speak with the president."

"What is it about?" Phillips replied. He was protective of his access to President Muller and he wouldn't let Mapother in if he didn't know in advance what subjects Mapother wanted to discuss.

"It's about a possible breach in the IMSI's cover."

DNI Phillips remained silent for ten seconds. "I see," he said. "All right, be here in ninety minutes. We'll leave together."

Mapother hung up and hurried to the interior-parking garage where his driver Russ Schneider was waiting.

He climbed in the Yukon. "Taylor Field Heliport, Russ. We're going to DC."

CHAPTER 87

Over the East River, New York

Colonel Asad Davari checked his watch. They'd been in the air for approximately fifty minutes. They had seen the Empire State Building, Central Park and had flown right next to the Statue of Liberty. Their pilot Jennifer, who also acted as their private guide, had provided excellent narration throughout the tour. For a few minutes, Davari had even forgotten that he was about to embark on one of the most perilous missions of his career.

They were now heading northeast over the Manhattan Bridge, putting them less than one mile away from their target. Davari hand signaled Mariwala and Mondegari.

It was time.

. . . .

Special Agent Jennifer Jordan had to admit she was confused. Were these four men really whom the FBI thought they were? If this was indeed a reconnaissance mission in advance of a new strike against one of New York's landmarks, Jordan expected them to ask more questions and enquire further about individual sights or even demand more flight time over certain areas. But they didn't.

Strange.

"The Manhattan Bridge is a suspension bridge and its main span is four thousand seventy feet. It's one of the four toll-free—"

The cold barrel of a pistol pushed into her neck made her stop mid-sentence. Her heart—which had miraculously slowed down—started pumping blood frantically again. A cold sweat formed on her back as she recognized what was happening.

They had been wrong all along. That wasn't a reconnaissance mission.

This was an attack.

. . . .

"What is—" Jennifer started, but Davari pistol-whipped her just above her right eye. Not hard enough to knock her out, but hard enough to break the skin and show her who was in charge.

"Jennifer," Davari said, "do as I say and you'll be fine. You're about to help us rob a medical warehouse. You're our way in, but also our way out. Understood?"

Jennifer nodded. Blood dripped from the gash on her forehead.

"Variyan, why don't you show our friend Jennifer where we need to go?"

While Sergeant Malegam showed her where she was to land the helicopter, Mariwala passed the MP5Ks around with extra magazines and stun grenades. Next were the SRX 2200 combat radios they would use to communicate with each other.

By the time everyone was geared up, they were on final approach.

. . . .

Jordan knew the FBI and NYPD were *en route* to her location. They had bugged the helicopter and could listen in even though she couldn't hear them. The NYPD had boats in the water. They'd be there in less than five minutes. She just had to keep it together until then.

The building they wanted her to land on was large enough to accommodate the AS350, but she had to bc careful with the antennas. There was a multitude of them but they were all cluttered in the same spot.

"Unidentified aircraft with number November-One-Four-Oscar-Romeo-Alpha, you're entering a restricted airspace." The voice in her headset startled her. By now the FBI should have alerted all the local authorities and asked them not to interfere. So why was she receiving this?"

"Hmm . . . This is Big Apple Tour November-One-Four-Oscar-Romeo-Alpha, I'm calling an emergency. We're landing—" she said, following the script the terrorists had given her.

"Negative Big Apple Tour. This is restricted airspace. I repeat, this is a restricted airspace."

Jordan turned her comms off. "This isn't a medical facility. What is it?" she asked the man seated next to her.

"Just land the helicopter, and watch those antennas."

CHAPTER 88

IMSI Headquarters, New York City

Mike jumped at the sudden shrill of the alarm. What now?

He had heard it three or four times in the past but they'd been mandatory security practice runs publicized forty-eight hours in advance. He didn't remember reading anything regarding a security drill today. That could only mean one thing.

They were under attack.

Mike sprinted down the hall toward the medical bay. He rushed into Sassani's room where Dr. Doocy and Lisa were arguing. Sassani was asleep in her bed. Attached to the back of her left hand was an intravenous pump. His wife had positioned herself between Sassani and Dr. Doocy.

"Lisa, what's going on?" Mike asked, his eyes on Dr. Doocy.

"He wants to medicate Sassani some more. If he does, you won't be able to speak to her for another five hours. We need to wake her up, not give her more morphine."

Dr. Doocy held a syringe in his right hand.

"What's wrong with you, Doocy?" Mike asked, unable to hide his contempt. "You're a real pain in the ass."

"This is my patient, not yours."

"Not only did Mapother gave me the nod to start questioning her, but can't you hear the damn alarms? They're ringing for God's sake. We might be under attack."

"None of this discharges me from my obligations toward my patient."

Mike took a couple steps toward Dr. Doocy while keeping an eye on the syringe.

"Give it to me, doctor."

"I'm not afraid of you, Mike Walton," Dr. Doocy said, nevertheless taking a step back. "I won't let you touch my patient."

Mike had had enough. In two quick steps he was on Dr. Doocy. He grabbed the wrist holding the syringe and twisted it away. For all his brave talk and acts of defiance, Dr. Doocy wasn't a fighter.

"What do you have in this?" Mike asked, showing him the syringe.

"Antibiotics."

"Get out of here, Dr. Doocy. Go make yourself useful somewhere else."

. . . .

Sassani heard the alarms first, and then Mike's voice. "Wake up, Tracy."

She opened her eyes slowly; her vision was blurred and took a few seconds to adjust. She blinked at the glare coming from the light. She had a terrible headache, her stomach still hurt like a bitch but she felt somewhat better.

"Can you hear me, Tracy?"

She nodded. Her mouth was too dry to speak. Lisa handed her a glass of water. She drank it in two gulps. She was so thirsty.

"Thanks."

"Tell me everything you know, Tracy. Everything."

"Why are these alarms ringing?"

"Don't worry about them. Focus on what you're about to tell me."

"Why aren't we doing this in the interview room?"

"Because there's no time."

Sassani's mind was spinning on overdrive. There was so much to say. What should she start with?

PERIWINKLE.

"I don't know what the ayatollah's final plans are," she said, "but here's what I can tell you."

. . . .

"So there were eight SAVAK colonels inserted in the United States?" Mike asked.

"And in Canada, just not the United States. And don't forget, only seven of these eight colonels were Iranians. My father told me number '8' was an American holding the rank of colonel."

"Yes, you've told me that."

"The Canadian prime minister was killed by one of us."

Yes, I know that too. Every single time it was mentioned on the radio or television, or even during a casual conversation with his teammates, Mike still got a pinching feeling in the center of his chest. As much as he disliked the former Canadian prime minister's domestic and foreign policies, he would have given his life to save him. The office of the prime minister was bigger than the man who occupied it.

On the bright side, Sassani was telling the truth. Everything she had said so far concurred with the intelligence they'd gathered.

"The primary objective of Ayatollah Khomeini was to have two generations of sleepers within North America," she continued.

"Were you asked to join specific police forces or government agencies?"

"Yes, the Secret Service in the United States and the Royal Canadian Mounted Police in Canada, or any political parties that would allow us to gain influence and authority. Initially, this is what the ayatollah wanted. But not all of us were able to. We had to adapt. Some of us had to join other police forces because our application was rejected. One of us became a well-known state politician, two others are well-respected reporters, and we also have a backup."

"Backup?"

"The female agent you killed at the hospital. She was the backup."

That made sense to Mike, and enraged him at the same time. As a former RCMP officer, he knew how the Canadian federal government had bent over backward to accommodate minorities into the organization. It had led to a lot of positive changes within the RCMP but, in Mike's mind, the drawbacks were also significant. Candidates to important positions within the organization were often selected based on their gender and skin color. Diversity was the key word. Candidates whose parents were born overseas with shaky family or professional ties were let through even though comprehensive background checks couldn't be performed. More often than not, these candidates became hard-working officers who boosted the RCMP's effectiveness. But there were undesirable effects too. Sergeant Khalid al-Fadhi was one of them.

"That's why you joined the NYPD instead of the Secret Service? Your application was rejected?"

"My dad's past . . . I failed the background check."

"What about the politician? Is he holding elected office?"

That would be terrible. Elected officials were those who could gradually transform the day-to-day lives of their countrymen.

Sassani coughed. She apologized and asked for more water. Lisa handed her another glass.

"Yes, he's an elected official," she said between sips of water. "His name is Maxim Ghasemi."

"The name rings a bell," Lisa said.

"He had his moment of fame six years ago when he was elected mayor of a small town in Michigan. He has an anti-police rhetoric that pleases his constituents. He's now a state senator and will probably be the next governor. He's aiming for even higher office."

Of course he is.

A sudden loud explosion resonated in the medical bay. The whole building shook.

"What was that?" Mike asked aloud. The lights flickered but stayed on. Then came the unmistakable chattering of automatic fire.

Mike looked at his wife. She seemed pissed off but she already had her pistol in her hand.

"Go," she told him.

"I'll be back as soon as I can. Keep her alive."

"Come back to me in one piece, Mike."

Mike pulled his compact Taurus from its holster and headed out the door.

CHAPTER 89

Ramallah, Palestine

The operational plan called for two hours of rest prior to the departure time. Zima made the best of it and fell asleep almost instantly.

"Hey, princess, time to go."

She opened her eyes, and there was Eitan, his face two inches away from hers. He kissed her lightly on the forehead before helping her up.

"Do what you got to do," Eitan said. "We're leaving in five."

Zima made her way to the bathroom and brushed her teeth. She drank a whole bottle of water and discarded it in the garbage can next to the sink.

By the time she came out of the restroom, the whole team was in the living room, double-checking their equipment. Most members were carrying M4s in slings but two had MP5s. All had their secondary attached to their chest. Zima wasn't a big fan of the thigh holster. She had two major problems with it. The first was that it was damn uncomfortable. The leg straps had a tendency to cut off circulation in the leg and to limit movement when climbing and running. The second was how easy it was to get disarmed with a thigh holster, especially from behind. So Zima opted for the chest rig too.

"The vehicles are two minutes out," Captain Burke said. "Get ready."

The target was a fifteen-minute drive across town. At this time of the morning, there would be almost no traffic. Burke had a man stationed at an OP—observation post—one block from where they thought Meir Yatom was being kept. The target building was a disused soap factory. It was mid-sized and spanned three floors. Intelligence collected by the man at the OP suggested that Yatom was in the basement.

Right on time, the garage door opened and two Mitsubishi Pajeros entered. The door closed behind them. The moment they were shielded from the street, Captain Burke and his team climbed in the back of the SUVs, with Zima and Eitan taking the front passenger seats.

The traffic was even lighter than anticipated, which worked perfectly. They still had forty-five minutes before sunrise. If everything went according to plan, they'd be in Israel in forty.

CHAPTER 90

Ramallah, Palestine

Meir Yatom fought to stay awake, as he feared he'd never wake up. Davari was long gone. The new crew was even worse than Colonel Davari. At least he understood Davari. He knew what the Iranian was after. Yatom wondered why he and his sidekick had been called away. He hadn't divulged enough stuff for them to go after anything. At least he hoped not.

The new guys were all Palestinians. Yatom was convinced they were with Hamas. He could tell by their lack of discipline. Twice, they'd nearly killed him. The first time was when they hit him on the side of the head with a tennis racket. The next time, only a few hours later, was when they suspended him by his feet for too long.

Without their leader's intervention—the only one with a brain, it seemed—he'd be dead. An hour ago, they had turned off the lights and prepared makeshift beds and cots. The majority of them were now snoring, while two Hamas fighters remained awake to stand guard.

Both had their eyes on their smartphones.

"My men aren't disciplined like yours, Meir Yatom," a voice said behind him.

Yatom recognized the leader's voice.

"And I apologize for the senseless beatings you had to endure at their hands."

Yatom didn't respond.

"But can you really blame them? You took everything from them, Yatom. E-ve-ry-thing."

Yatom's head was suddenly jerked back as the Hamas leader grabbed his hair and pulled back. He found himself staring upside down at the furious face of the Hamas leader. A knife appeared and Yatom felt its tip against his neck.

"You don't talk much, do you?"

Yatom groaned as his head was pulled back even more. A drop of sweat fell from the Hamas leader's forehead right into his left eye. Yatom blinked several times.

"I've been ordered not to kill you. It's a real shame."

Yatom could smell the man's breath, and it wasn't pleasant. It was a mix of stale onion and rotten meat.

"But I think I'm allowed a little souvenir, don't you?"

Before he could react, the Hamas leader cut off Yatom's left ear with one swift movement of his knife. Yatom opened his mouth to scream but the Hamas leader stuffed his mouth with it. He then clamped Yatom's mouth and nose shut using his two hands. Yatom's agony reverberated across his whole body and throbbed with every beat of his heart.

"Shhhh," the Hamas leader kept saying in his ear. "Make a sound and I'll cut off the other one too."

Yatom's entire body shook uncontrollably as warm tears streamed down his face. His lungs burned and screamed for air. Every muscle, every bone, every cell in his body was hurting.

It was time to go. They had pushed him too far. In a way, it was his way of saying, *Fuck you.*

CHAPTER 91

Ramallah, Palestine

Zima heard Captain Burke asking for a last-minute situation report from the observation post.

"Zima," Burke said a couple of seconds later, "we're good to go."

It was Burke's way to request her permission to proceed. He was too macho to ask properly, but Zima didn't mind.

"Let's go then," she replied. She took a few deep breaths.

"All elements, we're a go. I say again we're a go. OP reports no new activities and just took out the two exterior sentries. Team One will position on the left, Team Two on the right. We move in together. Team Two leader, acknowledge."

Zima heard Eitan's voice. "Team Two on the right, copy."

Fifteen seconds later, the two-car motorcade came to a stop in front of an abandoned building.

"That's us," Burke said.

Zima climbed out of the SUV and covered her team's movement by scanning the second and third floor windows for threats. Team Two arrived five seconds later and ran to the right side of the main entrance. A building this size would usually require a much bigger team to clear, but since they only had the basement to take care of they were hoping eight would be enough. That's all they had anyway. The drivers were support personnel, not door-kickers like the rest of Burke's crew.

"All teams, this is Team One leader, in ten secs, five secs. Stand by, stand by, stand by. Go! Go! Go!"

. . . .

Zima was the first to run down the stairs. There were supposed to be two flights of stairs leading down to the basement. Team One was charged with taking the one on the north side of the building, while Team Two was to take the one on the south side. Unfortunately, the southern staircase was no more, so instead of attacking the basement from two different entry points, Team Two was now playing catch up.

They had come equipped with NVGs but they weren't needed. There was enough light to operate without them, which pleased Zima as she always found it hard to aim properly with them. She pulled the MP5 firmly into her shoulder as she reached the first landing.

Her heart almost stopped as she came in contact with a huge man going up the stairs. By the expression on his face, he was even more surprised than she was. He carried an AK-47 slung across his chest. She double-tapped his center of mass and the man crumbled. She shot him once more in the head, in case he was wearing a bulletproof vest.

"One tango down, first landing, north-side staircase," she said over the radio.

She continued down the stairs and reached the basement without incident. She was sweating profusely. The sweat ran down her back and between her breasts. The air inside was humid and the tactical vest didn't help.

A small corridor led into a bigger room. She stopped short of the next room. She peered around the corner, trying not to stick her head out. There were a dozen men sleeping in cots. At the far end of the room, close to where the southern staircase would have ended, sat Meir Yatom. He was naked, tied to a chair. A man was behind him, talking into in his ear.

Zima was relieved but terrified at the same time.

"Visual on Yatom. He's on the south side. There are at least a dozen tangos. Most are sleeping."

"Is he alive, Zima? Is Yatom alive?" Eitan asked.

"Yes."

"When you're ready, Zima. Clock's ticking."

. . . .

The *whump* and flashes of a multitude of stun grenades blasting the air at the same time brought Yatom back to reality. The muffled sounds of the suppressed sub-machine-guns was music to his ears—or his ear. The Hamas leader, who was still standing behind him, let go of his hair, and, for a second, Yatom thought he had been killed.

To his dismay, he realized the terrorist wasn't dead at all; in fact, he was now firing at the assault team, using him as cover.

. . . .

Zima moved half a second after the first stun grenade exploded. The first target to appear in her iron sights was holding a cell phone. Was he simply a sentry passing the long boring hours playing a game of Candy Crush on his phone, or was he about to remotely detonate explosive charges hidden all around the building? Zima didn't wait to find out. She fired three rounds in quick succession from her MP5. Her target staggered backward.

Zima quickly moved deeper inside the room so the rest of the team could move in too. She moved her barrel left and right, taking shots at the men who, just a few seconds ago, were still sleeping. Most of them were unarmed, but they had their weapons within reach. That was good enough for Zima. To her right, she saw a terrorist roll out of his cot. She fired the last two rounds of her magazine at him but missed, her rounds piercing the cot's fabric. Zima got to one knee to make herself as small a target as possible. She locked eyes with her target, both knowing that one wouldn't survive the next three seconds. His hands were on his AK-47 and he was in the process of moving the barrel toward Zima. She let go of her MP5 and transitioned to her pistol.

She wasn't going to make it. She ducked and rolled to her right just as shots rang out over her head. Two muffled shots fired from behind her hit her target. She looked back.

It was Captain Burke. He nodded at her.

Then the top of his head exploded, and his body dropped to the ground.

No!

Zima fell to a prone position but her MP5 was making it awkward. She unslung it.

She looked back. Albert Manchester—the team medic—was already pulling Burke out of the line of fire.

There! To the right of Yatom. A man stood and fired a long salvo. Someone moaned in pain behind her.

Goddamnit! She had no shot. At that range—about thirty yards—she didn't trust herself with the Sig. Only a tiny portion of the man's body was uncovered. The coward was using Meir Yatom as a shield.

CHAPTER 92

Ramallah, Palestine

Eitan took a deep breath. Then another. He had trained for situations just like this all his life. He adjusted his aim slightly, having removed the suppressor for better accuracy. In his mind, this was just like target practice. It didn't matter that the hostage was Meir Yatom. That wouldn't change anything. He'd take the shot the moment he had the opportunity.

And it better be soon because with all the commotion the firefight had caused, the authorities were already on their way.

Burke was down. Manchester was down. This needed to end.

They were in a stalemate. Every second they wasted brought the authorities or the Hamas closer. Something needed to happen.

There. The terrorist was changing his magazine. To do so, the man angled his body differently, allowing Eitan a couple inches of exposure.

He pulled the trigger.

. . . .

The firefight had stopped. Yatom was alert enough to understand they were at a standoff. The Hamas leader behind him simply had to hinder the rescue attempt for a few more minutes and everything would be lost.

Yatom's heart jumped at the single unmuffled gunshot.

He felt the heat of the bullet whiz past him and heard a noise like that of a fist striking a pillow. A wet sucking sound confirmed a bullet had penetrated the terrorist's flesh.

CHAPTER 93

Ramallah, Palestine

Zima ran to Yatom, not bothering with the dying terrorist behind him. Burke's men would finish him off. She cut Yatom loose using her knife. Seeing him like this, she felt as though someone had ripped her heart out of her chest. His face was swollen almost beyond recognition. There were gashes and streams of dried blood below his knee. One of his thumbs was missing.

"My God, Meir, what have they done to you?" she said, her voice cracking. Tears shimmered in her eyes. Someone was going to pay dearly for this.

"Zima," Eitan said, "we have to go."

"Look what these bastards did to him."

"We need to go," Eitan repeated. "We'll avenge him later, I promise you. But first, we need to get to our extraction point."

Yatom carried his boss in a fireman carry while two other team members took defensive position around him. Two other men carried Burke and Manchester. Zima picked up her MP5 and inserted a fresh magazine. She jogged to the front of group and was first to climb the stairs.

It was still dark but the sun was just starting to rise.

"Chariot One and Two, this is Team Two leader. We're coming in," Zima heard on the radio as she reached the first landing. The body of the terrorist she had killed was still there.

"Copy that, team leader. We're green, but take note, there are civilians outside. Unarmed for now. Ready to receive."

She dragged the corpse away so the men carrying the casualties wouldn't trip on it. She hurried up the stairs. If hostiles were hidden among the civilians, waiting for them to come out, they'd know soon enough. Zima guessed they'd wait until most of the team was out in the open. Since the vehicles were parked less than ten yards away from the entrance, they had a good chance of making it.

Or maybe not, Zima thought, as she remembered the Mitsubishis weren't armored.

Here we go.

Zima came out with her MP5 up. She scanned the windows and the balustrades across the street. She put herself out in the open so she'd be the first to be engaged. She was aware she was being filmed but, at this point, she didn't care.

A man in the crowd shouted something. Someone else joined him. Within twenty seconds, the crowd had become wild. Then someone threw the first rock. It landed a few feet in front of Zima. Another rock, thrown directly at her, hit her between the shoulder blades. The tactical vest caught the brunt of it but she almost lost her balance.

In her earpiece she heard, "We're clear, Zima. Let's go!"

She started retreating toward the two-car motorcade when a glass bottle smashed into her head. A bright light exploded in her eyes and she lost her vision. Something warm dripped down the back of her head.

"Let's go, Zima!"

She tried to wipe away whatever was in her eyes but it only caused more discomfort and more brightness.

Fuck!

"I need help, Eitan, I can't see!"

A series of shots rang out and two rounds slapped her in the chest. She staggered back just as another round hit her in the back with a sickening thud. The wind was knocked out of her as she sank to her knees, her MP5 slipping out of her grasp. For a moment, she felt at peace. She turned her head and through the fog saw Eitan staring at her in disbelief through the Mitsubishi's windshield. She tried to tell him to go, to save Meir, that everything would be all right but, before she could, someone rammed her at full speed. And then, all at once, she fell on her back and was sucked down into blackness.

. . . .

Eitan was grateful that Zima had moved a bit further up the road. It allowed him and the rest of the team to climb into the vehicles.

"Let's go, Zima!"

It was time to leave. They had a rendezvous point to make and their window was closing fast.

Then came her distress signal. "I need help, Eitan, I can't see!"

Eitan looked through the windshield. Zima was holding her weapon with one hand while wiping her eyes with her forearm. Two muzzle flashes to the left followed by another on the right brought Zima to her knees.

Eitan never hesitated; he hurried out of the vehicle and ran toward her, unconcerned for his own safety. Before he could reach her, someone, revolver in hand, tore through the crowd and rammed Zima to the ground. The man had time to punch her twice in the face before Eitan kicked him in the head. The man rolled to his side and Eitan shot him twice in the heart just as someone else opened up on full automatic. Most of the bullets missed him but one round hit him in the thigh and another took off the end of one of his small fingers.

Fuck!

Eitan pivoted to his right and shot the man with a one-handed triple tap. The man reeled back, his chest ripped open by Eitan's slugs.

Eitan pointed his pistol toward the crowd and yelled in Arabic, "Who's next?"

The intense sting caused by the bullets made him feel even more alert. Slowly, the crowd scattered. Eitan holstered his pistol and kneeled next to Zima. Her face was white, creased in pain and glistening with sweat. Her breathing was shallow, her eyes closed. She moaned, as if having a bad dream.

"C'mon, baby, I got you." He took Zima in his arms, wincing at the agony of his own wounds. Blood ran from his thigh, down the back of his leg, soaking his combat pants. He took a step and swayed from the pain but continued toward the vehicle. He placed Zima in the front passenger seat and closed the door behind her.

"Go!"

He limped to the second SUV and sat on the backseat. The Mitsubishi accelerated away. Eitan snatched the satellite phone from one of his tactical vest pockets and contacted Matthias Sachar in Tel-Aviv.

"Matthias, this is Eitan. We have him. He's alive. Please tell me the choppers are on their way."

"They'll be at the extraction point on time, Eitan. Any casualties?"

"One dead, three critically wounded, including Meir," Eitan said, forgetting he was wounded too.

"There's a medical team aboard one of the choppers. I'll see you soon, Eitan. And please share my gratitude with Captain Burke's team."

CHAPTER 94

IMSI Headquarters, New York

They were still ten feet over the building when Davari saw a man emerging from the rooftop's trapdoor. The man was dressed in a black security guard uniform and carried a sidearm. For the moment the sidearm was still holstered, but the security guard was waving off the helicopter with his arms while trying not to fall off the rooftop. The helicopter's main rotor generated enough wind that the guard had to lean into it to keep his balance.

"The trapdoor is open. This is our chance," Davari said to his team. They gave him the thumbs-up. He switched radio frequency so he could talk to the pilot.

"Jennifer, bring it down."

The moment the skids touched the rooftop, Davari opened the door of the AS350. The security guard had his pistol out, but he was aiming at Jennifer. Before he could switch his aim to Davari, Mariwala opened up with his MP5K on full automatic, striking the man with multiple bullets. With the guard down, Mariwala jumped off the helicopter. Davari and Mondegari followed.

A head popped outside the trapdoor and Davari fired, the sound of his MP5K lost in the chopping of the helicopter blades. The man fell back into the hole but Davara wasn't sure if he had hit his target. With his MP5K at the ready, he peered into the trapdoor. A large ladder with thick steps led down to a locker room. The security guard lay motionless at the foot of the ladder.

"Cover me, Musa, I'm going down."

Davari hurried down the ladder by taking the steps two at a time. He jumped the last three and assumed a kneeling shooting position. The locker room was just that, a room with four dozen blue lockers. From his position, Davari could see only one point of entry, right in front of him. He signaled Mariwala and Mondegari to come down.

Davari activated his throat mike. "Malegam from Davari, radio check, over."

"Five by five, sir."

"Davari copy. Cover our six, Variyan. Keep an eye on that ladder on the south side. It leads to the front of the building."

"Yes, sir, will do."

Confident Malegam would cover their rear, Davari shared a few words with his two teammates.

"Let's create as much chaos as we can. If you see a computer or a server, destroy it. Remember, our objective is to give General Kharazi enough time to activate the final phase of his operation."

. . . .

Special Agent Jordan was shocked by what she had just witnessed. Two men were dead already.

Madness.

This was a fully fledged assault on the building. How come she had no idea what this building was? She'd been briefed on all the potential targets the terrorists might be interested in, but there had been no mention of this building.

Why?

Maybe this was one of those CIA "black sites" she kept hearing about? Could this be it? It had to be.

How long would it take for the police to arrive? From her vantage point, she could see numerous police cars racing down the Brooklyn Bridge and Manhattan Bridge. Three minutes? Four minutes?

That was too long. More people would die if she didn't act now. She had to do something. She couldn't stay still. Taped under the pilot seat was a small Colt Mustang XSP. If she could get to it . . .

Her peripheral vision caught movement. On her left, a guard was making his way to the rooftop using the ladder. The terrorist next to her saw him too and raised his arm to take a shot through the window.

Jordan didn't hesitate. She grabbed the barrel of his pistol and angled it toward the roof of the helicopter just as Variyan pulled the trigger. The bright flash made her blink. In that small space, the sound was deafening. Jordan struggled to keep Variyan from firing at the guard but he was much stronger than she was. He twisted his arm out of her grasp and smashed the butt of his pistol into the bridge of her nose with such force she almost blackout. Her head was spinning. She tried to reach the Colt taped under her seat but her safety belt and shoulder harnesses restrained her.

Variyan fired again. The window to her left shattered. Thousands of glass fragments were sucked back into the cockpit, cutting her neck and face. She couldn't be sure but she thought she heard him yelled in pain too. They were both shouting. He tried to hit her again, this time with his elbow, but only grazed her cheek. He started pumping rounds out the window so fast it sounded like an automatic weapon. She tried to grab his arm again, but he pushed her back and continued to fire.

The guard fell, clutching his leg. Another guard, who had just climbed onto the rooftop, ran to him and tried to pull him to safety. Variyan fired another round, and then the slide remained open.

His magazine was empty. She saw him reach for another.

It was now or never. Jordan unclipped her harness and seat belt and reached under her seat. She almost made it. She had her hand on the Colt when Variyan pressed the hot barrel of his pistol against her temple. It burnt her skin.

Then it dawned upon her that he couldn't shoot her. She was their exit strategy, their only way out. She went for it. She pulled the gun from under the seat and brought it up. She jerked the trigger just as Variyan deflected her arm away with his right forearm. Her shot went wide and punched a hole in the windshield. He chopped down on her wrist with his left hand. She dropped the gun.

In desperation, she grabbed the stick and pulled it hard toward her while opening the throttle wide. The helicopter lifted off. Variyan jumped on her. She tried to push him off but he was too heavy. He fought her for control. They were almost clear of the antennas when the rear rotor hit the highest one. The back blade exploded and came off the chopper. The engine spooled, building power. The whole chopper vibrated, and Jordan knew she was in trouble. The chopper pitched forward and up, its nose rising.

We're gonna stall. Fuck.

A second later, it came down, missing the rooftop by less than five feet. The chopper crashed next to the garage door and exploded on impact.

CHAPTER 95

IMSI Headquarters, New York

Mike ran up the stairs to the ground floor where the control room was located. For the time being, he wasn't worried about his colleagues working there. Since this was the spot from where the analysts and case officers ran all the IMSI's operations, the control room was the most secure location in the building. The minute the intrusion alarm rang, it locked itself and became impregnable from anyone on the outside. There was enough food, water and other supplies for a full contingent of employees to last five days. What worried him was the server room on the second floor. If the control room was IMSI's heart, the server room was its brain.

The issue at hand, though, was his pistol. He needed something with more stopping power. His Taurus was nice and compact but not the ideal weapon for taking down a group of well-armed assaulters.

How many were they?

By himself, Mike knew his chances were limited. He needed to link up with Sanchez or with the three security guards posted on the second floor to protect the armory and the server room.

Were they after the servers? What had prompted the Iranians to conduct such an attack in broad daylight? Why were they so desperate? Hopefully Anna Caprini had shut the server room down, but, to do so, she needed to be in the room. A breach there would be catastrophic. Since the majority of the IMSI employees working at headquarters were analysts and support personnel and most of the assets—the operators who were actually conducting the missions—were presently overseas, Mike could only count on Lisa and Sanchez to help him flush the intruders out. With Lisa on bodyguard duty, Sanchez's help was crucial.

The police were certainly on their way, but it would take them time to breach the security at the front gate. As per protocol, a skeleton crew would stay at the gate while the other guards would rush in from both entry points to secure the building. The objective was to sandwich the attackers and counter-attack them on two fronts.

His phone chirped in his pocket. Three long bursts, followed by two small ones.

Sanchez.

With his left hand, Mike pulled his phone out. He read Sanchez's message:

Where r u? Im in Charles office. Lost contact with security team. Anna up in the server room. Bout 2 go hunting. Believe bad guys came in through trapdoor.

Mike replied:

Don't move. On my way. I'll knock twice.

If he could link up with Sanchez, they had a chance. Mike put his phone in his back pocket and made his way to Mapother's office, making sure to clear every angle before committing to a new direction.

The corridors were empty. Mike was glad to see everyone had followed the protocols Charles Mapother and Sanchez had put in place for such an eventuality. Not only were the IMSI employees better protected in their offices, it made the security team's job much easier.

Mike knocked on Mapother's door twice. The door opened automatically from the inside.

"Jonathan, it's me," Mike said, loud enough to be heard.

"Come in."

Mike entered Mapother's office. Sanchez was standing in one corner, his pistol at the low, ready.

"How much ammo do you have?

"I have three mags of fifteen plus one in the pipe," Sanchez told him.

"I have twelve plus one, and a spare magazine."

"That's not much, buddy," Sanchez said.

"Agreed, but remember what they say: The battle isn't won with the first short; it's won with the first accurate shot."

CHAPTER 96

IMSI Headquarters, New York

Mike held his Taurus at eye level as he climbed the stairs to the second floor. Sanchez was on his heels. They were heading to the server room, hoping to link with Caprini.

Mike climbed slowly, arms extended in front of him with both hands firmly on the Taurus's grip. His sights were aligned with the opening at the top of the stairs. His eyes, his ears and his mind were alert for anything suspect.

There was a time when once the adrenaline had kicked in, Mike's senses would be enhanced, and his reactions sharpened. A detached sense of anticipation would envelop him and make him more efficient in every way. Now, nothing was the same. His throat had dried up and sweat formed on his forehead. It was already trickling down, stinging his eyes. His chest tightened, and his vision grew fuzzy at the edges. Mike had to hold on to the railing to steady himself. He took two deep breaths and forced himself to focus on the task at hand.

"You're okay, Mike?" Sanchez asked. "What are you doing?"

"Sorry, I missed a step. I'm fine," he replied.

Mike continued but stopped four steps from the top. He could make out the sounds of one or more people moving somewhere up ahead. Since all the IMSI employees were locked in their respective offices, Mike was confident the sound didn't come from friendlies—unless it was Caprini? Mike remained low and moved up one more step. With his pistol up and ready, he peeked above the last step.

At the opposite end of the hallway, three men armed with compact sub-machine guns walked down the last step of the staircase.

Mike was struck by their efficiency. Their guns were extensions of their arms, sweeping left to right and right to left, seeking targets. Mike stepped back and whispered, "Three tangos moving this way. Fifty yards and closing in. They're armed with sub-machine guns. No friendlies in sight."

They couldn't engage the three terrorists from this distance with their pistols and hope to win. He wondered where the three guards assigned to the second floor were. The comms had ceased working right after the explosion. Had they climbed to the rooftop to investigate? If so, it meant they were either dead or incapacitated since the Iranians were now on the second floor.

The unmistakable sound of a boot kicking in a door, followed by a single gunshot, resonated in the staircase. Mike risked another peek at the terrorists but quickly ducked back when two rounds whizzed over his head.

Shit!

They were effectively pinned down. They had no room to maneuver forward. More gunshots rang across the floor, chipping the wall behind them.

"Whoever is in the server room is getting slaughtered," Mike said, as more rounds ricocheted above.

They didn't need to say it. *Anna was in danger, if not already dead.*

Sanchez climbed up a few steps and fired only one shot before he had to scurry back.

Mike's mind was racing. It was surreal that they were being attacked right here in Brooklyn. He had never thought this would happen. The IMSI was piggybacking on many of the country's intelligence services. This was why the organization could quickly become a political hot potato if discovered. A private corporation with this kind of access—this was bad enough; but if the terrorists gained access to the mainframe, it could cripple the country.

"We need to get to Anna, Jonathan," Mike said.

"What are you thinking?"

"Forty seconds. In forty seconds, I'll pop him from behind. Make sure to keep his head down starting at second thirty-five."

"Got it."

Mike synchronized his watch with Sanchez's, and then he was off.

. . . .

Sanchez inserted a fresh magazine into his pistol and then glanced at his watch.

Ten, nine, eight . . .

He pictured Mike running up the stairs on the opposite side and knew his friend would be mowed down if he didn't provide cover fire at the right time.

Four, three, two . . .

Sanchez got up and started firing down the hall where he had last seen the Iranian soldier. To his surprise, the soldier had moved to the other side of the corridor and Sanchez lost a quarter of a second adjusting his aim. The Iranian, though, already had his sights on him and opened up with a three-round burst. The bullets whizzed to his left, one of them grazing his left cheek, and forced Sanchez to jerk the trigger before his sights were perfectly aligned. Sanchez missed but the Iranian didn't. His second three-round burst smashed into the marble floor just in front of Sanchez and ricocheted up. One of the bullets cut into his right shoulder, while another entered his body below his right nipple. They might have been ricochets, but the force of the impacts sent Sanchez tumbling down the stairs. He knocked his head against the wall. He could hear the firefight raging one flight above him. Mike was counting on him. Sanchez tried to move but it was as if shards of glass had shot through his entire body. The blistering pain stopped him cold. The staircase around him turned fuzzy. His shirt was damp with blood. He felt as though someone had shoved a burning sword into his lungs. He tried to breathe but couldn't find any air. Nothing came in, and nothing came out. Black and red dots slid across his vision and, despite the searing pain wracking his body, he clung desperately to consciousness, knowing that if he let go, he'd never wake up.

. . . .

Mike hurried down the steps and sprinted the entire length of the ground floor. He had to slow down to check his watch.

Twenty seconds left. He picked up speed again but couldn't stop thinking about Anna Caprini. Not only was she the best analyst the

IMSI had, she was a friend. He rushed up the stairs and heard Sanchez fire his first shot followed by the Iranian's riposte. Mike had to time this perfectly. He reached the second-floor hallway right after Sanchez had fired his third shot.

For reasons he didn't yet understand, instead of returning fire at Sanchez as Mike had expected, the Iranian soldier did a shoulder check. By the time Mike pulled the trigger, the Iranian was already facing him. Mike prayed his aim was true. His first shot ricocheted off the Iranian's weapon, sending sparks flying. In the background, Mike heard a weapon go off on full automatic.

It came from within the server room. Mike continued closing the gap. The Iranian didn't waver either; he kept his eyes fixed on Mike in a perfect firing position. He transitioned to the pistol he kept in a holster in the small of his back. Mike fired a second round and a third. The Iranian fell to his knees and then to his side, clutching his stomach and spitting blood. Mike took an extra second to aim his next shot and sent his round into the Iranian's head.

Mike waited for Sanchez to join him but his friend didn't come. Had he been hit?

Damn it! This was why the Iranian had done a shoulder check. He had seen his round hit its intended target and thought he was no longer a threat.

As much as Mike wanted to rush back to help Sanchez, he needed to secure the server room first. He'd love to have Lisa by his side, but there was no time to lose. He'd have to do this one solo.

CHAPTER 97

IMSI Headquarters, New York

The explosion startled Davari. He knew what it was and what it meant for him and his men the moment he heard it. A quick look in their direction told him they knew it too.

Since there was only one big empty space outside the locker room, they cleared the third floor in no time. There were two staircases, one at each extremity of the building. They came across a set of elevators but kept walking until they reached the staircase at the end of the hallway. They reached the second floor and faced a long, white marble corridor with half a dozen doors on the left side but only two on the right. Not a single living soul was in sight, but there was a subtle hum emanating from the entire right side of the corridor. There were no knobs on any of the doors, only black keypads. Davari tried the first door to his left but it refused to move. They continued down the hallway, scanning for threats, but the whole floor was like a ghost town.

They were halfway down the corridor when, to his immediate right, a slight vacuum-sucking *swoosh* attracted his attention. Someone had cracked open a door.

Davari didn't hesitate. He pivoted on his right foot and kicked the door open with his left. Somebody stumbled back and Davari walked in with Mariwala squeezing past him and turning left to clear his corner. In front of Davari, a guard lay on his back, his face registering shock, and then fear. He moved his hand to his backup but Davari shot him in the face. Just behind the dead guard, an attractive black-haired woman in her mid-thirties stared at him. She showed no fear. In fact, a defiant smirk came to her lips.

"Contact rear!" Mondegari yelled from the hallway as he opened up with his MP5K. For a fraction of a second, Davari had allowed himself to be distracted. The woman pounced on him. Caught off guard, he didn't move fast enough, and she slammed into him, knocking him off balance. Her forward momentum thrust him against the wall, his MP5K pinned between them. She kneed him in the balls with such force, his eyes watered and his knees weakened. She took a step back and, to his surprise, a gun appeared in her hand.

Where did it come from? His hand moved to his holster.

Empty.

The realization of what had just happened sent him into a fit of rage. The pistol belonged to him. He tried to deflect it, but she was out of reach. In slow motion, he saw her pull the trigger, and he wondered if he would feel anything. He closed his eyes.

The gunshot rang out, its earsplitting retort louder than usual. He felt a warm spray of blood mist across his face, but no pain. He opened his eyes. The woman in front of him had dropped the gun. Her two hands were now on her neck, blood seeping through her fingers. She looked at him in disbelief.

Mariwala was standing ten feet to his left, his MP5K raised, a wisp of white smoke escaping its barrel.

Davari brought up his MP5K and emptied the rest of his magazine into her. He ejected the spent magazine and inserted a new one.

"You're good, Colonel?"

Davari nodded and took in the rest of the room.

Banks of computer servers and communication interfaces lined the room on both sides. The room was kept chilly for optimum performance. In addition to all the fail-safe switches, there were also massive surge protectors in place to guard against power surges. In one corner was a backup generator to provide power in case of a major outage. This was the place they'd been looking for.

Mariwala had probably reached the same conclusion as he was already removing the C-4 explosives from his backpack.

"How long do you need?"

"One minute, sir. I'm setting the timer for two minutes."

Davari thought about it. With the chopper gone, there was no chance for them to escape. The explosion would obliterate the room and there was a possibility the floor would cave in. If they wanted to survive this, they needed to find a way to—

The distinctive sound of a grenade hitting and rolling on the floor interrupted his thought process. "Grenade!" Davari yelled, diving forward.

CHAPTER 98

IMSI headquarters, New York

Mike flung the stun grenade into the server room and rolled away from the door until it detonated. Mike rushed into the room before the flash faded. The first thing he saw was the dead guard, and then the chewed-up body of Anna Caprini.

No! I'm too late.

The sight—one he would remember until his death—wrenched his heart out of his chest. A few feet further, two men were on their knees, struggling to bring their MP5Ks to bear. Mike wasn't thinking straight. Instead of shooting center mass, he aimed to inflict maximum suffering. The first bullet hit the man on the left in the right bicep. He dropped his weapon and clutched his injured arm. His second, third and fourth shots all went to the other man. The first bullet broke his femur, the other two lodged themselves deep into his stomach. The man writhed in pain. Mike kicked both MP5Ks away.

"Who the fuck are you?" Mike asked, pressing his foot against the man's femur.

The man yelled and shouted something in Farsi.

"English."

"Fuck. You."

Mike shot him in the mouth.

He turned his attention to the other man. He didn't even have to ask a question.

"My name's Colonel Asad Davari. Quds Force. I surrender."

CHAPTER 99

IMSI Headquarters, New York

Lisa heard the faint sounds of gunfire through the ventilation system.

"What's going on?" Sassani asked.

"We're under attack," Lisa admitted. "I'll protect you."

A sudden and vicious episode of coughing took over Sassani. There wasn't much Lisa could do to help her. Sassani managed to get her breathing under control.

"You're okay?"

Sassani nodded. "I'll be fine."

"Talk now, Tracy. If you wanna help, you need to do it now."

Sassani's head fell back on the pillow. She sighed. "Okay."

Lisa dialed Mapother's number. She wanted to be sure he heard this live in case the intruders overran them.

Mapother answered on the second ring. "Are you okay, Lisa?"

"For now, Charles. We're under—"

"I know. I'm in constant communication with the control room. The NYPD and the FBI are already on their way. Hold tight."

"Charles, I'm with Sassani in the medical bay. I want you to listen to what she has to say."

"Wait a second, Lisa, I need to put you on hold."

Lisa couldn't believe it. She was about to share with him intelligence vital to the national interest of the United States, and he was putting her on hold?

What the hell?

CHAPTER 100

Oval Office, The White House, Washington, DC

Charles Mapother put Lisa on hold and looked at DNI Richard Phillips.

"I think President Muller will want to hear this, Richard," Mapother said.

"I'm sorry, Charles, I really am," Phillips replied. "You know we won't be able to sweep this under the rug, right?"

Mapother was no fool; he knew this was the end of the International Market Stabilization Institute. How many heads would roll, nobody knew. And if Mapother was asked to stand up and face the music, he would, without a hint of hesitation. He was proud of what they had accomplished.

"Frankly, Richard, this should be the last of our concerns right now. Protecting the lives of my employees and listening to what Sassani has to say should be our only priorities. Not politics."

"Easy for you to say."

"I'll stand before a Senate committee if you want me too. Heck, before a grand jury if you prefer. But let's get this information to the president."

The door to the Oval Office opened and one of the president's aides invited them in. "President Muller will see you now, gentlemen," she said.

Mapother and Phillips got up. "Okay, Charles."

. . . .

"You're still there, Lisa?"

"Goddamnit, Charles, what kind of game are you playing?" she replied, pissed off. "Someone could breach in here at any moment."

"Dr. Walton?"

"Who the fuck is this?"

"This is President Robert Muller."

Lisa's jaw dropped. She looked over at Sassani. She had heard it too and wore a look of disbelief.

"Are you still there, Dr. Walton?"

Lisa overcame her initial shock. "Yes, sir, my apologies."

"You're with NYPD Sergeant Sassani, correct?"

"Yes, Mr. President, but she's badly injured—"

"I know. Her father shot her," President Muller interrupted. "Can you hear me, Sergeant?"

Lisa moved the phone closer to Sassani, who made an effort to sit, her face contorted in pain.

"Yes, I can hear you, Mr. President."

"Good, that's good. I . . . hum . . . I understand you had a change of heart, Sergeant?"

"I guess you could say that. It kind of messes with your head when your father shoots you."

. . . .

Mapother and Phillips were seated in front of President Muller. Mapother had placed his phone in the middle of the Resolute Desk.

"Well, speak then, Sergeant. You have my undivided attention."

Sassani took a deep breath.

"Let me first say that I understand the plight of the Iranian people," Sassani started. "I'm not sure the economic sanctions are what's best for the American people either."

Phillips gave Mapother a peeved, almost angry look.

What the fuck, he mouthed to him.

"I share your concerns, Sergeant, I do," President Muller said. "And I hope to have a better working relationship with Iran very soon."

Mapother knew this was pure bullshit. Or was it? You could never be sure with politicians.

"Thank you," Sassani said, her voice cracking. The girl was clearly passionate about the country of her ancestors.

"What can you tell us about the threat we're facing?" Muller asked.

"You're about to be extorted, Mr. President, or you're about to get hit."

"I know about the extortion, but what do you mean by a hit?"

"Someone close to you might try to kill you, that's what I mean."

Mapother glanced at Muller. The president wasn't one to worry easily, but the assassination of the Canadian prime minister and the attack on Mayor Church had taken their toll on him.

"This was the plan all along, sir," Sassani continued. "They called it PERIWINKLE. They wanted you to fear that whatever happened to the Canadian prime minister, the mayor of New York City and to the New York State governor could also happen to you. They were going to leverage that fear for either financial support or foreign policy manipulation, and, if that didn't work, they'd kill you."

A stunned silence fell over the Oval Office as the impact of Sassani's statement hit home.

"How?"

For the next couple of minutes, Sassani explained how eight Iranian SAVAK officers were sent to the United States and Canada to breed a new generation of sleeper agents. They were to be the scalpel able to carve inside the heart of the West, with the ultimate objective being to have at least one of them close to an American president or Canadian prime minister, and one politician close enough to exercise some degree of influence at the national level. Those who weren't able to join the Secret Service, the RCMP or elected offices were to find jobs that could help sway American opinion to be friendly toward Iran.

"Do you have the names of these individuals?" Muller asked.

Sassani gave them the names.

"Myself, Tracy Sassani, NYPD sergeant attached to the protective detail of Mayor Church; Michigan State senator Maxim Ghasemi, who'll be running for governor next election; Khalid al-Fadhi, RCMP sergeant assigned to the protection detail of the Canadian prime minister; Savis Moria, senior editor at the Huffington Post; Radman Divecha, New York State Police sergeant assigned to the protection detail of the governor; Lara Firouzgari, trained assassin based in New York City; Nasrin Yazdanipour, reporter at CNN."

Mapother was floored. Savis Moria and Nasrin Yazdanipour were highly respected and well-known reporters. Both had millions of followers on social media and yielded considerable power.

President Muller pressed the mute button. "I want these individuals—those still alive—dealt with," he said, and then added as if it was an afterthought, "After a proper investigation, of course."

"That's only seven names, Mr. President," Mapother pointed out.

Muller pressed the mute button again.

"Didn't you say there were eight of you?" Muller asked.

"I'm missing one, I'm afraid," Sassani replied. "The one in the White House. I don't know who he is."

CHAPTER 101

Tehran, Iran

The American news media were all over the incident in Brooklyn. This and Mayor Church's assassination attempt were the only two subjects they talked about. Even the murder of the Canadian prime minister had been pushed aside for the time being. There was a panoply of police cars, fire trucks and ambulances on site, but, so far, the media were kept at bay. The only images coming in were from a couple of news choppers flying over the area, but even those were asked to move out.

Was Colonel Davari dead? Kharazi certainly hoped so. Despite his promise he'd be willing to do a prisoner exchange with the Americans if Davari was caught, he never intended on keeping it. The political blowout would be too high. Furthermore, Meir Yatom was worth more than Davari. Much more. So, until he was named deputy supreme leader, he didn't want to weaken his already tenuous position with the ayatollah.

In less than an hour, a team of Quds Force operators he had hand-selected would be arriving in Ramallah to take possession of the Israeli spy. Kharazi had lost contact with his man on the ground but he wasn't overly concerned. Poor communication with the Palestinians was a common occurrence. No one in Hamas would be crazy enough to defy his order. Not if they wanted to live.

As for the ayatollah's plan, there were twenty-four hours left before he gave his special asset the kill order. He had hoped that the attack on the covert facility would have prompted a call from DNI Philips, but it was radio silence on that front too. Part of him wanted to call his asset now to make sure he was still in play. Had Davari actually succeeded? By Kharazi's count, in addition to his special asset, there were still at least three single cells in operation. They weren't trained shooters like the others, but sometimes words were stronger than bullets. If the Americans had figured out who they were, they would have been arrested by now. Kharazi had checked their Twitter feeds half an hour ago and they were more active than ever.

But what about Divecha and Firouzgari? They hadn't checked in since he had activated them. And there had been no new announcement about Mayor Church. Should he assume the worst and scratch their names of the list for good?

His personal cellphone pulsed on his desk. Very few people had this number.

"Yes?"

"General Kharazi? This is Colonel Mizraei, sir."

"How did you get this—"

"He's coming after you. You need to get out. Now."

Mizraei's words struck a chord. *He's coming after you.* Kharazi swallowed hard.

"Slow down, Colonel," Kharazi said, with a calm and reasonable voice, even though his heart was racing. "What's going on? Who's coming after me?"

"The ayatollah."

Kharazi was in analysis paralysis; his mind was going one hundred miles an hour but wasn't making any decision. Why would the ayatollah come after him? Mizraei was still speaking but Kharazi wasn't listening.

Wasn't he the architect behind the ayatollah's plan, and a trusted advisor? Maybe a little less so since he had kidnapped Meir Yatom without authorization, but a trusted advisor nonetheless.

A couple words made it through the thick fog around Kharazi's brain.

"What? Say that again?"

"It's because of Meir Yatom, sir, he's . . . Well, he's gone, sir. Some kind of special forces team secured his release an hour ago. The ayatollah knows."

The news stunned him. *No, this couldn't be true. Mizraei was lying. He had to be.*

"I'm sorry, sir."

The line went dead.

Kharazi slouched in his chair and leaned his head back, trying to make sense of it all.

A knock at his door made him jump to his feet. The door opened before he had the chance to wipe the perspiration off his forehead.

"Major General Kharazi," said the newcomer. "May I?"

Kharazi forced a smile. "Of course, General Hajizadeh."

"Thank you. I promise not to take too much of your valuable time. I'm told you're quite busy at the moment."

Brigadier General Ali Hajizadeh was the commander-in-chief of the Law Enforcement Force or LEF. The LEF was the uniformed police force of Iran and counted over sixty thousand police personnel. Hajizadeh was tall, maybe an inch or two above six feet, and was dressed in an immaculate uniform. He was a favorite of the ayatollah. Hajizadeh's presence in his office was bad news. Although Kharazi held a superior rank, he had to tread carefully around Hajizadeh.

"What can I do for you?" Kharazi asked.

"I had the chance to dine with our supreme leader," Hajizadeh said, pausing for effect. "And your name came up."

Kharazi didn't say anything. He waited for his guest to continue.

"He shared something with me, and I thought I'd come to you first before, you know, ordering my staff to take action."

Kharazi felt his face turn red. He did his best to suppress the anger that was rolling up in his gut. He spoke only when he thought he could control his voice. "And what would that be?"

"I'm told you've launched an unauthorized operation against the Americans," Hajizadeh said, a tiny smiled appearing on his lips. "Something called PERIWINKLE. Isn't that so?"

Kharazi didn't need to hear more. The ayatollah had betrayed him. Why was he pulling out? There was still a chance the list General Adbullahi had leaked out had been destroyed by Colonel Davari's raid on the American compound. If this was indeed the case, PERIWINKLE had to continue. Not only did they have a shot at some much-needed cash influx, but the latest polls suggested Maxim Ghasemi would become the next governor of the state of Michigan. And who knew where he could end up ten years from now? The idea of the White House wasn't as farfetched as it once was.

Again, why was the ayatollah pulling out now?

"Is that true, Major General Kharazi?" Hajizadeh repeated, louder this time.

Kharazi sighed and rolled his shoulder like a broken man. "You know as well as I do the ayatollah was behind everything, Ali. But if he wants me to take the fall, I will, and with great honor. I'll do it for him, for Allah, and for the good of our country."

Hajizadeh seemed pleased by his answer. "I'm sorry it didn't turn out the way you wanted, Jalal. I'm glad you understand."

"What now?"

"Go home, get some rest, make love with your wife," Hajizadeh said. "You'll be arrested first thing in the morning."

Kharazi knew this was pure bullshit. One of Hajizadeh's men was probably sticking a bomb under his car as they spoke. That's what he'd do if he was in Hajizadeh's shoes. You didn't leave a powerful and resourceful man like Jalal Kharazi out of your sight.

"Thank you. I appreciate the gesture. May I ask you something?"

Hajizedeh looked at his watch and then nodded, as if he was doing Kharazi a huge favor.

"Why? We were so close to our objective. Our two most important assets are still in play."

"It doesn't matter anymore. The Russians withdrew their support, Jalal. If you were to go ahead with the last phase of PERIWINKLE, it would force the Americans into an all-out war. A war we couldn't win. You understand?"

Damn these Russians. Cowards of all them. The Americans must have promised them something the Iranians couldn't match. A loosening of the economic sanctions against Moscow, maybe? A back-channel deal regarding the North Korean threat? Whatever it was, Simonich's decision had placed the ayatollah in an unsustainable position and he had decided to cut his losses. *And blame me.*

"Yes, I understand."

"You had your chance," Hajizadeh said, getting up. "I'll see you in the morning."

In one swift movement, Kharazi snatched the silenced pistol from the holster Velcro-ed under his desk. He aimed it at Hajizadeh's heart and said, "No you won't."

The brigadier general opened his mouth, a look of terror on his face. Kharazi pulled the trigger twice. Two neat, dark crimson holes appeared on the general's tunic. He fell right back in his chair.

For a brief moment, Kharazi considered not going through with the last phase of PERIWINKLE. The Americans would respond in kind, and more. But he'd be far away by then.

Ayatollah Bhansali's betrayal couldn't go unanswered. The supreme leader shouldn't have tried to push him over.

He made the call.

CHAPTER 102

The White House, Washington DC

United States Secret Service Supervisory Special Agent Yash Najjar was in the White House mess eating a green garden salad when he got *the* call.

"Hello, Yash, it's your uncle."

Najjar didn't have any uncles, or aunts for that matter. He recognized the voice anyway. It belonged to General Kharazi. He swallowed hard, apprehension roiling his gut.

"Everything okay, Uncle? I wasn't expecting your call."

"The timing has changed, Yash. It has to be now. Will it be a problem?"

"What about my family?"

"I've already talked to your father. He's on his way to pick them up. There's a plane waiting for them at Dulles."

Najjar wished he could have spent one more day with them, but knowing they'd all be safe in Montenegro soothed his anxiety. His father had worked tirelessly for years preparing for this. Everything was in place. New identities had been created for his dad, his wife and his children. He even knew which school his kids would go to. He had built the perfect life for him and his family.

He had built the perfect lie.

"Thank you," he said, finally. "I'll do my part."

"May Allah bless you . . . And may He guide your hand."

Najjar and Kharazi had spoken a total of five times before. All of their talks had been face to face. His father, an Iranian American and former US ambassador to the United Arab Emirates, had been there during these meetings. Recruited in 1978 by Ayatollah Ruhollah Khomeini himself, his father had been the highest mole the Iranian government ever had within the United States. He had been granted the rank of colonel. But his record had been eclipsed by his son the minute Yash became a member of the Secret Service presidential protective detail.

. . . .

Najjar hadn't expected to be activated for another twenty-four to forty-eight hours, if at all. That didn't mean he wouldn't be able to accomplish his mission, but it wouldn't be as clean as he wanted it to be, or as easy. But Kharazi had said *now*.

He knew he was the most important asset of a grand plan crafted by the first supreme leader almost four decades ago. His dad had told him the truth about his real identity only once he had been accepted by the Secret Service. His father had used his significant influence to get reference letters for Najjar's application. Reference letters from former and current United States ambassadors and two ex-secretaries of state had played a role in getting Najjar noticed among the thousands of applicants.

Surprisingly, Najjar wasn't shocked when his father admitted he was working for the Iranian government, and that he'd been a personal friend to Ayatollah Khomeini. His father's spy stories fascinated him. His father had offered him a way out, not wanting to force his son into a life that wasn't of his own choosing. Najjar and his wife, also a young Iranian American, had agreed to move forward. Who were they to challenge the will of Allah? If the supreme leader needed them, they would answer the call.

Najjar checked his phone, which gave him access to the president's schedule, and realized that Charles Mapother and DNI Phillips were in the Oval Office. This was good news. These were powerful men and their deaths would only contribute to the overall success of the mission. He made his way from the basement, where the White House mess was located, to the Oval Office on the first floor. Two agents would be positioned right outside the Oval Office. It was standard procedure when the president met with his DNI. Hugh Thompson, one of the two special agents, was a good friend. The other agent's name was Jeffrey James. He was the youngest agent on the presidential protective detail. He was cocky, but he was currently holding the record for quickest draw. Najjar would use caution.

The knot in his stomach grew larger, tighter, with each step that brought him closer to the Oval Office.

This is it. This was so surreal. Najjar almost felt as though it couldn't possibly be him walking to the two agents standing guard. He knew what was going to happen, and they did not. The knowledge made him feel powerful, confident.

"Hey, Hugh," Najjar said, "need a break?"

"I'm good, Yash," Thompson replied. "Thanks."

"You're sure? The garden salad is spectacular down at the mess."

Thompson looked at him with disdain. "I hate salads, Yash, don't you know that?"

Without warning, Najjar pulled out his Sig Sauer and shot Thompson through the right eye point blank.

One down.

Najjar pivoted forty-five degrees to his right and fired two rounds into James' chest, pushing the young agent against the wall. To his credit, James' pistol was already out and he even managed to fire one round that grazed Najjar's right calf before Najjar's fourth and fifth rounds hit him an inch above his vest.

Two down.

James slowly slid down the wall, painting it dark with blood, a gurgle of aspirated blood the only sound he made as he slumped to the floor. Najjar didn't hear any of it; he was charging into the Oval Office.

. . . .

Charles Mapother stiffened when he heard the gunshot.

They're here. In the White House.

When the second and third shots rang, Mapother was already in the air over the Resolute Desk. He landed on top of President Muller—who was seated in his chair behind the desk—and both men fell when the chair tilted backward.

By the time the fourth, fifth and sixth shots were fired, Mapother had his Smith & Wesson firmly in his right hand and was pushing Muller's head down onto the rug with his left.

DNI Phillips was standing in front of the Resolute Desk, like a deer caught in the headlights. A second later, there was a knock on the door and Supervisory Special Agent Yash Najjar barged in, his gun pointing down in the low-ready position.

"Quick, Mr. President, we need to go."

He seemed in control of the situation, and Mapother would have probably listened to his commands if it wasn't for the intelligence Sergeant Sassani had delivered to them only a few minutes ago.

You're about to get hit, Mr. President . . .

Something wasn't right here.

. . . .

Najjar was running out of time. More agents were coming in. He could hear them in his earpiece. An aide had seen him shoot his colleagues and had identified him to the other agents. There was nowhere for him to go. He had about twenty-five seconds before they arrived. Charles Mapother had taken cover behind the Resolute Desk with the president. DNI Phillips was standing in front of them, his eyes fixed on Najjar's gun. Another second or two and the DNI would try something. Of that Najjar was sure. Somehow, they knew he wasn't there to save them.

Allahu Akbar.

Najjar raised his pistol and aimed at DNI Phillips who, to his credit, didn't even blink. He shot him once in the middle of the forehead. Phillips' head snapped back and he fell over backward, half his body resting on the Resolute Desk.

Najjar couldn't get an angle on Muller or Mapother so he moved sideways across the Oval Office, pumping rounds into the Resolute Desk to keep them pinned down.

. . . .

Splinters of wood flew everywhere around Mapother. The president was in fight or flight mode, and the flight side of his brain was winning. Half of Mapother's focus was on keeping Muller on the ground. The shooter was moving from right to left and soon would be in a position to hit something.

Where the fuck was the cavalry? Fuck this.

"Stay down, Robert!" yelled Mapother, before leaping to the side and firing his pistol while in midair.

. . . .

Najjar saw Mapother diving to the ground to his right, bright flashes coming from his pistol. A bullet whizzed over his head, another scratched his left knee and another missed to his right. Mapother had gotten out three shots at him before Najjar pulled the trigger. He hit Mapother high on the shoulder as Mapother's next bullet sliced against his neck, hot and sharp.

Then Muller made his move in a mad dash from the Resolute Desk to the closest exit door. Najjar spun on himself but could only pull the trigger once before Mapother's next round mushroomed in his brain.

CHAPTER 103

Oval Office, Washington DC

President Muller knelt next to Charles Mapother. Mapother was hyperventilating from the pain and gasping for breath. And he looked pissed. Muller had never seen him like this.

"You took one in the shoulder," he said to Mapother.

"What were you thinking, for Christ's sake," Mapother said. "You could have gotten yourself killed."

Muller thought about it for a second and then said, "Honestly, Charles, I had no idea what I was thinking. The only thing I knew was that you were down and about to get shot again. I didn't think. I only wanted to get his attention so could you shoot him before he shot me."

"He got one off," Mapother said. He winced in pain as Muller helped him to his feet.

"He did, but he missed, and you didn't."

A storm of agents rushed into the Oval Office and whisked the president to safety.

CHAPTER 104

Miami, Florida
Six months later

Mike was enjoying the cool breeze coming from the Atlantic Ocean. It had been a hot summer with way too many hurricanes.

"You think we should sell the penthouse, baby?"

"And go where?" Lisa replied, raising her eyes from the psychological thriller she'd been reading nonstop for the last four hours.

Mike tried to read the author's name.

James . . . Hankins. Mike had never heard of him but, if his wife was reading his books, he'd make sure to check him out.

"I don't know, but I'd like to try the Pacific coast," he finally said. "What about Seattle?"

"You'd hate the rain, Mike."

"Maybe, but think about all those wineries," he said, smiling.

The International Market Stabilization Institute was no longer operational. The official story behind the Brooklyn attack was that a catastrophic accident had happened when a private company had been hired to test the security procedures of a new Secret Service training facility.

The attack on the White House that cost the lives of DNI Richard Phillips and three Secret Service special agents dominated the news for a full month. It took three colossal category-5 hurricanes hitting the continental United States within the same month to have them talk about something else.

Mike knew Mapother hadn't forgotten Brooklyn, though. He was yet to fully recover from the loss of Anna Caprini. Mapother had taken her death personally. He loved her like a daughter, and her death had taken a major toll on his health. Still, he spent the weeks following the attack dismantling the IMSI, the organization he had built from the ground up. He did his best to find new positions for every IMSI employee by calling in favors he had accumulated during all his years at the service of the United States.

There was no denying the attacks that had taken place within the White House. So President Muller had addressed the nation in a speech that lasted close to an hour. He admitted that Iran had been responsible for the deadly attacks that had left the Canadian prime minister and his wife, the director of National Intelligence and countless brave law enforcement officers and civilians dead. He had vowed to pursue those responsible and to bring them to justice.

In a move that shocked Muller, the Russian government had condemned the attacks, which in turn had forced the Iranian prime minister to confess that a rogue element within its Quds Force had ordered an unsanctioned operation against the United States and Canada. He promised the guilty parties would be hunted down.

Mike didn't trust their efforts, but at least their confession cooled down the tensions between the two countries.

Sanchez's injuries, albeit serious, weren't going to slow him down for very long, which was surprising to Mike. He had visited his friend at the intensive care unit where Sanchez had lain motionless on a hospital bed. Mike remembered the tubes sprouting from every part of Sanchez's body. For a while, the former Delta operator had been incapable of breathing on his own. The bullet had taken out two ribs and half of his right lung. Bullet fragments now rested a quarter of an inch from his heart. The surgeons were able to fix his shoulder, but he would probably never regain one hundred percent of its use. The fact that he was alive was itself a wonder. That the man was running five miles a day, five days a week, six months after surgery was a miracle.

Eitan, though, wasn't as lucky. Even if the bullet had narrowly missed his femur, it was so deeply buried into his thigh that it had required numerous surgeries to remove it. Mike knew Eitan was feeling better, but once in a while his leg would flare up, and you wouldn't see him for a day or two. Mike had a private discussion with Zima about it, and she had told him that the doctors were confident that within the next year or so, these flare-ups would stop. Eitan's pinky hadn't fared much better. The bullet had torn through its flesh and powdered the small bone. As for Zima, her vest had stopped the three small-caliber rounds, but the cut she had received behind her head where the glass bottle had struck had necessitated a great number of stiches. Despite their injuries, Mike hadn't heard any of them complain.

In fact, today Sanchez had joined Eitan and Zima on Mike's new toy, a Mako 414 CC, to do a bit of fishing. Mike hoped they'd once again catch a couple of tunas, or, at the very least, a Mahi or two, so they could feast on fresh ceviche and carpaccio for dinner. And if there were enough fish, maybe he'd ask Lisa to grill the fillets on the barbecue.

"Hey, honey, where were you?" Lisa asked him. "You weren't here."

"I was thinking that if the weather holds, we should all go to Bimini tomorrow. What do you say?"

"You wouldn't ask if you hadn't checked the weather and knew it would be holding—"

Mike chuckled. He had indeed checked the marine weather. "So, you wanna go or not?"

"And sleep there?"

"Sure, why not?"

Bimini was a district of the Bahamas located approximately fifty miles east of Miami Beach. The beaches were gorgeous, and the marine life was fun to watch.

"You want something to drink, Lisa?"

"A beer would be great. An IPA if there are any left."

Mike closed the huge patio door behind him. He walked to the kitchen and opened the fridge. He grabbed a couple of IPAs and was about to head back outside when he noticed his smartphone's red light blinking.

Five missed calls? One voicemail.

He punched in his code and listened to the message. It was Meir Yatom. And Charles Mapother. They wanted to meet with the whole team.

Tomorrow.

Mike sighed. The weather was supposed to be perfect for a weekend in Bimini.

He had decided not to call back when it rang again.

"Hi, Meir."

"You got my message?"

"I just did.

"Why didn't you reply?"

"I told you, I just listened to it."

There was silence at the other end of the line.

"Hello?" Mike asked.

"I'm here, and I'm waiting for your answer."

Mike loved Meir Yatom. What he had gone through at the hands of Asad Davari was inhuman. The skillful hands of the plastic surgeons had done their best to rebuild his ear and hide the deep lesions that covered his body but there was only so much they could do.

"I'm not sure we'll make it, Meir. Why don't you come over? The beach will do you some good, old man."

"My work isn't done, Mike," Yatom hissed. "And yours isn't either."

"Listen, Meir—"

"No, you listen, Mike," Yatom said, his voice shaky with rage. "When you're done playing Baywatch, get your collective ass in gear and get over here. We found Kharazi."

EPILOGUE

Nassau, The Bahamas

Everybody was present. Meir Yatom had taken care of the logistics. He had rented four two-bedroom suites at the Reef at Atlantis located just across from Nassau on Paradise Island. He had converted half of one suite into a meeting room.

Yatom and Mapother had flown from Heathrow, while the rest of them had traveled by boat from Miami. The major advantage of arriving by boat was that it was much easier to enter the country incognito and bring the equipment they would need to conduct a covert operation. With Mike's new boat, it had taken them just under five hours to run from Miami Beach to the Marina at Atlantis.

"Thanks for coming," Yatom said from his wheelchair.

The best doctors in the world had tried to rebuild his knee, but the damage Davari had inflicted with the power drill had been too extensive. In a few months, there was a chance he'd be able to walk, but never for more than a few minutes at a time. The wheelchair was there to stay. Zima had told him Yatom was fine with that.

Yatom signaled Mapother to proceed. Mapother opened a blue folder and placed it in the middle of the small conference table they had gathered around.

"Who's this?" Lisa asked.

"You're looking at the ugly face of General Jalal Kharazi. He now calls himself Kurt Abedi," Mapother said.

"I'll be damned," Zima said. "He dyed his hair?"

"And he lost a lot of weight too," added Sanchez. "How did you find him?"

"While you were building sand castles by the beach, I spent two months debriefing Davari. He never said a word. Tough sonofabitch, if you ask me."

"But he did end up talking, right? We wouldn't be here if he didn't," Mike said.

"You wanna know why he finally broke?" Mapother asked.

"C'mon, man, spit it out," Sanchez said.

"This guy," Mapother said, pointing at Yatom with his index finger. "And please, somebody ask me how?"

"How?" Sanchez said, playing his game.

"Just by seeing him. Davari told us General Kharazi had agreed to do a prisoner exchange in case they were caught. So when he saw Yatom, he cracked."

"Where are you keeping Davari?" Mike asked, though he had a feeling what the answer would be.

"He's in good company. Let's leave it at that," Mapother said.

"He's with the Sheik, isn't he?" Mike insisted.

"Yes."

"As long as they don't become pals."

"Trust me, Mike, this isn't happening anytime soon."

Mike hoped they were both rotting in hell. If he knew Yatom and Mapother as well as he thought he did, the two terrorists weren't living the somewhat cushy lives regular federal prisoners were entitled to.

"What do we know about Kurt Abedi?" Sanchez asked, getting back to why they were there.

"Enough to take him down," Yatom answered. "He's by himself, no bodyguards. He really thinks he slipped past the radar."

"So, are we *taking* him or *killing* him?" Zima asked. "Personally, I'd much prefer if we were here to kill him, but that's just my two cents."

"I'm sorry to disappoint, Zima, but we've been hired to take him," Yatom said.

They all looked at each other, their confusion apparent.

"What are you talking about?" Mike asked. "Did you say *hired*?"

Hired would mean Mapother and Yatom had an employer. That seemed very unlikely.

"Let just say that Meir and I started our own consultation firm," Mapother said. "We're entrepreneurs now."

"MOSSAD knows about this?" Eitan asked, unimpressed. Everybody knew Yatom had retired from the Israeli spy agency, but no one believed for a second he was really out.

"Not only does MOSSAD know, it will be a major client of ours."

"Same with Donald Poole over at the CIA," Mapother added. "Director Poole is the one who hired the IMSI's services for this operation. In exactly twelve hours, we will deliver Major General Jalal Kharazi to a CIA political action group in Fort Lauderdale."

"Sounds good, Charles," Mike said. "But did you say IMSI? We were all under the impression the IMSI had shut down its activities. I'm not following."

"We should have mentioned this sooner. Our apologies," Mapother said, smiling for the first time in a long time. "Our new firm is called the International Mobile Service Institute. We specialize in extraordinary renditions. You guys like the name?"

About the Author

Simon Gervais is a former federal agent who was tasked with guarding foreign heads of state visiting Canada. Among many others, he served on the protection details of Queen Elizabeth II, US President Barack Obama, and Chinese President Hu Jianto. He has also protected the families of three different Canadian prime ministers. Prior to this, Simon spent five years in an anti-terrorism unit and was deployed in many European and Middle Eastern countries. He now writes full-time and is a member of the International Thriller Writers organization. He is the author of two previous Mike Walton novels, *The Thin Black Line*, which was an international bestseller and *A Red Dotted Line*, as well as the Mike Walton novella, *A Long Gray Line*. He lives in Ottawa with his wife and two children. Find Simon online at SimonGervaisBooks.com, facebook.com/SimonGervaisAuthor, and Twitter.com/GervaisBooks.

Acknowledgments

Writing the acknowledgements is always fun. It means that the book is finished and I get to say a big "Thank you!" to everyone who helped me along the way. For me, the first word of gratitude should always go to my readers. Whether *A Thick Crimson Line* is the first book you read in my Mike Walton series or you've been with me since *The Thin Black Line*, I thank you for your support.

Thanks to Lou Aronica, my editor at The Story Plant, for his mentorship and friendship. Lou is a true author's editor. He's supportive, engaged and he sincerely cares about his authors. Thank you for making *A Thick Crimson Line* the best book it can possibly be. Thanks also to my friend and remarkable literary agent Eric Myers of Myers Literary Management. I can't thank him enough for his work ethic and dedication.

Finally, thanks to the most critical members of my team: my family. I love you all. I'm especially indebted to my amazing wife, Lisane, whose unwavering support is my most prized possession.

You are my strength, *mon amour*. My love for you, Florence and Gabriel knows no bounds.

A Letter from the Author

Dear Readers,

I have exciting news to share with you. I recently finished writing *Hunt Them Down*, the first book in an electrifying new series featuring DEA special agent Pierce Hunt, a former Army Ranger who isn't afraid to step over the line if it gets the job done or keeps his team safe.

When his thirteen-year-old daughter Leila is kidnapped while at sleepover at her friend's house—the residence of Tony Garcia, the head of Miami's most violent crime family—Hunt has forty-eight hours to find her before she's executed in real time on social media. To rescue Leila, Hunt goes dark and is forced to team up with his archenemy's own daughter—a woman he once loved but who now vows to see him dead. With the walls closing in on him and the minutes ticking away, Hunt's only chance is to become the man he swore he'd never be again.

The Real Book Spy—the #1 reference when it comes to thrillers—had this to say: "Get ready for a new awesome series..."

Hunt Them Down will hit bookstores in February 2019. I hope you'll check it out.

It is a privilege to write for you, and I'll never take that for granted. Your entertainment options are many, and yet you chose to take a chance on me and my books. For that, I'll always be grateful.

Warmest,
Simon